"If ye didn't come for the thimble, then ye must have come to see me," Drew said with a grin.

"Look, Highlander," she bit out, punctuating her words with jabs of the tankard. "I'm runnin' a beer-wagon. I didn't come for that. And I certainly didn't come for ye. Just because we shared a kiss or two—"

"Three," Drew corrected.

"Fine. Three."

"Ye shared three kisses?" one of the crowd asked.

"In some parts o' the Highlands," another onlooker said, "a kiss is as good as a betrothal, and three kisses—"

"Can ye not mind your own affairs? This isn't the Highlands, and I'm not his damned betrothed. Aye, I kissed him thrice. But I'll bloody well ne'er do it again."

There was a long silence, and Josselin lifted her chin.

Then someone from the back of the crowd said, "Five shillin's says he gets a fourth kiss..."

"Ever so sensual and emotional...caught me off guard with its romantic intensity."

—YankeeRomanceReviewers.blogspot.com

"An entertaining, fast-paced sixteenth-century historical romance...Historical readers will enjoy this exciting, twisting tale as love arrives when you least expect it."

—Harriet Klausner,
GenreGoRoundReviews.blogspot.com

"It takes a good writer to take the reader to a place and time and have them feel as if they are there with the characters, and Ms. Morgan does just that with ease and entertainment."

—MaryGramlich.com

"A sensual adventure...The quick pace and engaging characters alongside the colorful history make this an entertaining and winning novel."

—*RT Book Reviews*

"A tantalizing story of love set in an era filled with traitorous people. The characters are well developed and the author's talent shines on every page. I foresee a rewarding career in this author's future."

—HuntressReviews.com

"I was completely enthralled...A refreshing love story with a new plot. Kira Morgan is an extremely interesting novelist with a terrific imagination for a great story."

—FreshFiction.com

"A page-turner...written with depth and details...It has betrayal, romance, sensuality, wit...will capture your heart from page one to the end."

—MyBookAddictionandMore.wordpress.com

"Kira Morgan has an exciting way of telling her tale and creates both a rich setting as well as interesting characters."

—Tweezlereads.blogspot.com

"A fast-paced story with a nice blend of mystery and romance that will keep you interested page after page."

—"DK's Book Reviews,"
dkay401-bookreviews.blogspot.com

"A fantastic story...Florie as the female lead is just wonderful and strong."

—"Book Hounds," maryinhb.blogspot.com

"Fascinating...The mysterious elements of the plot were well constructed, but the romance was front and center. Rane is my newest literary crush...I can promise his actions will make you swoon."

—TheFictionEnthusiast.blogspot.com

"Packed with suspense plus tumultuous emotions...plenty of steamily passionate desires...an unforgettable couple. Kira Morgan makes the intriguing sixteenth-century Scottish time period come alive with originality and accuracy...Emotionally charged throughout, the heart-warming romance in *Captured by Desire* will not soon be forgotten."

—SingleTitles.com

"Fans of historical romance won't want to miss this fun romp...full of interesting characters that will pull you in and have you rooting for them from page one. Excellent romantic escapism!"

—Marta'sMeanderings.blogspot.com

"Enjoyable...humorous...suspenseful."

—ArmsOfASister.com

"Once the romance really started cooking—wow! This was one sigh after another, a super-sweet romance...a can't-miss book!"

—IntheHammock.blogspot.com

"This historical romance is a surefire winner for every romance fanatic. The title says it all!"

—YouSayToo.com

Seduced by Destiny

KIRA MORGAN

FOREVER

NEW YORK   BOSTON

Forever
Hachette Book Group
237 Park Avenue
New York, NY 10017
Visit our website at www.HachetteBookGroup.com

Forever is an imprint of Grand Central Publishing. The Forever name and logo is a trademark of Hachette Book Group, Inc.

The publisher is not responsible for websites (or their content) that are not owned by the publisher.

Printed in the United States of America

First Printing: March 2011

10 9 8 7 6 5 4 3 2 1

ATTENTION CORPORATIONS AND ORGANIZATIONS:
Most HACHETTE BOOK GROUP books are available at quantity discounts with bulk purchase for educational, business, or sales promotional use. For information, please call or write:

Special Markets Department, Hachette Book Group
237 Park Avenue, New York, NY 10017
Telephone: 1-800-222-6747 Fax: 1-800-477-5925

For all the Kathy's
who've made a difference in romance:

Kathleen Woodiwiss, Mother of Historicals
Kathryn Falk, Queen of Readers
Kate Duffy, Fearless Editor
Kathy Baker, Bookseller Extraordinaire
Kathe Robin, Gifted Reviewer
Kathleen Givens, Irreverent Angel

Special thanks to:

Frances Jalet-Miller and Helen Breitwieser
for their support

Lori Royal-Gordon and Karen Nesbitt
for sharing the adventure in Scotland

Richard Campbell
for taking a third wife

Robin McGregor
Secretary of Musselburgh Links
for his generosity, patience, and vivid tales

David Hamilton
author of *Golf—Scotland's Game*
for his depth of expertise and his enthusiasm

James McAvoy and Reese Witherspoon
for their inspiration

Fair Maiden Lilliard
Lies under this stane
Little was her stature
But muckle was her fame
Upon the English loons
She laid monie thumps
An' when her legs were cuttid off
She fought upon her stumps

—Inscription on gravestone
near Ancrum Moor,
in the Borders, Scotland

Seduced
by Destiny

Prologue

February 27, 1545

The three battle-weary Scots slogged across Ancrum Moor. In spite of the devastation surrounding them, their spirits were at ease, for most of the blood spilled upon the sod was that of their English foes.

Earlier, when they'd beheld the scores of enemy troops marching toward them across the moor, the three comrades-in-arms had exchanged grim farewells, sure 'twas their last day alive.

But to their amazement, the traitorous Border Scots who'd chosen to ally themselves with the English had finally come to their senses. In the middle of the fighting, they'd heeded the plaintive call of the pipes and turned coat on their English captains, assuring a Scots victory.

Now there was nothing to do but bury the dead, return home, and brace for the next skirmish. The English never tired of war, it seemed, and the Borders bore the scars and scorched earth to prove it.

The three men crossed the trampled grass, solemnly

picking their way through the fallen, giving more than one mortally wounded English wretch a final blow of mercy with a misericordia.

Then Will paused over one of the dead bodies and frowned, poking it with the tip of his sword. He crouched down to take a closer look.

"Sweet Mary, Mother o' ..." he breathed.

"What is it?" Angus grunted.

Will rolled the body over, and all three took a shocked step backward. They recognized the bonnie Scots lass from their village of Selkirk. Her name was Lilliard. But her once-soft honey curls were caked with blood, and her rosy lips were ashen. One fist still clutched her sword with a death grip, but she'd been unable to block the last fatal blow—a blade thrust beneath her ribs that had stopped her heart.

"English devils!" spat Angus. "She was but a maid."

Will shook his head. "Poor lass didn't have a chance against them."

"Wait." Alasdair narrowed his keen eyes. "Who'd let a lass on the battleground?"

The question gave them all pause. No Scotsman worth his dirk would allow a helpless woman near a field of war.

Will rubbed his grizzled jaw. "Wasn't her husband killed by the English?"

"Aye, I think so," Angus said, "two years back, at Solway Moss."

Alasdair nodded at the bloody linen shirt and gray jerkin draping her poor lifeless body. "Those are his clothes."

"And his blade, no doubt," Angus added. "She was likely lookin' to avenge his murder."

"But the poor lass had no idea o' the danger," said Will.

They stared in thoughtful silence for a while. Then Alasdair cleared his throat. "We should carry her home."

When they lifted her small body to place her on a plaid, they discovered her arm was broken and both of her legs had been gashed to the bone. The lass hadn't gone down without a fight.

With their tragic burden, they traversed Ancrum Moor and continued several miles to Selkirk, to the isolated stone house where the lass had lived.

As far as they recalled, Lilliard had no family in the village. The men didn't even know her surname. Still, Alasdair could read, and there might be some missive in the woman's house that would help them locate her kin. If nothing else, they could at least give a proper burial to the brave lass.

The cottage appeared empty. No one answered their knocks. When they pushed the door open, no fire burned on the hearth.

'Twasn't until they lowered the maid's broken body gently to the floor that they spied a small lass in the corner of the room, a flaxen-haired beauty with wide green eyes and her thumb in her mouth.

They froze, speechless, as the tot studied them with stern appraisal, one by one. After a moment, she popped her thumb out of her mouth and toddled forward a step, then stuttered back, plopping onto her bottom with a startled blink.

The men winced, expecting a piercing wail. Instead the lass opened her mouth and uttered one loud, distinct, emphatic word.

"Da!"

*   *   *

Edward Armstrong was halfway home before the wrenching sobs stopped racking his body. He'd fled through the forest, tears streaming down his cheeks, unable to face his fellow soldiers. He didn't know whether they'd won or lost the battle at Ancrum Moor, and he didn't care. He wasn't fit to defend the English crown. Jesu—after what he'd done, he wasn't fit to muck out King Henry's stables.

He leaned against an oak trunk, fighting a dizzying wave of nausea. Every time he closed his eyes, he saw her face—her fair cheeks, her innocent eyes, her pleading lips—just before...

He stumbled to his knees and retched into the bushes, but nothing could purge him of the hideous memory.

He hadn't meant to hurt the lass. He hadn't meant to hurt anyone. Violence was against his nature. But his brothers had expected him to fight alongside them, and he'd joined the battle at their prodding.

They'd never told him he'd be killing women.

He shivered, then rose on shaky legs, wiping his damp brow with the back of one trembling hand.

He had to get home. Everything would be fine if he could just get back home.

God's wounds! What had the lovely maid been doing there? Her angelic face didn't belong in the midst of such a massacre.

When he'd first glimpsed the Scots lass wielding a blade, Edward's instinct had been to retreat. He'd had little enough desire to engage the Scots soldiers, none at all to battle a Scots *maid*.

But then she'd turned a dewy, stunned gaze up to him,

and her lips had moved in silent prayer. As he lowered his eyes, he saw that her left arm hung limp at her side, and blood had begun to soak the bottom of her oversized shirt like a rapidly blossoming scarlet rose.

She was too weak to lift her sword, and 'twas a miracle she was still standing, for he could see both thighs had been deeply slashed by a blade. She was going to die—she was losing too much blood to survive.

Death would come slowly and painfully, and she seemed to know it. What she begged of him with her glance was mercy.

Without hesitation, he did what he thought was right. While the battle raged ruthlessly around them, he granted her the mercy she requested.

Only after he pulled the blade out of her frail chest and watched her sink lifelessly to the ground did he realize what he'd done. God forgive him, he'd slain a woman.

He pressed his palms hard against his eyes, then ran a shaking hand back through his hair. He had to get home. He had to go somewhere familiar, where he could remember the gentle soul he'd been and not the monster he'd become.

'Twas nightfall when Edward at last staggered through the door of his cottage, a safe three miles across the border.

His six-year-old son Andrew knew at once that something was wrong. The lad was perceptive and bright, as curious and interested in life as Edward had been in his youth...before his brothers had pressured him into taking up the sword.

Andrew would grow to be a better man than he was. The lad was blessed not only with his departed mother's piercing blue eyes and rich brown hair, but also her brilliant mind, her even temper, her strength of character. Andrew would succeed where his father had failed.

Edward knew what he had to do. He stirred the fire to a cheery blaze and lit all the candles in the room, chasing away the dark shades that haunted him. Then he asked the lad to pour him ale while he fetched a scrap of parchment, ink, and a quill from the cupboard.

The ale did its work. His hands stopped trembling, his stomach settled, and his mind cleared. He dragged a candle close and, with a steady hand, scrawled out all of it in plain terms—his sin, his shame, his atonement.

When he was finished, a strange peace settled over him. He rolled up the parchment and gave it to Andrew, kissing his son's head and bidding him take the missive to his uncles' house.

Andrew may not have understood what was wrong, but he sensed his father's urgency. He ran the whole mile in the moonlight, breathlessly giving the note to his Uncle Thomas, who read it aloud to Robert and Simon. The more Thomas read, the more upset they all became.

His uncle finished the missive, then flung open the door, and the three of them raced with Andrew all the way back to his father's house, dragging him along until his sides ached.

They burst in through the door, making the candles in the room flicker wildly. Uncle Thomas gasped and tried to block Andrew's view, but 'twas too late. Andrew saw his father swaying from the rafters, just like the outlaws that were sometimes hanged from the town gallows.

While Andrew regarded them in stunned silence, his uncles swore and sobbed. They cut his father's body down, cursing the Scots with words Andrew had never heard before, saying the Scots were to blame for his father's death. He wasn't sure, but it sounded like his uncles were angry at the Scots for giving swords to lasses.

They buried his father in the yard by the light of the moon and spoke a few words over his grave. Then they looked down at Andrew, and Uncle Simon placed his hand on Andrew's shoulder.

He said that today the uncles were going to make Andrew's father a solemn promise. They'd take care of Andrew from now on. They'd feed him, clothe him, shelter him, and, most importantly, train him. The Scots would regret slaying his father, they said, for they intended to turn Andrew into an unrivaled swordsman and a fierce killer— a man of whom his father would have been proud.

Chapter 1

August 19, 1561

Andrew... Drew... scowled as he eyed his opponent across the field. He'd trained long and hard for this duel. He didn't intend to lose, especially not to the cocksure Scots nobleman who was currently brandishing his weapon with all the grace of a crofter chopping wheat.

Drew seldom lost. He'd earned his reputation on the tournament field as a master. He was lithe, strong, and intimidating. His arm was powerful and his aim deadly. He'd left his last two opponents gasping on their knees and the one before that cursing into the dust.

Ian Hay would likewise prove an easy conquest. The barrel-chested Scot was currently making a great show of flexing his arms, adjusting his trews, and gauging the position of the rising sun, which was nearly invisible on this unusually gloomy summer morn. But it seemed to Drew that Hay was merely delaying his inevitable demise.

The motley mob of peasants and merchants and nobles who crowded around them, shouting and shoving and

placing hasty wagers on the match, did not agree. By the
loud cheers they sent Hay's way and the nasty aspersions
they hurled at Drew, 'twas apparent most of them had bet
heavily on their local hero.

Unable to stall any further, Hay mopped his brow,
cleared his throat, and approached, gripping his weapon
so tightly that it seemed as if he meant to throttle the life
out of it.

The crowd hushed, their gazes locked on the
combatants.

Drew took a calm breath and waited.

Despite the man's poor form as he swung, there was
a tap as he managed to connect with the ball, sending it
bounding well down the green, where it arced to the left,
bounced four times, but somehow landed at the far edge
of the grass, a good two dozen yards past the hole.

Nonetheless, his supporters roared with gloating satisfaction, and Hay let out a triumphant cackle. He bowed,
inviting Drew to do better.

Drew lifted the corner of his lip in a grim smile. Oh,
aye, he'd do better. He hadn't left his home, changed his
name, and risked his life, roving through the land of
enemy Scots, just to lose to a smug Lowlander with a distinct hook in his swing. Drew might not be spilling the
Scots' blood as his uncles would have wished, but he was
definitely doing his part to drain their coffers.

Ignoring the raucous bystanders, who tried to rattle
him with insults, Drew made a small mound of sand and
placed his elm ball upon it. He glanced at the blades of
grass in the rough to gauge the direction of the breeze. A
light wind normally blew in from the North Sea, which
was visible from the links, just past the rise, but today the

air was still and veiled with fog. He could only faintly discern the imposing rock of Ard-thir Suidhe, which rose above Edinburgh like a fortress wall.

Drew chose the spoon from among his clubs, earning him a scornful bark of laughter from Hay, which was echoed by the crowd. Apparently no one realized how short the hole was. Drew balanced the club easily in the fingers of his left hand as he set the head down with calculated precision behind the ball, then clasped lightly with his right hand.

Ironically, much of his golfing aptitude came from the training his uncles had given him with a sword. His grip was solid, yet not too tight. Flexibility, whether holding a blade or a golf club, was the key to control and accuracy. The rest of his skills he'd learned from Lowland golfers who were more than willing to show a stranger a thing or two about golf for a few pints of beer.

Drew glanced up once toward the hole, which was slightly to the right on the rise ahead. 'Twas hardly necessary—he could have played the Musselburgh links blindfolded.

The Scots who'd wagered on Hay gathered as closely around Drew as they dared, yelling and stomping and waving their hands in an effort to break his concentration.

Taking an even breath, Drew shifted his weight back then forward, swinging the club with smooth power. It whistled and connected with a solid crack. The ball shot straight ahead, rolling and bounding down the green like a hound on the hunt, slowing and settling directly in front of the hole.

Hay made a pained, strangling noise, which he quickly disguised with a cough, and his constituency groaned in collective disappointment. Then he waved to his servant to bring along his satchel of clubs as he shuffled off toward his ball.

Drew always carried his own clubs. He refused to engage a servant to do something he could do just as well himself. Besides, he preferred to keep the Scots at arm's length, and that included the serving class. He was an Englishman masquerading as a Highlander, and the fewer who knew his secret, the better.

As they ambled down the course, trailed by the disgruntled crowd, Hay tried to strike up a probing but friendly conversation. "So, MacAdam, have ye played much at Musselburgh?"

"A time or two." The truth was he'd played at Musselburgh enough to know it like the back of his hand. This might be the country of his foe, but he liked it well enough to spend a good deal of time here. There was a wild quality about the eastern coast of Scotland that pleased him.

Hay's servant, upon reaching his ball, extracted a fairway club from the satchel. Drew cleared his throat, wondering if the servant had made a mistake in his choice. After all, the ball wasn't *that* far from the hole.

But the servant arched a knowing brow at Drew. The crowd hushed, and Hay lined up behind the ball, wiggling his backside to get the proper posture. When he finally swung forward, the servant's choice proved to be a prudent one after all, for Hay all but missed the shot, only narrowly clipping the top of the ball, which rolled forward to end up, by fool's luck, beside Drew's.

The Hay faction cheered, and Drew let out a whistle of disbelief, which Hay mistook for admiration.

"Aye, we Lowlanders have golf in our blood," Hay

boasted, resting his club on his shoulder and marching happily forward. "Tell me, MacAdam," he said loudly enough for the onlookers to hear, "do they even play the sport where ye're from?"

In England? Drew thought. Not anymore. Golf had been outlawed there. But that wasn't what Hay was asking. As far as anyone knew, Drew MacAdam was born and bred in the Highlands. No one here had heard of the Englishman, Andrew Armstrong. Still, these Lowlanders had almost as much contempt for their northern brothers as they did for their English foes.

"In Tintclachan?" Drew replied in his best Highland brogue. "Nae. There's naught but rocky ground and lochs so deep ye'd drown chippin' your way out."

"Indeed?" Hay nodded to the crowd, as if to confirm that a Highlander couldn't possibly have the experience to win this match.

"Aye." Drew nodded out of courtesy to indicate Hay could play first. "And ye'd be lucky to swing a club without hittin' a cow." He gave the bystanders a wink, and the few of them who'd wagered on Drew to win chuckled in response.

Hay took a putting cleek from his servant, who then spread a cloth on the grass before the ball and helped his master to his knees. Hay doubled at the waist to line up his shot, his hands flat on the ground, his arse in the air. He cocked a wild eye at the hole as if to threaten it into submission. Then he straightened, and with three practice swings, he knocked the ball forward, missing the hole by more than a foot.

"Damn!"

The crowd's oaths were somewhat coarser. Some of them had wagered a week's earnings on Hay to win.

The servant helped Hay struggle to his feet while Drew waited without comment. Just as he'd expected, this was going to be an easy match. Hay was already losing his temper on the first hole. By the seventh, he'd doubtless be apoplectic and completely unable to control his shots.

Drew advanced toward his ball. With scarcely a wasted motion and before the onlookers could distract him with their taunts, he tapped it neatly into the hole.

Hay started in surprise. "Oh." He added grudgingly, "Well done, MacAdam."

After that, it took the man not one, but two more attempts to sink his ball. By then his ears were red, and the onlookers were growling in irritation.

"Your drive," Hay muttered.

Drew nodded and walked past the green to tee off. The path to the second hole was much longer, with a marshy patch in the middle. On a sunny day, he could do it in five strokes. Today, with the mist heavy on the course, 'twas hard to tell.

He lined up the shot with his longnose club while the mob closed in, whistling and jeering. Ignoring the detractors, he swung back, but as he swung forward, an overly enthusiastic Hay supporter waved out his arm, and Drew's club caught on the man's sleeve, destroying the shot. The ball sliced to the right, landing near the edge of the rough.

Half of the crowd cheered in approval, willing to seize on any advantage. The other half, recognizing the man's behavior as unsporting, shoved and rebuked the offender.

Drew frowned. He'd seen men cheat like this before. 'Twas one thing to bellow and stamp and cast aspersions. 'Twas another to physically interfere with a man's shot.

Hay, however, was a man of some character. "Ye can take the shot o'er, MacAdam," he offered.

Drew nodded his thanks. But to be honest, he didn't want to take *all* of the challenge out of the game. "Nae, let it lie."

Hay seemed unsure whether to be grateful or insulted. He nodded in deference to Drew's courtesy, then took the club from his servant and groused at the onlookers, "I'll play my own game, if ye please."

While they moved down the course and Hay carried on about unruly crowds, Drew grunted, only half listening. He was distracted by the sight of something odd upon the waves in the distance—strange shadows shifting through the veil of mist. As he scanned the horizon, the dark flank of a ship emerged from the fog. Ghostly white sails billowed on its three masts as it sailed toward Leith Harbor. Behind it another vessel materialized.

Hay, oblivious to the ships, chattered away as he struggled to keep up with Drew. "'Tis a foul day for this time o' year—not golfin' weather at all."

Drew stopped, squinting to try to make out the colors of the flag flying from the highest mast.

"I suppose it could be worse," Hay blathered on. "It could be rain—"

He suddenly crashed into Drew with an "oof," but Drew was too preoccupied to take notice. Ships came into Leith Harbor all the time, but there was something different about this pair.

"Those galleys," Drew said, "whose colors are they flyin'?"

Hay sputtered, then shaded his eyes with one hand to try to make out the ships.

His servant joined them. "They're French, sir."

"French." Two French galleys sailing up the Thames in London would have presented a threat. But here, Drew reminded himself, there was a strong alliance between France and Scotland that went back centuries.

"Aye, right ye are," Hay chimed in, pretending he could see that far. "They're French. Ye can tell by... Wait." He straightened abruptly. "French? *French?* Is it..." He elbowed his way past Drew and scrambled through the rough to get a better look. "Nae. It couldn't be. She wasn't due to arrive for another two days!"

"She?" Drew asked, turning to the servant.

The crowd began murmuring in wonder as the servant gazed into the distance with curious adoration. "The new queen," he breathed.

Chapter 2

Ye'll not best me this time, old man."

Will scowled at his young protégé and pushed back his sleeves, revealing his thick, hairy forearms. "Will ye ne'er learn to respect your elders?" He raised his dagger and shook his head, muttering, "Old man indeed."

The two had sparred together so often that they'd memorized each other's strengths and weaknesses, ploys and habits. But this week, Will's favorite student had learned a new trick from Angus. Today the master would taste defeat at the hands of his apprentice. The stakes were high, the prize priceless.

Will's first advance came, as always, across and down from the right in a diagonal slash. 'Twas predictable and easy to dodge.

His second strike was always a return from the left. It might come in low or high. Today the arc was at shin-height, low enough to jump over.

The advance had to be quick then. There was only a second or two to reply.

One immediate forward thrust sent the old man

scuttling back, followed rapidly by a downward slash, which forced Will to dodge to the side.

Once a man was on the defensive, Angus had said, he'd reply with hasty desperation, and his blows might be incautious. 'Twas then the risky move would have to be made.

When the old man's awkward, defensive slash whistled from left to right, his opponent needed precise, lightning-quick calculation and sheer nerve to step sideways into the blade's path. Thankfully, the measurement proved accurate. Will's dagger sliced superficially through cloth and flesh, not enough to cause too much damage, just enough to sting like bloody hell.

As predicted, Will dropped his weapon in shock at what he'd done. "Jossy!" he cried.

Just as Angus had suggested she do, Josselin played up the injury. She gave a feminine gasp, winced, and staggered, letting Will get a good look at her wounded left arm, but never letting go of the blade in her right.

With horror in his eyes, Will stepped forward. "Jossy, lass, are ye—"

"Aha!" Before he could finish, she swung the tip of her dagger up to rest it at his stubbled throat. "I win."

"What?" His bewildered gaze almost made her regret her trickery. Almost.

"I win." She gave him a grin of triumph.

His confusion turned rapidly to anger. "Win, my arse," he spat. "Ye cheated, brat."

"I didn't cheat," she said with an injured sniff. "Ye can see the blood."

"I can't believe ye'd do that on purpose," he scolded. "I could have cut ye badly, ye fool wench." He shook his head. "Who taught ye such deceit?"

" 'Tisn't deceit," she said, avoiding the question. After all, 'twould make Will jealous if he knew he wasn't her only teacher. " 'Tis cleverness."

He batted her dagger away. "Cleverness, my ballocks," he grumbled. "Ye'll get yourself killed with such cleverness."

"But I win, right?" she said. "I get to go to Edinburgh to see the new queen."

He muttered something under his breath that sounded suspiciously like an expletive.

"Ye promised," she warned.

"Aye, that I did. Never let it be said I'm not a man o' my word. But," he said, wagging his finger at her nose, "ye're goin' to promise me somethin' in return."

Josselin's heart was beating so fast with the thrill of winning the wager that she didn't care what his promise was. "Aye?"

"Ye'll go as a lad."

"What?"

"Ye heard me."

"What do ye mean?"

"Ye'll get yourself some trews, a baggy shirt, and boots," he told her. "And a hat big enough, Mistress Goldilocks, to hide your hair and those connivin' green eyes."

Josselin furrowed her brows. "Why?"

"For protection."

She brought her blade up swiftly. "I've got this for protection."

"Don't argue with me, lass, or ye'll not go at all."

"But ye swore. Ye said if I bested ye, I could go to Edinburgh."

"So I did, and I'll be true to my word...even if ye did cheat."

"I did not—"

He held up a hand to silence her. "But if ye don't agree to my terms, I can't promise I won't have a slip o' the tongue in front o' Kate about the mischief ye've been up to these past few years."

She whisked her dagger back down and looked at him in hurt disbelief. "Ye wouldn't."

He folded his arms over his stocky chest. "Only if ye force me to it."

She huffed out a vexed puff of air. "Oh, fine. I'll go as a bloody lad."

She sheathed her weapon and unbuckled the belt from her hips, handing it to Will. As they walked back toward the tavern, Josselin smoothed her skirts and loosed her braid, letting the waves fall around her shoulders and down her back, then tied on her linen coif. Kate mustn't know she'd been fighting. 'Twould break the woman's heart.

Will brought up Kate Campbell any time he wanted to keep Josselin under his thumb. Kate, a prosperous brewster, had taken Josselin in when she was twelve years old, claiming 'twas unseemly for three unwed men to raise an orphaned lass, pointing out that they'd taught her nothing but sparring, spitting, and swearing.

But despite the woman's kindness, Josselin had burst into tears as she'd been forced to leave behind the three men she called "Da" to move her things into the room over Kate's tavern.

Will had taken pity on her. He'd whispered to her that if she promised not to tell Kate, he'd continue sparring with her every Monday morn. After all, he'd sworn on her mother's grave that he'd teach Josselin how to defend herself properly.

What Will didn't know was that her second da, Angus, had made a similar arrangement. They met to cross swords on Wednesday afternoons, to honor the memory of her brave father, killed in battle.

And neither Angus nor Will knew about her engagements with her third da, Alasdair, who dedicated Fridays to teaching Josselin how to read, do sums, and, if nagged enough, how to wield a dagger with lethal grace.

As far as her foster mother knew, Josselin went off for several hours a week to gather flowers, do embroidery, or visit with friends. That was in addition to her regular work, which was serving beer at the tavern and managing the brewster's accounts.

"Ye'd better keep your wits about ye in Edinburgh," Will muttered as they crossed the field toward town. "'Tisn't Selkirk, after all."

"I'll keep my wits *and* my blade about me, Da." She called all three of her fathers "Da." It got confusing sometimes, but none of the three would surrender the title.

"Half o' Scotland is determined to get a peek at the new queen," he said with a shudder, making his graying beard quiver. "There's bound to be an enormous crowd."

Josselin's heart raced, imagining the grand procession...hundreds of people waving scarves and cheering...French soldiers on horseback and lairds from all over Scotland marching through the streets...musicians and players and dancers making festive displays. And floating like an unruffled goddess above the din and ceremony would be Queen Mary with her constant companions, the Four Maries.

"Get that glimmer right out o' your eyes, lass," Will

groused. "'Tis a dangerous place, the city. And not everyone will be so glad to see the queen."

"How could they not?" Josselin broke off a purple thistle growing beside the path. "She's been gone for twelve years. 'Twill be a triumphant return." She smiled, tickling Will's cheek with the blossom.

He scowled and brushed it away. "She's a Catholic, and there are those who don't much care for the old religion."

Josselin thought that was silly. What did it matter where a person worshipped on Sunday? Scotland was finally going to have her own real queen. And from all reports, Mary was beautiful and powerful, intelligent and charming.

"Mary is strong," she decided. "She can defend herself."

"Not accordin' to Knox."

"Hmph." Josselin had heard men in the tavern talking of John Knox, the Protestant zealot. It seemed many were swayed by his charismatic speeches. "I hardly think one nasty old man with a waggin' tongue can wield much influence."

"Perhaps not, but he has powerful friends."

Josselin straightened with pride. "Well, so does the queen." More than anything, Josselin wanted to live up to her mother's legacy, to fight the foes of the crown, to triumph where she had fallen. "Who was it taught me," she added pointedly, "that the best defense is a strong offense?"

Will stopped in his tracks, grabbed her by the shoulders, and spun her to face him. In that one instant, his fierce frown took all the wind from her sails. "Ye'll not tangle with the likes o' Knox, do ye hear me?"

Josselin gulped. She wasn't afraid of Will, but she did respect him.

"He's a dangerous man," Will said. "All fanatics are. Ye can go do your merrymakin', watch the hurly-burly, and steal a peek at young Mary from a distance. But ye steer clear o' Knox and his ilk."

She wriggled loose of his hands. "I've no interest in the man anyway. Ye fret too much, Da."

"Ye give a man much to fret about," he said, shaking his head and sighing unhappily as they continued down the path. "What are ye goin' to tell Kate about that gash on your arm?"

She shrugged. "I'll say I fell off the beer cart."

He arched one grizzled brow. "Again?"

Chapter 3

September 2

Drew grumbled under his breath. He didn't know why he'd come. He usually avoided crowds like the pox. Already he'd been jostled by drunks, elbowed by peddlers, pushed aside by filthy urchins trying to get a better view, and aye, even patted on the arse by a wench looking for a bit of business.

But he was currently staying in Edinburgh, and the whole city seemed to be in a feverish fervor over their new monarch, Queen Mary. He hadn't been able to persuade any golfers to play today, even with the offer of weighting the game in their favor. So he'd decided, since the links were deserted, and since he'd missed the coronation of his own Queen Elizabeth three years ago, perhaps he'd venture down to the Royal Mile to see what the clamor was about.

So far, Queen Mary had been nothing but an inconvenience to him. Her early arrival at Leith Harbor had interrupted one perfectly good golf game, and her homecoming festivities today prevented another. True, he'd been paid handsomely for the forfeit of his match with Ian Hay. But lately, he was driven as much by his love of the sport as by coin.

He frowned, beginning to regret his decision to come. The hubbub was inescapable. The crowd was packed in at Lawnmarket as tightly as herring in a barrel. People were cheering and singing and shouting and laughing in a deafening commotion. And the queen hadn't even arrived yet.

He scanned the crowd with an uneasy scowl, wondering how quickly the Scots would string him up if they found out he was English. Fortunately, he'd played the part long enough to be fairly certain he could convince even the most dubious Lowlander that he'd been born and bred in the Highlands. And the rare Highlander who ventured this far south had never heard of his hometown of Tintclachan—which was no surprise, since Drew had invented the village and placed it in a vague, remote part of the country.

'Twas a necessary deception. Traveling as a Highlander along the eastern coast of Scotland, he could steal from the purses of those who'd stolen his father from him, exacting a fitting but bloodless revenge.

His uncles, of course, would have preferred he join the English army and kill every Scot in sight. Drew had considerable skill with a blade, thanks to his uncles' training. But like his father, he'd never had the heart for violence. Besides, with King Henry dead and Queen Elizabeth on the throne, battles along the Borders were rare. Still, to keep his uncles content, Drew let them believe the coin he earned was won on the English tournament circuit with a sword rather than on the Scots links with a golf club.

He thought his disguise was reasonably convincing. He'd let his hair grow a bit shaggier than was fashionable, and he usually went a day or two without a shave. He owned a pair of sturdy knee-high boots and a long, belted saffron shirt with a short leather doublet, beneath which he wore dark tartan trews, even in summer, for he'd never quite accustomed himself to the Highland habit of going bare-arsed. When the weather grew cold, he tossed a Scots plaid over one shoulder.

He'd spoken so long with a brogue that he could hardly remember how to speak proper English. After three years of living the lie, he almost believed it himself.

"And ye have the ballocks to call yourself a Scotsman!" cried the lad beside him unexpectedly.

Drew stiffened.

But the lad was yelling at someone else, a half-drunk redbearded fellow who was carrying on about the new queen in a loud bellow. "I'm more Scots than some Catholic tart who's been livin' in France all her life!"

The lad gasped, then spat, "Ye take that back!"

"I won't!" snorted the redbeard.

The lad gave him a hard push.

The man stumbled back a step, spilling a few drops of his ale, but continued his tirade. "What gives the wench the right to sail into my harbor and tell me how to say my prayers?"

The youth raised a puny fist and spoke through his teeth. "Ye'd *better* say your prayers."

The redbeard was too drunk to recognize the threat. "I won't be takin' orders from ye, nor from that French trull."

The lad growled a warning.

Drew groaned inwardly. The last thing he needed was to get caught in a brawl. This wasn't his fight. He wasn't Scots. And he didn't care a whit about the queen. He was already having a miserable day. He didn't need to make it worse.

But the lad was half the redbeard's size. A strong wind would blow him over. Drew couldn't just stand by and watch the young pup get his arse kicked. He laid a restraining palm on the lad's shoulder. "Easy, half-pint."

"He's right!" a third man chimed in from Drew's other side, suddenly placing Drew squarely in the middle of the battle. "No Scot should have to kiss the derriere of a French wench."

The lad shrugged off Drew's hand. "Mary was born here, ye lobcocks!" he insisted, his voice breaking with his vehemence. "She knows our history. She speaks our tongue."

"Ye're a daft grig!" the redbeard crowed, raising his cup of ale. "No sensible Scotsman would let a hen rule the roost, eh, lads? Even John Knox says so!"

Drew grimaced as the surrounding men cheered in accord.

He could practically feel the heat rising off of the angry youth beside him as the lad ground out, "John Knox is a bloody blockhead."

Drew had heard the preachings of John Knox, who was an infamous misogynist, and he had to agree with the lad. But he couldn't afford to be trapped in the midst of a rabid pack of battling Scots. He leaned down to murmur a few words of friendly advice to the reckless youth. "Careful, lad. Ye're outnumbered."

The lad whipped his head around, facing Drew

directly, and answered him with all the fearless passion of youth. "I'll gladly fight them all in Mary's defense."

Drew recoiled, not from the youth's bold boast, but from a startling revelation, a revelation that the men surrounding him had not yet had.

All at once, the crowd began cheering wildly, and the debate was forgotten as everyone turned toward the road. The procession had arrived at last. People clapped and shouted and waved their arms. Some chanted—whether in welcome or mockery, Drew couldn't tell.

Nor did he much care. He was far more interested in his new discovery. He stepped back a pace and let his gaze course down the back of the youth beside him. 'Twas hard to tell with the ill-fitting shirt and the oversized hat, but Drew would have wagered his putting cleek that the brazen half-pint standing beside him, making bold threats and swearing like a sailor, was a lass.

Chapter 4

Josselin was so caught up in the excitement of Mary's arrival that she forgot all about her quarrel with the drunken redbeard. She stood on her toes to try to get a better view as a loud fanfare sounded to announce the procession through Lawnmarket.

This was what she'd come for—to see the Queen, to lay eyes on the ambitious lass who, though not much older than Josselin, had already forged for herself a powerful legacy.

As Alasdair had explained to her, Mary, the descendant of both King Henry VII of England and King James II of Scotland, had not only been wife to the Dauphin of France, but would also now be Queen of Scotland, and might well inherit the English crown from Elizabeth.

Josselin admired Mary's spirit and ambition, for she knew what 'twas like to be a woman, fighting for a significant place in the world of men. This new queen was going to change things. She was sure of it. And Josselin wanted to be a part of that change.

As she peered over the shoulders of the people in front of her, she spied the first wave of the procession. Dozens of yellow-robed Scotsmen disguised as Moors—their limbs blackened and their heads covered with black hats and masks—cleared the way through the flowers the townsfolk had strewn in the wide street. Behind them came the Edinburgh officials, who carried aloft a purple canopy embroidered in gold with French lilies and Scots unicorns.

French soldiers and Scots lairds made up the bulk of the impressive entourage. Behind them, four lasses of Josselin's age rode shoulder to shoulder, and she knew they must be the Four Maries. Seeing their lavish velvet gowns and rich jewels made Josselin curse her guardian all over again for forcing her to disguise herself in his drooping trews and baggy shirt.

Then, beneath the canopy, riding upon a white palfrey, came Queen Mary herself, more magnificent and beautiful than Josselin had imagined. Though Mary had recently lost both her mother and her husband, today she'd discarded her white mourning shroud in favor of a more festive gown of purple velvet with gold embroidery. Jewels twinkled from her neck, waist, and wrists, but they couldn't outshine the charming sparkle in Mary's eyes. As Josselin looked on in awe, the queen nodded regally to the crowd, her face lit up by a serene smile.

A huge, brightly painted triumphal arch had been erected across the road at Lawnmarket, and from the gallery above, a choir of children began to sing. Riding forward, Mary waved to them in greeting.

As she passed beneath the arch, a mechanical globe painted like a cloud slowly opened to reveal a child dressed as an angel. Josselin watched in amazement as the angel was lowered on a rope to hand the queen the keys of the gates.

Then the child began to recite an eloquent welcome to Mary in verse. But as the words became clear, the Catholic queen's smile faltered. Buried in the prose was a thinly veiled reference to the Reformation.

Some in the crowd gasped, and some, including the men Josselin had been arguing with, sent up bellows of approval.

Josselin's blood simmered. Who dared insult the new queen with such obvious blasphemy? She rounded on the redbearded oaf who'd earlier called Mary a tart and shoved him.

Someone gripped her elbow. "Not now, lass," a man murmured into her ear.

It didn't occur to her that he'd called her "lass" at that moment. Her hackles were up, and she was itching for a fight. She wrenched her arm free and shot him a scathing glare over her shoulder.

Then she cast her gaze back to the spectacle before her. The child angel was handing the queen two purple velvet tomes now, a Bible and a Psalter, and Josselin knew without a doubt that they were Reformer books.

"A fittin' gift," the redbeard muttered to his friend, "for the Whore o' Babylon."

"Aye," another added. "'Twill show her she'd best leave the Pope in France."

"Shut your mouths, ye jackanapes!" Josselin fired back, her blood now seething.

Once more, the man behind her seized her arm, this time more forcefully, hissing in a strong Highland accent, "'Tisn't worth it, lass."

Again, she twisted away.

John Knox must be behind this travesty, she decided.

'Twas rumored the Reformer meant to meet with the queen personally very soon in order to challenge her faith. That might be, but by God, Josselin didn't intend to let anyone humiliate Mary today.

"Refuse the books, Your Majesty!" she shouted in encouragement over the crowd. "Go on! Toss them away!"

The Highlander made a choking sound. "Cease, lass. Are ye daft? Don't draw attention—"

The redbeard yelled up at the child suspended from the arch. "'Tis no use tryin' to court Mary, wee angel! She's already wed to Rome!"

The men nearby howled with laughter.

Josselin had had enough. 'Twas bad enough that the new queen had to hold her own against the bloody English without having to deal with detractors among her own countrymen. With a roar, she unsheathed her dagger and faced the redbearded dastard. "Defend your slander with a blade!"

Behind her, the Highlander swore in exasperation.

But the redbeard took one look at her dagger, threw down his cup of ale, and went for his weapon.

"Aye, that's it," Josselin goaded, beckoning him with the fingers of her free hand. "Come on!"

The Highlander stepped suddenly between them to address the drunk. "Ach, man, ye don't want to be doin' that."

"Out o' my way!" the redbeard bellowed.

"Aye," Josselin agreed. "Out o' the way, Highlander, unless ye want to get skewered."

The Highlander turned to her then, filling her vision and sternly commanding her gaze, and for one stunned instant, she couldn't breathe. She hadn't paid much heed to him before, but now she saw he had the face of a dark angel—strong yet sweet. His eyes were the clearest blue she'd ever seen, like the sky on a warm spring day.

His heavy brows lowered as he said pointedly, "Ye can settle this... later."

The redbeard shoved him aside. "Stay out of it, man. 'Tis between the lad and me."

Rattled, Josselin nonetheless managed to raise her knife and face her opponent, eager to resume the duel. "No one insults my queen, ye traitor. Ye'll answer to me for your offense."

"Oh, I'll answer ye," the redbeard assured her. "I'll carve a cross into your flesh to remind ye o' your misbegotten faith."

"Ye won't get the chance," she promised.

"Put your blades away, both o' ye," she heard the Highlander mutter. Nobody paid him heed.

They faced off, and the crowd gave them room.

"Sheathe. *Now*," the Highlander insisted.

She ignored him, waving her dagger at the redbeard like a taunt. But before she could get off a good swipe, the Highlander stepped toward her.

"Fine," he said.

She half-wheeled in his direction, thinking he meant to attack her as well. Instead, he snatched the hat from her head. She gasped as her curls spilled over her shoulders like honey from a crushed comb.

The redbeard's eyes widened, and he retreated, dropping his knife.

Josselin tossed her head, angry that her secret was out. But she wasn't about to call off the fight. Her heart was pounding now, and she was primed for battle.

"What, ye sheep-swiver?" she sneered at the redbeard. "Are ye afraid to fight a woman?" She twirled the dagger once in her fingers. "Pick it up, coward! Pick up your knife."

The crowd had suddenly grown quiet.

"What's wrong with ye?" she challenged. "Is there not a single champion among ye poltroons?" No one moved. "And ye call yourselves men!" she scoffed. "Who stole your tongues and cut off your cods?"

No one answered. There was nothing but tense misgiving and wide eyes in the faces around her.

She frowned in sudden confusion. Then she realized the entire street had grown silent. 'Twas more than a silence of surprise. 'Twas a silence of warning.

The back of her neck began to tingle with apprehension. Slowly, cautiously, she lowered her dagger and turned toward the procession.

Staring at Josselin from atop her noble white steed, a curious, inscrutable half-smile playing upon her royal lips, was Queen Mary herself.

Chapter 5

Josselin gulped. As she stood there, breathless, the queen gave her a thorough inspection, perusing her from her tangled blond hair to her dusty leather boots. After what seemed an eternity, Mary finally passed the Bible and Psalter to her captain, then waved her fingers in a beckoning motion.

Josselin instinctively started to step forward, but the Highlander dug his fingers hard into her shoulders, holding her back.

Mary's gesture hadn't been meant for her, but for one of the royal officials. The distinguished-looking man approached the queen, who bent to whisper something in his ear, nodding toward Josselin.

While Josselin watched with bated breath, Mary gave her a slight dismissive nod, then urged her mount onward down the road, and the procession resumed.

Meanwhile, the official straightened his belt and strode directly toward Josselin. The crowd parted to make way for him.

He was French, tall and thin, perhaps a dozen years older than Josselin, and he looked mildly displeased. He had perceptive brown eyes, a neatly trimmed beard, and a long nose that he probably found useful for looking down on people.

With a curt nod, he introduced himself. "I am the queen's secretary, Philipe de la Fontaine. The queen has commanded that you make yourself known to me. You and I are to have a rendezvous today at The White Hart. You know the place?"

Josselin tried to speak, but her voice refused to come out. Faith, she'd received a command from the queen herself!

The Highlander answered. "I know the inn."

"Very well," the secretary said. He gave Josselin a belittling frown. "I expect to see you there this afternoon, Madame...?"

"Josselin," she managed to croak.

"Zhos-a-lahn," he repeated, using the French pronunciation. Then he gave her a brief, contemptuous inspection. "See if you can stay alive long enough to make the appointment."

The secretary hastened off to catch the royal entourage, and gradually the crowd resumed their chattering. But Josselin's pulse was still racing when the Highlander gently pried the dagger from her white knuckles.

"Ye aren't from around here, are ye, lass?" he murmured.

"Nae," she answered in a daze. "I'm from Selkirk. Holy saints, did ye see that? Did ye see how she—"

"Who brought ye to Edinburgh?"

She stared in wonder after the procession. "I came alone."

"Alone?"

"My da said I could," she said dreamily. The queen was well down the road now, but Josselin kept watching. "As long as I don't talk to strangers. Or go to taverns. Or lose my temper." She smiled. "Ach! Wait till I tell Da that the queen herself—"

"A piece of advice, lass," he confided. "Hie home to Selkirk straight away." He scooped up her hat, dusted it off, and pressed it into her hands. "Ye could be halfway there by afternoon."

She snapped out of her stupor and frowned up at the man with the dark hair and the clear blue eyes, who really was quite handsome . . . for a Highlander. "Home? Why would I want to go home?"

He looked at her as if she were barmy. "Ye aren't thinkin' o' keepin' the appointment?"

"O' course I am. The queen herself commanded it." The sound of that sent a shiver of excitement through her. "The *queen*." She couldn't wait to tell her guardians.

He arched a stern brow. "Look, lass, before ye get your trews in a twist, I don't expect ye're bein' invited to supper."

Supper! That idea hadn't even occurred to her. Was it possible? She tucked the corner of her lip under her teeth, imagining it. Then she recalled, "She smiled at me."

"Royals always smile whilst they're sharpenin' their swords."

She lowered her brows. The damned Highlander was ruining her good mood. "Ach! What would *ye* know?"

"I know ye brought the procession to a halt." He shook his head. "I don't imagine the queen's too pleased about that."

She bit the inside of her cheek. He had a point. Josselin

had made an impression on the queen. But what if 'twas the wrong impression?

"I did draw a blade," she admitted.

"Aye."

"And I *was* brawlin' in the street."

She looked at him uncertainly.

"I've heard in the French courts," he said, eyeing her garments, "they even have strict laws about dress."

She looked down at the overlong hem of her linen shirt, clutching a fistful of it. "Do ye think I offended her?"

He gave her a maddening shrug.

Her shoulders sank. "I didn't mean to offend her."

Then she narrowed her gaze at the Highlander.

"This is all *your* fault!" she decided, swatting his chest with her hat. "If ye hadn't stolen my hat, none o' this would have happened."

His lips curled into a smirk that was half-smile, half-frown. "Oh aye, lass. Instead ye'd be wheezin' at me through a knife hole in your chest."

She scowled at him, jamming the hat back over her head. "Ye've obviously never seen me fight with a blade."

"I've seen enough to know ye've got a hot temper that likely ruins your aim." He handed her dagger back to her, hilt first.

She snatched it from him in irritation and slid it back into its sheath. Her Da Angus had told her the same thing a hundred times. She didn't need to hear it from a bloody Highlander, no matter how handsome he was.

Chapter 6

The crowd began to disperse. Mary's procession was moving toward the Tollbooth. Drew could easily make his escape now, retreat to the comfort of his lodgings, settle in front of the fire with a frothy pint of ale, and forget about the whole upsetting debacle.

But something prevented him. Something with flashing green eyes, wild honey hair, and a filthy mouth. Something that was quickening his pulse and rousing the beast in his trews.

As a rule, Drew kept his distance when it came to exchanges with the natives. The less they knew about him, the better. His dark scowl kept most people away. For those to whom he had to be civil, he'd learned to affect Highland charm to steer the conversation away from personal matters. As for intimate encounters, he employed discreet wenches who charged for their services and their silence.

Why he felt drawn to engage a wee, fiery-tempered, trews-wearing lass who was a danger to herself and others, he didn't know. Surely it had nothing to do with her rosy pink lips, the rough whiskey timbre of her voice, or the thought of what bewitching charms might lie beneath that baggy shirt.

Lord, he thought, shaking his head, he'd spent too many days of late on the links and not enough feeding his carnal appetites.

The lass might be beautiful, but she was trouble. 'Twas a mistake to intervene in the affairs of quarrelsome Scots. And the last thing Drew needed was to draw the notice of their queen.

But he supposed he was obliged to help the maid. She was partly right—it *had* been his idea to expose her. The queen might never have noticed her had it not been for the waving pennant of her dazzling curls.

Besides, be they Scots or English, he'd never been the sort who could walk away from tiny, helpless creatures. Especially ones with sparkling eyes and tempting lips.

He'd at least get the lass out of immediate danger and on the road home. He owed her that much.

He studied the departing entourage to measure its progress.

"Look, lass," he offered, "I'll take ye as far as Roslin." With the current speed of the procession, they had about an hour's advantage.

"I'm not goin'."

"We should leave before the . . ." He swung his head back to her. "What?"

"I'm not goin'." Her arms were crossed stubbornly over her chest.

He checked quickly for witnesses, then lowered his head to whisper, "If ye leave before the procession's o'er, ye can escape ere they know ye're gone."

Her eyes narrowed with disdain. "Spoken like a true

Highlander." She looked him up and down. "If ye get into a scrape, ye just scamper off into the hills, don't ye, never to be heard from again."

He blinked. He believed he'd just been insulted.

"I'm no coward," she told him, "and I'm a woman o' my word. I told the man I'd meet him, and meet him I will."

Despite her brave vow, she was still a wee, naïve country lass from Selkirk who was about to get herself into more trouble than she realized.

He told himself 'twasn't his duty to set wayward innocents on proper paths, particularly not *enemy* wayward innocents.

'Twas folly for an Englishman to traffic with Scots.

'Twas madness to traffic with Scots royals.

And 'twas the height of insanity for Drew to endanger his entire mission of vengeance for an impertinent, foolish, hot-tempered brat of a lass he'd just met who clearly didn't want his aid.

But, God help him, the words rushed out of his mouth before he could stop them. "Fine. I'll escort ye to The White Hart then."

She lifted her impertinent, pointy chin. "Nae, ye go along. Shoo. Run off into the hills. 'Tisn't your fight."

'Twasn't his fight. The people here could worship the Pope, the Heavenly Father, or the ancient Celtic gods as far as he cared.

But now the lass had insulted his honor and issued a challenge. He straightened proudly, fixing her with a stern gaze.

"I'm no coward either, lass," he bit out. "Let's go. 'Twas me who sliced ye into the rough. I'll be damned if I won't chip ye out of it."

Her forehead creased in mild confusion.

He smirked. He *had* spent too much time on the links.

"Come along, lass," he said with a resigned sigh, offering his arm. "Whatever the queen's intent, after sufferin' the sneers of her high and mighty secretary, we could both use a pint."

She refused his arm, but let him accompany her as they weaved their way down Lawnmarket, past the tall buildings that stood shoulder to shoulder along the street. They made an admittedly odd pair—an Englishman in the guise of a Highlander escorting a lass in the guise of a lad. For someone accustomed to blending in with the crowd, Drew felt dangerously exposed as they ambled down the Royal Mile.

Still, he'd sworn to accompany the lass to the inn. He supposed if he was marching to his execution, he might as well do it with a pretty wench at his side.

Josselin grew curiously quiet as they walked past the crowded shops. When Drew gave her a sidelong glance, he saw that she was worrying her bottom lip with her teeth. The closer they got to their destination, the tighter she knitted her brows. Apparently, the stouthearted maid wasn't quite as stouthearted as she pretended to be.

In golf, when Drew was faced with the prospect of a particularly daunting match, he found it best not to dwell on the game too much. A bit of distraction was beneficial. Perhaps he could distract the lass from her worries with his Highland charm.

"So tell me, lass . . . Jossy, is it?"

"Josselin."

"Tell me, Jossy," he said, ignoring her disapproving scowl, "where did ye get your trews? From your father?

Brother? Lover?" He cocked a brow. "Or is that what all the lasses are wearin' in Selkirk?"

She gave him a long-suffering glare. "My da."

"Ah, the same da who warned ye away from strangers... and taverns... and losin' your temper?"

She sighed. "Aye."

"Did he also teach ye to fight with a knife?"

"Nae, that was my other da."

That stopped him in his tracks. "Your *other* da? How many do ye have?"

"Three."

"Three?" *That* she needed to explain. He reached for her elbow, hauling her around to face him.

She instantly wheeled on him with her dagger drawn. "Get your bloody—"

Before she could finish, he'd seized her wrist and plucked the blade from her.

Her jaw dropped.

He, too, was startled. He hadn't needed his defensive reflexes in a while. It appeared they were still in good working order.

After a moment of mutually shocked silence, they spoke at the same time.

"What the...?"

"How did...?"

"Sorry."

"I didn't mean..."

"Reflexes."

"Instincts."

They avoided one another's eyes, finally exchanging brief sheepish smiles.

He returned her dagger.

She sheathed it.

After an awkward moment, they resumed their journey, turning left down Grassmarket.

In the prolonged silence, Drew stole sideways glances at Josselin, who looked strangely adorable in her floppy hat and her baggy trews. 'Twas hard to believe such a sweet-faced kitten had such sharp claws. He wondered if she possessed sinuous feline curves as well beneath that voluminous clothing.

Before long, the lass started biting nervously at her lip again, and Drew was struck with the most profoundly mad urge to kiss her fretful mouth. Indeed, he decided that if he weren't sure she'd run him through, he'd be glad to distract her from her worries with a kiss. Seduction was the best diversion he knew.

Lord, what was he thinking? He was already taking far too many chances in escorting the lass. The wise thing would be to bid her a quick farewell at the inn and, considering the wicked bent of his thoughts, perhaps take himself to the nearest bawdyhouse.

In the meantime, he'd continue with the second-best diversion he knew—conversation.

"Knife-fightin', eh? I suppose 'tis a good skill for your three da's to teach ye," he said with a shrug, adding pointedly, "if they're goin' to let ye wander loose on your own."

"Wander loose?" she echoed. "I'm not a bloody sheep. I'll be damned if I need watchin' o'er."

"Ach, lass!" he said, wincing. "Did ye learn the filthy language from your fathers as well?"

She pierced him with a glare.

"Nae?" He shook his head, allowing a gleam of

mischief to enter his eyes. "Well, I've never heard such words from a lass... at least not outside o' the Canongate stews."

Her eyes widened at his wicked suggestion, then closed to smoldering green slits. Apparently unable to think of a vile enough retort that wouldn't further prove his point, she resorted to giving him a hearty punch in the arm.

Drew figured he deserved it. Josselin was no more a harlot than he was the Archbishop of St. Andrews. The way she whipped out her blade at the slightest provocation, 'twas surely a rare man who got within arm's reach of her. And with three fathers hovering about, he doubted the lass had so much as been pecked upon the cheek.

He rubbed at the place she'd struck him. "Marry, ye've got a strong arm on ye, Jossy," he said, his eyes twinkling. "Maybe ye're a caber-tosser then."

She gave him a sarcastic smirk. "Aye, that's it. So ye'd better beware, Highlander. One wrong move, and I'll toss ye on your bloody arse."

He clucked his tongue at her swearing. "Dreadful."

The White Hart was just ahead. He almost regretted arriving so soon. No matter that she was Scots, Josselin was surely the most refreshingly forthright and entertaining lass he'd met in a while. He'd almost be sorry to leave her.

"What about ye?" she asked. "Shepherd or cattle thief?"

He chuckled. Lowlanders assumed all Highlanders were one or the other. "Neither."

"Then what's your trade?"

"I golf."

"Golf?" she scoffed. "'Tisn't a trade."

"'Tis if ye win."

They stopped below the sign of The White Hart—a green background with the head of a white deer painted on it.

"And I suppose ye win all the time?" she asked, freeing the tankard from her belt.

"Most o' the time."

"Good." She pushed her way through the door of the inn. "Then *ye* can buy the beer."

Chapter 7

The instant Josselin stepped inside, a sense of ease came over her. Though she'd never set foot in The White Hart before, everything was familiar: the dim, crowded room with a crackling fire on the hearth, the clatter of dice, the chatter of tipplers, the pungent aromas of strong ale, mutton pies, and aged leather.

She'd spent a good part of the last seven years working in Kate's tavern. 'Twasn't exactly the safest place for a young lass, but Will had always been a whistle away, and he'd taught her at an early age to defend herself from drunken patrons with straying hands.

Poor Will. She realized now that she'd broken all three of the promises she'd made to her loyal guardian.

She'd lost her temper.

She'd trafficked with a stranger.

And she was about to spend the afternoon in a tavern by herself.

No, she corrected, not by herself. The stranger had insisted on coming with her.

She didn't mind too much. He was pleasant enough to look at, despite his dearth of Highland charm.

Besides, the truth was her purse had grown dangerously light. The cost of the inn where she was staying had been unexpectedly exorbitant, especially considering its absence of a level floor and proper shutters. She had just enough coin left to purchase one night of lodging, one loaf of bread, and one jack of ale for the trek home. As long as he was paying, she could use an extra pint to steady her nerves.

"Two beers," the Highlander called out to the tavern wench, unhooking his own tankard and banging the two cups on the counter.

"Your finest!" Josselin amended as they headed toward a small table in the corner. "And don't be waterin' it down."

The Highlander arched a brow at her.

"'Tis my trade," she explained dryly, "between tossin' cabers. I work at a tavern in Selkirk."

"Ah."

They took their seats, and when the beer arrived, Josselin took a cautious sip. 'Twasn't bad. Not as good as Kate's, of course, but passable. She wasn't about to complain. The Highlander had paid for it, and she knew better than to look a gift horse in the mouth.

She lifted her tankard in a salute and took one healthy swallow. Then another. And another. Once begun, she couldn't stop. She hadn't realized how badly the morn's events had rattled her. The bracing drink seemed like a magic elixir.

"God's bones!" the Highlander whispered in alarm. "Slow down, lass."

With an embarrassed sniff, she set her half-empty tankard on the table, wrapping her hands around it possessively.

"Don't ye want your wits about ye?" he asked.

Actually, she was tempted to drink herself into oblivion.

He shook his head, and one corner of his lip turned up in merriment. He reached into the small satchel at his waist, producing a linen handkerchief. He motioned her forward.

Wary of his intentions, she leaned tentatively toward him.

Before she could compose herself to resist, he captured her chin in one hand and, with the other, began dabbing with the handkerchief at her frothy upper lip.

Maybe 'twas the shock of the morning. Maybe 'twas the half-pint of ale she'd just quaffed. But instead of telling him to keep his hands to himself and blackening his eye, she let him attend to her.

His fingers were warm against her cheek, and his touch was surprisingly gentle. He was so close she could discern the stubble on his face and the half-amused, half-irritated glitter in his eyes.

"There," he said, finishing and tucking the handkerchief away. "Ye don't want to look like a mad dog, foamin' at the mouth, when Mary's man comes."

Josselin glanced down at her beer, wishing more than ever she could gulp down the contents and order another. The prospect of meeting the queen's secretary wasn't half as unsettling as the notion that she'd allowed the Highlander to put his hands on her.

The Highlander. Lord, she didn't even know the man's name.

"Thank ye..." She glanced up expectantly.

"Drew."

"Drew."

He saluted her with his tankard and took a few swallows. "So tell me, Jossy, how is it ye come to have three da's?"

She shrugged. "My mother and father both died when I was a bairn. The three men who found me looked after me."

"I'm sorry."

She took a sip of beer and wrinkled her nose. "I don't remember my parents, not at all."

He stared into his beer, and an inscrutable sweet sorrow came into his eyes. "Maybe 'tis better that way."

She wondered what had saddened him, but she didn't ask. Her Da Alasdair had taught her 'twasn't polite to pry. Besides, the man would likely be gone in an hour, and she'd never see him again, so what was the point?

Instead, she finished her drink, careful not to leave foam on her lip this time. Then she set the tankard down, tapping idly on its rim and eyeing the tavern wench.

"Can ye handle another?" Drew asked.

"Are ye buyin'?"

He smiled and summoned the maid.

Josselin knew she probably shouldn't drink another. She'd had nothing for breakfast, and on an empty stomach, she'd soon be feeling the full effects of the beer.

But every time she relived the events of the morn and thought about their possible consequences, she felt like she needed a good swallow of something to wash away the taste of fear in her mouth.

What she'd told Drew was true. She'd never run in her life. She'd never let fear master her. And she didn't intend to start now.

Still, another fortifying pint wouldn't be unwelcome.

"Another ale for my friend here," Drew told the tavern wench.

The maid smiled coyly, giving the Highlander a thorough perusal, then picked up Josselin's empty tankard without sparing her a glance. If she had, she might have noticed that Josselin wasn't the lad she appeared to be.

Instead, the wench sidled up to Drew and said in a silky voice, "We don't get many o' your kind here. I've oft wondered, what is it ye Highlanders wear under your saffron shirt?"

"I assure ye, lass," he said with a suggestive lift of his brow, "there's nothin' *worn* under my—"

"Ach!" Josselin spat in disgust, "If I hear that jest one more time..." She smirked at the maid. "Don't ye have beer-pourin' to do?"

The maid was so astonished, she almost dropped the tankard. Josselin waved her away.

Halfway through her second beer, Josselin began to feel its soothing effects as her shoulders relaxed and a pleasant buzzing filled her head. She gazed casually over the top of her cup at the Highlander, who was staring into the fire with a faraway frown.

He resembled some beautiful, dark, wild avenging angel that might grace the wall of a chapel. His hair was in need of taming, and his jaw was shaded where he hadn't shaved for a few days. His nose was straight, broad, and strong, and his mouth had a sweet curve to it, as if he were on the verge of a grin. But his eyes were most remarkable. They were deep-set and intense, shaded by heavy brows that seemed to be set in a permanent scowl, and their color was as clear and pure as a bluebottle blossom.

She wondered what he was thinking about as he gazed into the flickering firelight. Was he imagining his Highland home? Plotting a cattle raid? Pining for some long-lost mistress?

His gaze never left the hearth as he told her flatly, "Ye shouldn't stare, lass. 'Tis rude."

She averted her eyes, which wasn't easy, considering how languid they'd suddenly become. "I wasn't starin'. I was...glancin'."

He brought his gaze around. A twinkle lurked in his eyes. "Aye? And what were ye glancin' at?"

"Nothin'. I was just..." Her glance caught on his tankard. "I was wonderin' if ye were goin' to drink the rest o' that?"

"In time," he said.

She tried to raise a brow in challenge, though, in her condition, it may have only given her a quizzical look. "I'd heard Highlanders could outdrink Lowlanders, three to one."

"So they say. But do ye know why?"

"Why?"

He leaned toward her. She leaned toward him. His eyes danced with mirth.

"Highlanders can't count for shite."

Chapter 8

The unexpected laughter that bubbled out of the lass was as charming and infectious as a merry madrigal. Seeing her bright smile and her shining eyes, Drew forgot for a moment that she was his foe.

But as he glanced around the tavern, he saw that her giggling had drawn the interested gazes of several other patrons, and his grin faded. Attention was the last thing he wanted.

He'd intended to bid the lass good-day at the door, but she'd practically dragged him into the inn. So he'd chosen the darkest corner of the room in the hopes of avoiding notice.

Now it seemed that wasn't to be. Josselin, with her radiant looks and her unbridled spirit, couldn't help being the center of attention.

His only hope then was to distance himself from her as soon as possible.

But the way the wolves in the room were perusing her now—narrowing their eyes and licking their lips as if to devour her—he couldn't very well abandon the little lamb, especially not in her present state. She might not be fully sotted, but Scots beer was markedly strong, and she was definitely tipsy.

Maybe a bit of food would temper her intoxication.

"Are ye hungry?" he asked.

"If ye're buyin', I'm famished."

He snorted. The lass certainly had no qualms about spending his coin. But then she was a Scot. Notoriously close-fisted with their own purses, they had little trouble squandering away the wealth of others. He'd learned that more than once on the golf course, trying to collect his winnings.

He waved the tavern wench over and ordered two servings of whatever skink was simmering on the fire.

Once the stew arrived, Josselin proved as straightforward in her supping as she was in her speech. She didn't pick at her food, as most maids did. She dove in eagerly without wasting a drop and finished before he was halfway done.

For a small thing, she could certainly pack away a respectable meal.

"More?" he asked, indicating his own portion.

She paused, considering his offer, then politely shook her head.

"I had an enormous breakfast," he lied. Actually, he'd had two buttered oatcakes and a cup of ale, but since he wasn't golfing today, he wasn't very hungry. "I don't think I can finish it."

Her tongue flicked out involuntarily, and he pushed the bowl toward her.

"If ye insist," she said.

While she polished off his barley skink, he glowered in threat at the men in the inn, hoping his black looks would dissuade them from coming anywhere near the lass, even after he was gone.

He was about to tell Josselin that he had to be off when she happened to glance toward the door behind him, and a flicker of recognition lit her eyes.

" 'Tis him," she breathed.

Drew cursed silently, but didn't turn around. How the devil had the man gotten here so quickly? Drew had hoped to be long gone by the time the secretary arrived.

Now what would he do? 'Twas difficult enough to maintain his anonymity among common Scots. But to sit across from a bloody French noble...

He tensed, prepared to bid the lass a swift farewell and make his escape. Then he made the mistake of glancing up at her again.

She'd raised her chin a notch, putting on a brave face as she watched the man approach. But her lower lip trembled slightly, and she gulped as her fingers tightened around her tankard.

He couldn't just leave the poor lass. That would amount to desertion.

With a sigh of self-mockery, Drew reached out to squeeze her hand. "I won't let him have ye."

Even *he* didn't know what that meant. But the words seemed to soothe her. She nodded and loosed her hand to lift it in greeting to the Frenchman.

The man was no friendlier than he'd been on the Royal Mile, acting as if whatever task he'd been set to was far beneath his station.

"I would speak to you alone, Madame," he informed her, giving Drew a pointed glare.

She looked uneasy for an instant, but quickly masked her fears. "O' course." She gave him a tremulous smile.

Drew assailed the man with his most charming Highland grin, assuring Josselin, "I'll wait near the door, darlin'. If ye need anythin', just give me a wink."

He winked at her, then stood to give the secretary his seat. 'Twas tempting to pull it out from under him, but Drew resisted the urge.

What madness had possessed Drew to pose as Josselin's guardian, he didn't know. Nor did he much care to ponder it.

'Twas the height of recklessness. He had no idea what the secretary intended. But if the sneer on the man's face was any indication, the lass wasn't going to like his news. All Drew knew was that if he threatened Josselin, if he laid one bony finger upon her...

What? Drew wondered as he commandeered a table by the door. Would he box the man's ears? Pull a dagger on the fellow? Challenge Queen Mary's personal secretary to a duel?

Hopefully 'twouldn't come to that. In the meantime, he'd watch the man like a hawk.

When Philipe de la Fontaine took the seat across from her, Josselin had two simultaneous opposing thoughts. One was that she shouldn't have drunk so much beer. The other was that she wanted nothing more than to seize her tankard and gulp down the rest of its contents.

'Twasn't that the pinch-nosed nobleman frightened her. She wasn't easily intimidated by men. Her da's had trained her well. What troubled her was that she'd wanted so badly to make a good impression on the new queen. And she was deathly afraid she'd ruined her chances.

"You may have noticed," the secretary intoned, "that you caught the eye of the queen."

She swallowed hard. "Aye."

"Her Majesty was quite..." He searched for the word. Disgruntled? Offended? Enraged?

"Intrigued by you."

Josselin blinked. Intrigued? That wasn't bad, was it? "I see," she said carefully.

Behind Philipe's shoulder, she glimpsed the Highlander, seated by the door, scowling as if he could burn a hole in the secretary's back.

Philipe continued, oblivious to Drew's smoldering stare. "Her Majesty likes your spirit, your loyalty, your..." He shuddered. "Attire."

Josselin's gaze snapped back to the secretary. "My attire?"

He shrugged, as befuddled by the news as Josselin was.

"It is not my place to question the queen," he said, indicating with a sharp look that 'twasn't hers either. "Her Majesty has sent me to make you an offer of employment."

Josselin's heart skipped. "Employment?"

The tavern wench came briskly to the table, and the secretary asked, "You have French wine?"

"Nae, m'lord," she said, "only beer and ale and a wee bit o' Madeira."

Philipe shooed her away, muttering, "Dozens of taverns in this city and not a drop of good French wine."

"An offer, you said?" Josselin reminded him, breathless with anticipation.

"Yes, yes. The queen desires to reward your loyalty. She has sent me to find out your qualifications." He sniffed in scorn. "I already know you have a penchant for wreaking havoc. Do you have any other skills?"

Josselin was stunned silent. The very opportunity she'd hoped for—to serve the new queen—had fallen into her lap.

Thrilling images flashed through her mind... accepting a commission from the queen... leading a charge on the battlefield like a Scots Jeanne d'Arc... celebrating victory over the English at a royal dinner...

"Cooking?" the secretary blandly inquired. "Sewing? Spinning wool?"

Josselin frowned in disappointment.

He pursed his lips in distaste. "Or do you make your husband keep the house?"

"He's not my..." She took a deep breath. She had to make her intentions clear, which wasn't easy when her brain was swimming in beer. "I'm not a servant."

He stiffened. "In the court of Queen Mary," he announced regally, "we are all servants."

This wasn't going well at all. "I didn't mean... That is to say..."

He spoke slowly, as if he were addressing a child. "What is it you do all day, Madame? Besides inciting riots."

"I serve beer at a tavern in Selkirk." Then she straightened proudly and added, "But I'm good with a blade and my fists. Both of my parents fought in battles against the English—my father at Solway Moss, my mother at Ancrum Moor. I've held a sword since I was three years—"

He held up a hand to stop her, taking a sudden keen interest. "You're a tavern wench?"

"Aye," she said cautiously.

"And how long have you been employed?"

She shrugged. "Seven years." She didn't want to talk about serving beer. She wanted to talk about swordfighting.

"Seven years," he repeated.

"Aye. I started when I was twelve."

"Ah, you know your numbers." He nodded, impressed. "I don't suppose you are able to read as well?" he asked doubtfully.

"Aye. I keep the accounts for the tavern."

"Indeed?" He leaned back and studied her, stroking his neatly trimmed beard in speculation. "I may have a suitable position for you, after all."

Josselin waited for him to elaborate, but he only continued to peruse her, narrowing his eyes, pursing his lips, pensively tapping his cheek.

"Aye?" she blurted.

"Tell me," he said. "Can you keep a secret, or are you one of those maids who cannot stop her jaws from flapping?"

Josselin answered stonily. "I can keep a secret."

"On pain of death?"

Now he was speaking a language she could understand. "Aye."

"I wonder."

She furrowed her brows. The beer made her less cautious than usual. She leaned forward and bit out, "Ye can ask me that after what I did on the streets? Ye doubt my devotion to the queen? I defended Her Majesty against—"

"Reckless violence is not the same thing as devotion.

I need to know if you would give your life to keep the queen safe."

"In the beat of a heart." She'd been trained from the time she could barely walk to do just that. She'd fight with her last breath and die if she must. But she didn't intend to die. She intended to succeed where her mother had failed.

"So he is not your husband," Philipe said, gesturing with a nod of his head over his shoulder. "Who is he?"

She glanced at Drew. In her excitement, she'd almost forgotten about the Highlander. He was leaning back against the wall now, but his eyes were fixed on the secretary with a steely stare, and he was drumming his fingers on the table with calculated impatience.

"Nobody," she said.

"You're sure?"

"He knew the way to the inn, that's all."

He studied her eyes, as if to gauge the truth of her words.

"Do ye wish me to send him away?" she asked.

"No. That would arouse suspicion. But you must tell no one, *no one*, what I am about to tell you."

Josselin nodded soberly. If there was one thing at which she excelled, 'twas keeping secrets. The secrets of Queen Mary she would take to her grave.

Chapter 9

Drew sat back with feigned indifference, all the while watching Philipe de la Fontaine's every move. He wished he'd chosen a closer table. Unable to hear over the rolling dice and cheering players, the best Drew could do was watch for trouble.

Why he should worry, he didn't know. The lass might look as pretty and delicate as an English peach, but she was more lethal than a thistle tipped with poison. If Philipe made any wrong moves, she'd likely pull a blade on the poor fool.

Still, from what he'd seen of her so far, Josselin of Selkirk seemed to attract trouble, and this might prove to be more than she could handle alone.

They were talking rather animatedly, and so far Jossy was holding her own with the royal secretary rather than cowering in fear or misplaced humility.

But when the man pulled out a scroll of vellum and a quill from his penner and uncorked his inkhorn on the table, Drew straightened.

The secretary began writing something on the page while Jossy grimly looked on.

Still, the lass didn't seem to be in distress. She didn't try to garner Drew's attention. She didn't wave. She didn't wink. She didn't so much as glance his way.

Finally, the secretary reversed the page and handed her the pen, and Drew fought the urge to bolt forward and tear the vellum out of her hands.

What was she signing? A letter of apology? A writ of guilt? Her own death warrant?

He tried to read her face, but 'twas nigh impossible to read the face of a stranger. Was her expression calm stoicism? Resigned defeat? Silent dread? When she passed the paper back to the secretary, her countenance was as solemn as the grave.

The secretary fanned the ink to dry it, then rolled the document and slipped it inside his doublet. He scrawled something on another small scrap of paper and handed it to Jossy, who nodded and tucked it covertly into her knife sheath. Finally, to Drew's astonishment, the secretary counted out several silver coins into her palm.

Drew decided the lass had an uncanny knack for relieving men of their riches.

The Frenchman rose to go then, sketching an elegant bow of farewell.

Drew's instincts told him not to confront the man. If Philipe de la Fontaine intended to harm the lass, Drew reasoned, he wouldn't be leaving her unguarded, nor would he have paid her silver. So as Philipe turned, Drew dropped his head onto his arms atop the table as if he'd passed out and began snoring loudly.

He didn't look up again until the door closed behind Philipe. Then he cast a quick glance at Jossy, who sat deep in thought, staring at the age-warped planks of the floor.

He approached her, tempted to demand what the bloody hell she'd just signed. But knowing he'd catch no flies with vinegar, he summoned up his Highland charm.

"So," he said with a wink, "the Frenchman didn't come to drag ye off to gaol after all."

She looked startled, but recovered quickly. "Nae." She gave him an evasive smile. "He only wished to convey the queen's appreciation."

"Appreciation?" he asked, lowering himself to the vacant chair.

"For my loyalty. For defendin' her name."

"Ah."

He signaled the tavern wench for another beer. He hadn't intended on staying, but now that the immediate danger was past, his curiosity got the best of him.

Jossy elaborated. "With John Knox and his ilk tarnishin' her good name, the queen is grateful for loyal subjects."

"Is that so?" He tapped a finger twice on the tabletop in front of her. "And was that a document of appreciation ye were signin' then?"

His question rattled her, but she managed an answer. "'Twas a...'twas an invitation." He noticed, however, she wouldn't look him in the eyes.

"An invitation from the queen," he said with a low whistle of amazement. "To dinner?"

"Nae."

"What then?"

He could almost see the gears whirring in her head as she tried to come up with a suitable lie. In the end, she forfeited.

"I'm not at liberty to say," she told him haughtily.

Drew's beer arrived at that moment, and he was glad of the interruption, for it gave him time to ponder her words.

What would she have signed that she didn't want him to know about? What kind of deal had she made with the devil? Had the man blackmailed her? Indentured her? Or worse? And what had he scribbled onto that scrap of paper?

Whatever he'd written, 'twas apparent that Philipe de la Fontaine wasn't finished with the lass.

Drew had to get a look at that note.

Even while a small voice in his ear told him that he was a fool, that he should look after his own affairs and leave the lass to hers, he couldn't shake off the fear that Jossy had somehow just signed away her life, that she'd trapped herself in some royal intrigue that was far more perilous than anything she'd encountered in the sleepy village of Selkirk, and that 'twas his fault.

Josselin's head was spinning. She felt as if she were balancing at the edge of a cliff, peering down at the loch below, about to plunge into unfamiliar waters. The current might carry her safely, or she might drown in the murky depths. But now that she'd committed to the leap, everything was in the hands of fate.

Philipe had made her the most amazing, dangerous, exciting offer. As unbelievable as it seemed, he'd asked Josselin to serve as part of the queen's network of spies. Philipe had told her that women were often employed in intelligence-gathering because they were least likely to arouse suspicion. Not even the queen herself would be aware that Josselin was her spy. Mary would simply believe that Philipe had found work for Josselin selling beer.

The secretary had already enlisted male spies in the field to infiltrate John Knox's ranks and gather information about the Reformation uprising, but he had to have a secure method for collecting that information. He needed someone who appeared harmless, who could move easily in various circles, who could make contact with the queen's agents beneath the noses of the most dangerous Reformers.

The men of Scotland, Philipe had told her, had two great passions—golf and beer. In Edinburgh, when there was a golf match afoot, every man with five pence in his purse would buy a pint with four pence and wager his last penny on the game. Peasant, noble, merchant, clergyman—it made no difference. When there was gambling to be done and beer to be drunk, all Scots partook equally.

In the diverse crowds that attended golf matches, clandestine contacts could be easily made. And a beer-wagon set up beside the course was the perfect contrivance for the exchange of encrypted messages. The queen's spies need only buy a pint of beer from Josselin to slip her their missive, which she could later deliver to Philipe at this very inn.

"Another pint to celebrate disaster averted?" offered the Highlander, proving Philipe's point about Scots and their drink.

"What?" she said distractedly. "Oh, nae, thank ye." There was much to do, and she had to order her thoughts.

"I'm buyin'," he tempted.

"Nae, I've had quite enough." With effort, she turned her pensive scowl into a wide-eyed smile. Philipe had warned her to do nothing to arouse suspicion.

"Somethin' more to eat then?"

"Nae." She needed to make several purchases. Philipe had said he'd provide a horsecart and driver for her, as well as taking care of her lodging here at the inn. But she'd have to buy provender and clothing—women's clothing—and settle up with her current innkeeper. She also needed to find someone to carry a missive to Selkirk so her da's wouldn't fret over her. She couldn't reveal many details, of course, but she'd tell them not to worry, that she'd secured a position in the queen's service and was living safely in Edinburgh.

"At least let me walk ye to your lodgin's," the Highlander offered.

"That won't be necessary," she began, then realized her swift dismissal might seem suspicious. After all, the man had brought her to the inn, bought her food and drink, and offered to protect her. He'd expect a little gratitude. "I mean, ye've done so much already."

" 'Twas nothin'," he assured her.

"Ye really needn't trouble yourself."

" 'Tis no trouble."

"I wouldn't dream of askin' ye to—"

"I insist."

Somehow she'd known he'd say that. The Highlander seemed to enjoy insisting. First he'd insisted on escorting her to the inn. Then he'd insisted she finish his meal. Now he was insisting she let him accompany her to her lodgings. And that coy little wink of his didn't make his insistence any less irritating.

"Fine," she said. "But I don't intend to dally."

Taking her words to heart, he saluted her with his tankard, then upended it, guzzling the beer with all the untempered expedience she'd expect from a Highlander, and banging it down on the table. "Shall we?"

She shook her head, wondering if he'd make it to the inn before he passed out. The Highlanders' reputation notwithstanding, the man clearly had no capacity for beer. She'd stolen a peek at him a moment ago, and he'd been slouched over the table, snoring into his tankard.

Chapter 10

Glancing down at the delectable lass beside him as they ambled down the streets of Edinburgh, Drew thought he might have made a mistake, downing that last beer. If ever he needed a clear head, 'twas now. But every time he caught the glint of sunshine on Jossy's curls or watched the confident swing of her arms or glimpsed the upper curve of her creamy breast when her oversized shirt happened to gap away, as it did just then...

'Twas surely the beer causing the buzzing in his head. Ordinarily, he'd not give the wayward lass a second glance. Aye, she was pretty, the same way a wicked faery or a thistle blossom was pretty. She was far too full of fire and mischief for his taste. He preferred his women agreeable, predictable, and English. Didn't he?

"'Tis just up the lane," she said dismissively. "I'm sure I'll be safe now."

He frowned. How had they traveled so far so fast? He still hadn't had so much as a glimpse of that note. He'd have to move more quickly.

"I'll see ye to the door," he told her, glancing down at her knife sheath, where he knew the missive was hidden.

" 'Twould be a travesty to have come so far, only to be accosted by—"

The words stuck in his throat as she turned and her baggy shirt slipped off of one shoulder, exposing supple flesh that looked as smooth and delicious as honey.

She smirked. "Who would accost *me*—a lass clad in men's clothing?" She shook her head as if he were a dolt, then turned to start down the alley.

He had to think fast, which wasn't easy when the blood was rushing from one's head to one's nether regions.

"Wait," he said, loping up to her.

Her smile was bright, if a little strained. "Thank ye, sir, for bein' a gentleman. 'Tisn't somethin' I'd expect from a...well, a Highlander. But now that I'm home safe, I must *insist*," she said, borrowing his phrase, "that ye be on your way."

The lass was right. A real Highlander wouldn't bow politely and let his quarry escape. A real Highlander would damn well take what he wanted.

Silently cursing the desperation that made him act so ignobly, and praying his reflexes weren't completely dulled by beer, Drew reached out, caught Jossy's arm, and hauled her into an embrace.

The instant his lips touched hers, he heard her sharp intake of breath and feared he'd shortly feel the prick of her knife. But it didn't come.

What came instead felt like a brand searing his soul.

She tasted like summer—warm and ripe and sweet. Her mouth was soft and much more yielding than her dry wit and caustic tongue had led him to expect.

Still she didn't stab him.

He increased the pressure of his lips, sinking into the

kiss like a child tasting his first peach—surprised, then pleased, then intoxicated by the sweetness. He began to feel delightfully drunk, a sensation that had nothing to do with beer.

Still, by some miracle, Jossy let him live.

True, her left fist, which pushed ineffectually at his chest, was trapped between them. But as he'd hoped, she'd drawn her knife with her right hand, likely dislodging the missive, and that hand was perfectly capable of killing him.

Emboldened by her lack of violent response, Drew pulled her closer against him, deepening the kiss. He tangled one hand in her silky curls, knocking off her hat, and slanted his mouth across hers as if claiming her for his own. The blood flowed hot in his veins, sang in his ears, rushed to his loins.

'Twas madness, what he was doing, and in a moment he was sure he'd be skewered. But he couldn't stop himself. Whether 'twas the strong Scots brew, the sultry September afternoon, or his long abstinence, Drew felt incapable of tearing himself away from the pleasure of the moment. He was drowning in a sea of desire, and there was nothing he could do to resist the Siren dragging him down.

Then she made that sound.

'Twasn't anything, really. Just a small moan. The kind of sound a child might make in her sleep, as soft as the mew of a nursing kitten.

But that innocent sound struck at the sweet spot of Drew's lust, driving him straight toward the point of no return.

He answered with a groan that came from the depths of his manhood, and, fueled by his own primitive response, he feasted upon her with increasing urgency, nudging her lips apart to taste the fruit within.

If she were going to kill him, she'd surely do it now. And he'd probably never even feel the prick of the blade.

Josselin knew her hand was around her knife. She could feel the worn leather grip in her palm. And there was no mistake that the Highlander was overstepping his bounds, committing the most grievous insult upon her person. She should by all means use her blade on him.

'Twas what her da's had prepared her for—defending herself against the improper advances of a wicked stranger.

But somehow, though the knife was in her hand and she knew how to use it, she couldn't force herself to plunge the blade into the Highlander's gut.

In fact, at the moment, she couldn't force herself to let go of the man's shirt. Or twist out of his arms. Or tear herself away from his mouth.

Some devil had a hold of her, and she'd be damned if she could resist his temptation.

With a savage groan, the Highlander pressed her back against the stone wall, pinning her there with his mass, devouring her with the desperation of a starving animal.

She should have been terrified. No one had ever taken such liberties with her, cornering her and kissing her with such blatant possession.

At the very least, she should have been furious with the brute. Seduction was a low form of betrayal.

Instead, she felt wildly alive. Her heart raced, and heat unfurled in her body like a blossoming rose. She gasped against his mouth, which was rough and foreign and male.

They were not gasps of pain, but a curious breathlessness that kept her hungering for more.

The Highlander must have slipped some intoxicating poison into her beer, she decided, one that stole her will-power, dizzied her senses, and made her throb in places no man had ever touched.

Worse, it made her respond in kind, clinging to him like ivy to a wall, slaking her feverish thirst upon his lips, moaning as if he somehow tortured the sound out of her.

'Twas the clatter of her knife on the cobblestones, dropped from her slack fingers, that broke the enchant-ment. She gasped, and they both drew back in horror.

Rattling his head as if to clear it of cobwebs, the High-lander bent to seize her dropped weapon.

Flustered, Josselin wiped the back of her mouth with a trembling hand. She tried to snap at him, but her voice came out in a hoarse whisper. "I should skewer ye for that."

He lifted a brow over one languid eye. "Probably." Despite confiscating her knife, as he hunkered there before her, the Highlander seemed as curiously vulner-able as she felt.

"Is that all ye have to say?" she demanded. Lord, his eyes smoldered like live coals. And his mouth looked absolutely...delicious.

He came slowly to his feet. "If ye think I'm goin' to say I'm sorry," he said, passing her the knife, hilt-first, "I'm not."

She bit her lip. She wasn't exactly sorry either. She'd never felt anything quite so thrilling. But 'twas very unchivalrous of him not to accept the blame.

She sheathed her knife. "I was right," she bit out. "Ye're

nothin' but a savage Highlander, swivin' anythin' that'll stand still. I should have jabbed ye while I could. And I will if ye follow me. Go on now. Go back to your sheep."

She swept up her hat, jammed it back on her head, and turned on her heel. Then she stomped off in the direction of the inn before Drew could see the confusing glow of arousal and humiliation coloring her skin.

He may not have followed her, but she felt his hot gaze tracing her all the way down the lane. She swore she wouldn't look back at him. And she didn't. Until she arrived at the door of the inn.

The Highlander was standing just where she'd left him. But now he leaned with cocky arrogance against the wall, waving something over his head like a taunt.

Suddenly, her heart seized and her eyes widened. She clapped a hand to her knife sheath. The note from Philipe!

She narrowed her eyes, steeling herself for the worst.

"Ye lose somethin'?" he called out.

She mouthed a silent oath.

Damn the rake! How had he...?

Transfixed by the incriminating scrap of paper grasped between his careless fingers, Josselin worried her lip. The Highlander had no idea what he possessed or how important 'twas.

He continued to wave the note with maddening negligence. "I believe ye dropped this!" he yelled.

Josselin flinched. Did men have to bellow everything?

She glanced about for witnesses, then forcefully gestured for him to come to her.

"Oh, nae!" he shouted with a shake of his head. "I've no wish to be skewered! Don't follow me, ye said. I don't need to be told twice!"

His voice attracted the attention of a man staying on the second floor of the inn, who leaned out from his window.

"Come *here*!" Josselin hissed.

"If ye want it," Drew yelled, "ye'll have to come and get it!"

The housekeeper appeared at another window, opening the shutters to see what all the shouting was about.

The last thing a spy wanted was attention. Josselin hadn't even started on her first assignment, and already her vow of secrecy was being jeopardized.

Though it chafed against every fiber of her being to come at the man's beckoning, Josselin had no other recourse. As quietly and calmly as she could, she retraced her steps. But under her breath, she cursed the smirking Highlander every step of the way.

Of course, she was nearly as vexed with herself as she was with Drew. Entrusted with a task by the queen's secretary not two hours ago, she'd already lost her first message and endangered her first mission. What kind of a spy would she make if she let frivolous passions distract her from the queen's business?

Sobered by her own lapse of judgment and with newfound resolve, Josselin stopped before Drew and held her hand out for the missive.

The Highlander, too, seemed to have collected his wits since she'd stormed off. He was back to his grinning, cocksure, irritating self.

"I knew ye couldn't stay away," he teased.

She arched a brow. "And I knew ye couldn't leave without stealin' somethin'."

He coughed as if she'd punched him, then snickered and shook his head. He placed the note in her palm, closing her fingers gently over it. To her mortification, she actually shivered at his touch.

"Ye'd best hold on tight, lass," he murmured with a knowing smirk. "I'd hate to see ye lose your 'invitation to the royal supper.'"

His sarcasm gave her pause. Had the cad read the missive, *her* missive?

Of course he had. Who would be able to resist? How else would he know it belonged to her?

She glanced uncertainly at the Highlander, whose eyes danced with mirth.

'Twas no laughing matter. She'd signed an oath of allegiance to Queen Mary. She'd sworn that if ever she were compromised, she'd take her own life rather than reveal her identity as the queen's spy. If he'd read the note...

"Go on, lass," he urged, his gaze grazing her suggestively from head to toe, "ere ye lose both your note *and* your trews."

Josselin fumed. He was a vile, vile man. She couldn't believe she'd let him... let him...

'Twas too terrible to think about.

"Mind your own bloody affairs," she snapped, shoving the note into her belt, and whipping smartly about to march back toward the inn. "All o' ye!" she shouted to the small mob of curious onlookers that now leaned out of the windows over the lane, chasing them back inside.

Halfway to the door, she turned back toward Drew to fire off one last warning. "If ye know what's best for ye," she hissed, sliding her knife halfway out of its sheath in threat, "ye'll forget what ye read in that note."

He turned away with a grin, tossing a lazy wave of farewell over his shoulder.

"Silly lass," he called back. "Highlanders can't read."

Chapter 11

Drew liked to think of himself as a lone wolf, roaming the woods of Scotland on his own, keeping to the shadows, never forming attachments, never staying in one place too long. At choice spots, he'd emerge to feed on the native prey, then return to the sanctuary of the forest.

So the fact that he'd been in Edinburgh long enough for the innkeeper at The Sheep Heid to start calling him by name and for the tavern wench to have memorized his favorite brew was completely against his usual conduct.

He'd lingered for two weeks after the queen's procession, playing consecutive golf matches at Musselburgh, Berwick, Carnoustie, and St. Andrews, and winning most of them. To his chagrin, the wagering crowd was beginning to think of Drew MacAdam as a local favorite.

He justified his loitering, saying 'twas foolish to leave while he was on a winning streak.

He even half-convinced himself that simple curiosity compelled him to remain until the date mentioned in the mysterious missive from Queen Mary's secretary, particularly since the rendezvous was set for a location he knew so well.

Neither of these were the real reason he was still in Edinburgh. The real reason stood about twenty yards to his left at the edge of the Leith links, serving beer to thirsty Scotsmen.

He wouldn't have seriously wagered on seeing Jossy again. Edinburgh was a big city. Jossy was a wee lass. She'd left the inn she was staying in, and no one knew where she'd gone. Probably home like a sensible lass. Even if she hadn't gone home, Drew imagined the queen's secretary had more important things to do tomorrow than keep a vague appointment with a lowly tavern wench from Selkirk.

But the improbable odds hadn't kept him from loitering about till that date, watching for her on the streets of Edinburgh. And it hadn't stopped his pulse from quickening at the sight of any wench with long blond tresses.

Less than an hour ago, he'd decided 'twas an unhealthy obsession, some imagined attraction based on the distorted memory of a kiss that had only *seemed* to move the earth.

He'd determined to leave Edinburgh tonight. Today he'd play and beat Leith's champion, Campbell Muir. Then he'd return to the inn, pack his things, and head north.

'Twas for the best, he told himself. The lass had a curious effect on him, and he didn't much like curious effects. They could interfere with his concentration and throw off his game.

But to his chagrin, no sooner had he vowed to leave than the lass suddenly appeared out of nowhere in the midst of the Leith course, hawking beer from a wagon to the wagerers at the match. In that instant, all of Drew's well-laid plans went awry.

Faith, the lass looked even more beautiful in women's clothing. She might be small-boned, less than voluptuous, and able to pass for a lad. But she wore no oversized man's shirt today. Her snugly laced bodice accentuated the subtle curves she possessed. Muted green skirts flared over her gentle hips. And the soft puff of her white linen chemise floated atop her breasts. As he stole a glance, a breeze caught the edge of the sheer fabric, revealing a glimpse of tempting flesh that took his breath away.

He couldn't take his eyes off of her as she chatted with her customers. Her honey hair, peeking out from the linen coif perched on her head, gleamed in the morning sunlight. Her smile sparkled like a rippling stream. Her eyes shone with merriment and mischief. And his body responded with all the poise of a rutting deer.

Clenching his teeth against a wave of disconcerting lust, he turned his back, waiting for Muir to start the match.

The attraction he felt to her was inexplicable. Jossy wasn't at all what he preferred in a woman. He could list several things that were wrong with her already, and he scarcely knew her.

First of all, she was Scots, therefore his enemy.

Second, she was blond, and he generally favored brunettes.

Third, she was scrawny, and he liked his women pleasantly plump.

Fourth, she was headstrong, and everyone knew that headstrong lasses were trouble.

Fifth...

"MacAdam."

Fifth...

"MacAdam!"

"Aye?" he murmured.

Muir had taken his swing. 'Twas Drew's turn.

With a sobering shake of his head, Drew selected his club and placed his ball. But try as he might, he couldn't focus on his swing. It had nothing to do with the boisterous shouts of encouragement and discouragement fired his way, the aggressive goading and cajoling, the cacophonous praise and insults, or the inevitable shoving that occurred in any crowd of drunks. He was distracted by the comely lass he could glimpse out of the corner of his eye.

Even his opponent's secret weapon, the enormous hound Muir had trained to menace his opponents, was no match for Drew's fixation. Though the dog snapped and barked and lunged at him in deadly threat, 'twasn't the animal's antics that interfered with Drew's drive, but the fact that his gaze kept drifting to the beer wagon.

He desired the lass. That was all. Surely there was nothing more to his fascination. She was like a beautiful, mysterious, challenging course he had yet to play, a course that, once conquered, would no longer hold appeal for him.

'Twas simple, then. All he need do to curb his obsession was to give in to it. Once he'd satisfied his curiosity, played upon her field and learned the hazards and sweet spots of her particular landscape, he'd doubtless be cured of his lovesickness.

'Twas decided, then. He'd court the lass.

He glanced over at the tempting maid, who was tying on her apron, preparing for the incoming onslaught of patrons. He wondered why she was still in Edinburgh, why she'd decided not to return to her sleepy village and her three da's after all. Had she indeed indentured herself to the queen's secretary? Was she working off a debt to the crown as a tavern wench?

While Muir lined up his next shot—his dog presently by his side, as docile as an orphaned lamb—Drew was able to study Jossy further from the refuge of the crowd.

The lass definitely knew her trade. Not only could she fill a tankard without spilling a drop, but she could take coin for one beer, tempt a man into buying a second, and dance out of a third's grasp all at the same time.

"MacAdam, stop droolin' o'er your next beer," Muir scolded, "and get your head in the game!"

The crowd laughed, and at that very moment, Jossy spotted him.

Chapter 12

For an instant, time stood still as Josselin stared in disbelief. Then the tankard she was filling overflowed onto her hand.

"Bloody..." she exclaimed, handing the patron his brimming cup and wiping her hand on her apron. When she ventured a second glance, the Highlander had turned away and was making his way to the next hole.

Perhaps 'twas only her imagination. Perhaps the golfer had only borne an uncanny resemblance to that other man, she thought as she stared over the heads of the patrons clamoring for beer.

Nae, she decided, studying the man's backside as he strode down the green. That was definitely the Highlander's cocky swagger.

"Hurry up, wench," a grizzled merchant grumbled. "They're movin' down the course."

Josselin bit back a retort, hastily filling the man's cup and pocketing his coin.

Tankards were shoved her way as the mob vied to get their cups filled before play resumed. She worked with the fluidity of habit, no sooner topping off one foamy cup before starting another and never dropping a penny as she collected payment.

Meanwhile, her brain raced in mad circles as she tried to imagine what had happened to cause the Highlander to cross paths with her again.

The crowd thinned as the onlookers, their cups replen-ished, scrambled off toward the action. Then a small, wiry man with swarthy skin and fierce, dark eyes came up and expectantly handed her his wooden tankard.

"Four pence," she told him, taking the cup and prepar-ing to place it under the tap. But as she turned, her glance snagged on the rim of the cup, into which three curious notches were carved.

He was her contact.

Philipe's instructions had been clear. She was never to acknowledge the contacts by word or deed. She would not learn their names. And she'd do her best to forget their faces. They had the most dangerous tasks of all, and 'twas up to Josselin to protect them.

So without saying a word, while her back was turned, she reached under the hollowed bottom of the wooden cup. Just as she expected, a folded missive was lodged there, stuck fast to the cup with a blob of wax. She quickly popped the wax loose and tucked the note into the con-cealed pocket in the waist of her kirtle.

The missive would be written in some sort of secret code, the encryption of which was a closely guarded secret. It might give times and locations of Reformation meetings, provide bits of news about the movements of Knox's follow-ers, or establish lists of those loyal and disloyal to the queen.

But the note would appear to be a love letter, some-thing sappy and innocuous that a tavern wench like Josselin might carry about, something that would arouse no suspicion should she be discovered with it.

Filling his cup from the tap, Josselin returned it to the man and took his coin, but avoided looking at him. 'Twas easier to forget a man's face if his face wasn't too familiar.

He walked away, and already she couldn't recall the color of his eyes or what he'd been wearing.

His wasn't like the face of the Highlander, which seemed burned into her memory, much to her dismay.

Damn! she thought, briskly swabbing the counter with her rag. She'd figured the Highlander was long gone, half-way to Aberdeen by now, and that she could forget about her lapse in judgment and slip of propriety and focus on her new work.

But Drew's mocking grin, laughing eyes, and stormy brow seemed to haunt her at every turn.

She told herself 'twas because she'd been vulnerable when she'd met him—new to Edinburgh, fresh from her encounter with the queen, caught off-guard by his improper advances.

But that didn't explain why she felt the way she did now, why her heart fluttered and her breath stopped at the sight of him, why her blood warmed under his gaze.

"Ah, ye couldn't stay away from me, could ye, darlin'?"

Startled, she stared blankly into the unforgettable grinning face of the Highlander, who had materialized at the beer wagon as if by magic. A golf club was slung across his shoulder, his brow was beaded with sweat, and he was out of breath.

Hoping he couldn't see the blush rising in her cheeks, she frowned, muttering, "What are ye doin' here?"

"At a beer wagon?" He raised an amused brow as

if 'twas obvious. "Well, unless ye're sellin' somethin' besides beer…"

"Nae, I mean here, at the links?"

"I'm a golfer. Remember?"

Remember? Aye, she remembered. Her gaze caught on his lips, lips she remembered all too well, and she felt her blood warm dangerously at the memory. Lord, she had to get rid of the man before she made a wanton fool of herself.

She held her hand out brusquely. "Your cup."

He unbuckled his tankard and placed it in her hand, but didn't release it immediately, leaning forward to confide, "Ye know, Jossy, all dressed up like a lady, ye're quite a distraction. Faith, ye're ruinin' my game."

"Is that so?" She ignored his flattery, snatching his tankard away and raising her chin. "Well, your game might go a wee bit better if ye stayed on the course," she told him, nodding toward the crowd. "'Tis how 'tis played, I'm told."

He glanced over his shoulder as if gauging how much time he had left. "The truth is, darlin', ye're much more pleasin' company."

"I'm not your darlin'," she said, wheeling away to fill his tankard before he could see how his words had rattled her.

In the distance, she heard cries of "MacAdam! MacAdam!"

"I think someone's callin' ye, MacAdam," she told him over her shoulder. "Maybe that hound o' Muir's wants a bite o' your Highland arse."

"Ach, lass," he teased, clapping a hand to his heart, "'tis flatterin' to know ye're lookin' after my arse."

She bristled. How did he always manage to twist her words against her? She turned back to him, a scathing oath on her lips, but he was already loping away.

"Your beer!" she yelled after him.

"I ne'er drink durin' a match!" he called back.

She thumped the full tankard down on the counter, slopping foam over her hand. She might not have time for a biting retort, but her gaze nipped at his departing Highland arse all the way across the green.

She threw down her rag like a challenge. Who did the Highlander think he was? And what was he doing on *her* course, interfering with her work? He may suppose he had some stake in the links because he could push a wee ball about with a stick, but Josselin was here by royal decree.

Of course, she couldn't tell him that. She was sworn to secrecy. Which made the situation unbearable.

She picked up her rag again and narrowed her eyes at the wicked scoundrel across the course. Ruining his game, was she? He must be a terrible golfer if he was so easily distracted.

She patted the pocket at her waist. She had the missive now. She could pack up the cart and return with the driver to The White Hart, deliver the missive, and have the casks refilled for her important assignment at Musselburgh tomorrow.

But the stubborn streak in her, bred of her father's determination and her mother's indomitable will, made her decide to stay till the match was over. Drew MacAdam had upset her, thrown her off-balance, and left her feeling like a tongue-tied fool. She rather relished the thought of seeing him humiliated by the Leith champion.

She picked up the brimming cup, saluted the irksome Highlander with a mock toast, then downed half the beer. Only when she wiped the foam from her mouth did she remember the tankard she'd put her lips all over was Drew's.

Chapter 13

Now that he'd confronted the lass who'd been dogging his thoughts, now that the seeds of seduction had been planted, Drew could focus on his game. He was already behind by four strokes, and nervous gamblers who'd bet on him to win were starting to mutter about withdrawing their wagers. But if anyone could snatch victory from the jaws of defeat, 'twas Drew MacAdam.

First he made quick work of Campbell Muir's hound. Before his next drive, Drew turned and growled at the dog with such menace that the beast whimpered, tucked his tail betwixt his legs, and lay silent for the rest of the game.

As for his golfing, Muir might have grown up on the shores of Leith, but Drew knew the course like the back of his hand. Soon he was making up for lost strokes and hitting improbable drives that would be the talk of the Edinburgh taverns tonight.

'Twas only when they'd reversed their way through the course and climbed the shallow hill in its midst that Drew spied the beer wagon again. He'd half expected Jossy to be gone.

Courting a lass who pretended to despise him was

going to be a challenge. Still, she'd told him herself she wasn't the kind of woman to flee in fear. Nor was Drew the kind of man to walk away from a difficult course.

When he got close enough to detect the hostile cross of her arms, the smug tilt of her chin, and the haughty arch of her brow, he decided 'twas time to show the lass what he was made of, to reveal his talents and earn a place, both in her heart and in the important match tomorrow.

He shaded his eyes, pretending to study the distant hole. "Ach! I've *spit* farther than that!" he announced, loud enough for Jossy to hear. "That hardly warrants a longnose. I could make the distance in three strokes of a fairway club and sink it in four," he bragged, setting off a flurry of fresh single-hole wagering.

"And would ye be backin' that boast with coin o' your own, MacAdam?" Muir challenged.

"Let's make it a gentleman's wager. If ye win, Muir, I'll buy ye a beer."

All parties seemed satisfied, and Drew crouched to dribble sand into a pile for his tee.

What Drew neglected to reveal was that he planned to lose the wager. And when he did, Muir would collect his brimming tankard of beer, gulp it down like any manly, self-respecting Scot, and move on to the next hole, where Drew would again overestimate his abilities, wager Muir a tankard of beer, and intentionally lose.

In three more holes, Muir would be as drunk as a mackerel, lucky to connect with the ball at all, and Drew, while losing his single-hole wagers, would make up the strokes on the last holes and win the match by a mile. Best of all, Josselin from Selkirk would see just who held court on the Leith links.

*   *   *

Josselin smiled to herself. All the Highlander's bluster would only make his trouncing that much sweeter. She wondered how long his self-satisfied grin would last when he tasted bitter defeat.

She didn't know much about golf, just that grown men with nothing more productive to do chased wooden balls with sticks through fields, trying to force them into rabbit holes. It seemed a ludicrous preoccupation. But the fervid wagering that accompanied the pointless game was even more inane. And now that the Highlander had made that incredible boast, the stakes had been whipped up to a ridiculous frenzy.

Drew's club made a loud crack as it struck. The ball shot like a cannonball across the green. The crowd exclaimed in surprise.

Josselin shook her head. She might have known the Highlander was too ham-fisted for his own good. He'd probably send the ball into the firth with his next drive.

Muir clipped his ball, and it veered slightly to the left, quite short of the hole.

As he made his second drive, Muir belched, setting off an animated argument about whether the stroke should count. It did.

Drew's second swing was less forceful than his first, and he managed to place his ball within a respectable distance of his target.

Muir swung again, and his ball rolled to a spot near the rough. Two short drives got him within putting range.

With careful control, in two more strokes, Drew also tapped his ball to within a few feet of the hole.

Muir scored in two putts.

Drew took two as well, which left him one point closer to Muir, but disappointed those who'd wagered on his single-hole boast, leaving them groaning.

Josselin shook her head. 'Twould teach the braggart. Now he'd disappointed his supporters, and he owed Muir a beer. And when Drew came loping up to buy that beer, she couldn't resist pointing out his mistake.

"Ye were right," she told him. "Highlanders *can't* count for shite."

"Are ye sure, love?" he asked, giving her a wink. "Seems to me I'm catchin' up."

"There's a lot o' catchin' up and not much green left," she said smartly. "Ye can't do it, Highlander."

She filled Muir's tankard and handed it back, and he saluted her with it. "Watch me."

As much as she wanted to resist, she couldn't help but steal a glance as he lined up his shot at the tee.

Why watching Drew swing a stick at a wee ball held her interest, she didn't know. 'Twas only a silly sport, after all, a silly sport played by uncouth ruffians.

Yet there was something about that particular uncouth ruffian that made her breath catch, something that made it near impossible to look away.

There was nothing terribly remarkable about the Highlander's physique. He wasn't particularly tall or short, fat or thin. He didn't have the enormous shoulders of a caber-tosser or the agility of an acrobat.

But his concentration was astounding, and there was controlled strength and a sensual grace in his swing that made it seem he commanded the flight of the ball from the moment he addressed it on the grass.

Watching him was like watching a master swordsman do battle, Josselin realized. The intensity of his focus, the balance of his body, the elegance of his movement, the power of his stroke...

'Twas breathtaking. Observing such perfect form made her heart pound as if she were watching an expert dueler wield a blade, and her face flamed with mortification as she realized she was staring.

Drew MacAdam had a gift. There was no denying it. Too bad he couldn't count.

He was already up to his self-destructive tricks again. No sooner had Muir downed his prize beer for the previous hole than Drew began making outrageous claims about the next one.

"Nobody can make it in six!" someone spat.

"It has never been done," another verified.

"I can, and I will," Drew stated.

He didn't.

He made it in seven. But Muir took nine.

Josselin frowned in amazement. Drew seemed a damned fine golfer. So why was he intentionally making bets he knew he'd lose?

When he came trotting up to fill Muir's tankard a second time, several other thirsty spectators joined him.

She pulled Drew aside and whispered, "What game are ye playin' at?"

He smiled. "'Tis called golf, lass. I thought ye knew that."

"Ye know what I mean." She took the tankard and filled it again. "Ye could easily outplay Muir. Why are ye teasin' him like a cat dabblin' with a mouse?"

"Teasin' him? Maybe ye hadn't noticed," he told her,

tossing four pence on the counter as he left, "but I'm the one payin' for the beers."

The game moved on to the next hole, and the combatants became distant specks on the rolling rise. But Josselin could tell by the sound of the crowd that Drew was making another unbelievable claim, and once again the drunken fools were falling for it.

Suddenly the truth struck her like a bolt of lightning.

Drew was getting Campbell Muir drunk. The Highlander might be losing his wagers on the individual holes, but his overall score was improving, while Muir's was getting steadily worse.

The sly devil was cheating!

She was prepared this time when he raced up to the beer wagon just before the last hole.

"I know what ye're up to, Highlander," she said, ignoring Muir's tankard and folding her arms, "and I won't be a party to it."

"What are ye talkin' about?" he asked.

"Ye're tryin' to get Muir drunk."

"He plays much worse when he's drunk," he admitted.

"Well, I won't take part in such cheatin'."

"Cheatin'?" He chortled. "And where were ye when Muir's hound was tryin' to bite me off at the knees?"

"That's...different."

He shook his head. "Be a good lass and fill Muir's tankard."

She lifted her chin in refusal.

In the distance came Muir's drunken cry of, "Where's my pint, MacAdam?"

Drew wiggled his brows at her, his pale blue eyes all innocence.

Giving him a glare that would frost fire, Josselin muttered a curse, snatched the tankard, filled it, and shoved it back into his hand.

He flipped her a bawbee to pay for it, which she caught in midair. Before she could give him change, he nodded his head in farewell.

"I'll be back for another after the game," he called back.

She stuffed the coin into her purse. "Ye'll need it," she yelled. "I hear beer is good for drownin' one's sorrows."

"Oh, I won't be drownin' my sorrows, love," he promised. "'Twill be a victory pint."

Victorious or not, she didn't intend to loiter around to serve him beer, nor would she give him his change. The extra coin would be a gratuity for having to put up with his roguery.

Besides, she had much more important things to think about than who won a silly golf game. Tomorrow she was going to her appointment with Philipe at Musselburgh. After two weeks of patient waiting, Josselin would finally receive an official introduction to the queen and the Four Maries. Tonight she'd make sure that she had a bath, the beer wagon was in order, and all thoughts of that troublesome Highlander were as far from her head as possible.

Chapter 14

Will shrank in his boots. Kate Campbell's scowl could do that to a man. Even bold Angus and upright Alasdair were shuffling their feet and hanging their heads in the face of Kate's wrath.

"Ye let her do *what*?" Kate demanded, untying her brewster's apron and smacking it across the tavern counter.

Fortunately, 'twas after hours, so no one else would witness Kate hauling the three of them over the coals. Will supposed they deserved her sharp tongue-lashing. Not only had they let Jossy go to Edinburgh on her own, but they'd lied to Kate about it, telling her the lass was off visiting some long-lost cousin. They'd never dreamed Josselin would decide to remain in Edinburgh.

'Twas inevitable that Kate would eventually find out. Sure enough, though the three da's had managed to keep Jossy's missive secret for over a week, Kate had finally seen through their deception, forced them to surrender the note, and was now demanding an explanation.

Will swallowed hard and tried to sound reasonable. "The lass is the same age as Mary, after all."

"Ye mean the *queen*," Kate bit out, "who has the Scots army at her beck and call to defend her everywhere she goes?"

Will reddened.

Kate narrowed her eyes. "*That* Mary?"

He shuffled his feet. "Ye don't understand. I couldn't tell her nay. 'Twouldn't have been honorable."

"Honorable?"

"Aye," Will said, straightening with pride. "She won the fight, fair and square."

"Fight?"

Will winced. Perhaps he shouldn't have mentioned that.

"*Fight*?" Kate shouted, making the candle beside her flicker wildly.

Will realized he was too deep in the mud to claw his way out. He might as well admit the truth.

"Aye," he said. "Listen, Kate, I know ye wanted to make a proper lass out o' Jossy, but I couldn't let her grow up helpless like her ma. So I taught her how to use a blade." He added, "But she only sparred once a week."

After an uncomfortable silence, Angus grumbled, "Twice."

Will raised a surprised brow.

"Ye, too?" Kate asked, incredulous.

Angus kicked at the floor. "The lass has a natural talent. 'Tis a shame to waste."

"A shame," Kate said in disgust. "And what about ye, Alasdair? What did ye teach our young lass?"

"Readin'. Writin'. Sums." He cleared his throat and murmured, "And duelin'. But only after her other studies were done."

Kate planted her hands on her hips and shook her head. "Ye know, I'd knock your three heads together if I thought ye had half a brain among ye."

Will frowned, but he knew Kate was right to be upset. The three of them had unwittingly fed Jossy's hunger for war until she was obsessed with it. Now, because of them, she might have come to harm.

"Read it again, Alasdair," Kate commanded, stabbing a finger at the missive clutched in his hand.

He read, "Dear Kate and Da's, It is with great pride that I send you the happy news that I have entered into the service of the queen. I cannot say more, but if you wish to send me correspondence, I am staying at The White Hart Inn in Edinburgh. Yours faithfully, Josselin."

"The service o' the queen," Kate repeated, turning an accusing gaze on Will. "And ye said she was dressed as a lad, aye?"

He slowly nodded.

Kate's shoulders drooped, a gesture far more terrifying than her accusing finger. "Ye old fools," she growled. "Don't ye know what she's done?"

They frowned.

"What do ye think?" Kate sighed. "She's joined the queen's army."

Angus and Alasdair scoffed in disbelief, but Will knew Kate was probably right. It had always been Jossy's dream to fight in battle like her mother. 'Twas only a matter of time before she pursued that dream.

Still, Will didn't think Kate could blame them entirely. They'd done what they thought was right.

"Well, at least she's well-trained," he told Kate. "At least she won't go into battle unprepared like her ma."

"Lilliard?" Kate said with a humorless chuckle. "Her ma didn't die from lack o' trainin'. She died from lack o' judgment. From what I can see, 'tis a flaw she's passed on to her daughter, and a flaw ye've done nothin' to fix."

Will considered her words. Jossy had always been impulsive, a lass of action, not words, and she tended to overestimate her strength, her reach, her endurance, and her capacity for patience. Was it possible? Had she done so rash a thing as to use her disguise to earn her a spot in the ranks of the Scots army?

'Twas a sobering thought.

Of course, she'd be found out eventually. A beauty like Josselin couldn't pose as a lad forever. But what if she got herself into trouble and came to harm before anyone was the wiser?

Will shivered at the vivid memory of the poor, pale corpse they'd found so many years ago on the battlefield, the maid with the same fair face and honey hair as her daughter.

Dear God, what had he done?

"Ye're a sorry lot," Kate scolded. "But ye're goin' to fix this. In the mornin', the three o' ye are goin' to set off for Edinburgh." She dug several silver coins out of the till. "Ye'll go to The White Hart and settle up her account. Then, I don't care if ye have to drag her, kickin' and screamin', but ye're goin' to bring her back home. Do ye understand?"

All three of them nodded. The lass would be as angry as a cornered kitten when they showed up to haul her back to Selkirk. But Will knew Jossy's temper, as fierce as 'twas, was no match for Kate's.

Chapter 15

The sun dawned bright on the links at Musselburgh. The game wouldn't begin for another half hour, but Josselin wanted to be prepared. This was a championship match. Only the best would be invited to play. Philipe had told her that the queen, who was a devotee of the game, wished to see how skilled the local players were, and this match had been secretly arranged for her benefit.

Indeed, 'twas the promise of this meeting that had convinced Josselin to sign the document for Philipe that first day. She would be introduced to Mary and her court. 'Twould be a day she'd never forget.

Her hands trembled as she counted out the stacks of coins she kept ready for change. This was her chance to repair the bad first impression she'd given the queen, and she didn't want to mess anything up.

She smoothed her skirts and tucked stray wisps of her hair under her freshly washed white linen coif, then took a deep breath and stared off across the green. 'Twas a fine day to be outdoors. The grass was jeweled with dew, and the fluffy clouds that outlined the crags of Ardthir Suidhe in sharp relief promised to temper the warm

September sun. The sea was calm, the wind was gentle, and she could already see a lone golfer in the distance, practicing his swing at the edge of the rough.

She narrowed her eyes. Something about the man's stance, his stature, the fluidity of his swing...

"Nae," she whispered.

It couldn't be. Not here. Not at Musselburgh, where the queen would be arriving any moment. Not when Josselin had to be at her best, unperturbed by the perturbing winks of a cocksure Highlander.

This was not going to happen. She had to get rid of him.

"Hey!" she yelled.

Her voice was as jarring to the quiet morn as a dog barking in the middle of church. But he didn't seem to hear her.

"Hey!" she tried again.

Nothing.

Then, to make matters worse, she began to hear the faint conversations of groups of golfers and spectators arriving at the course.

"MacAdam!" she tried.

Nothing.

"Drew!"

He calmly swung his club, waited to see where his ball landed, and finally turned toward her expectantly. He'd heard her all along. The cad had just chosen to ignore her.

"Come here!" She motioned to him.

With an intentionally languid stride, the Highlander made his way to the beer wagon.

"What the hell are ye doin' here?" she demanded.

He lowered one brow. "Weren't ye callin' me?"

"Not here. *Here.* At Musselburgh." Her gesture encompassed the course.

"Ah," he said, casually laying his golf club atop the counter. "Playin' golf."

She pushed his club away. "Ach, nae, ye're not."

He winked. "Aye, I am."

"Give me your damned tankard," she said, thrusting out her hand.

He shook his head. "I told ye, darlin', I don't drink while I play."

"Ye're not goin' to play. Give me your tankard."

"If this is about the beer ye owe me, I'll collect it after the game."

"There isn't goin' to be a game," she insisted. "Ye're goin' to hand me your tankard. I'll fill it with beer. And then ye're goin' to take your big wood sticks and wee wood balls and go home."

He chuckled. "Ach, lass, what is it ye have against golf?"

"Nothin'. But this is a very important game between the local champions. Ye have no right to be—"

"I *am* a local champion."

"What?"

"I won the game yesterday. If ye hadn't scampered away like a frightened rabbit, ye'd know that."

That came as a surprise, but he *had* cheated after all. Still, it didn't change anything. She wanted him gone—before Queen Mary showed up.

"Ye can't play here," she told him, handing him his club.

"Is that so?" He wrinkled his nose doubtfully and used the head of the club to scratch his back. "And just how are ye thinkin' to prevent me?"

She bit the corner of her lip. A dozen options went through her head, most of them involving some form of hand-to-hand combat. But before she could suggest anything, a large group of golfers arrived on the course, and in their midst, she glimpsed Philipe.

There was no time to battle the Highlander. She had to get rid of him now before Mary showed up.

"Ach, very well," she said, throwing up her arms. "Play your bloody game then. But do it over there," she said, pointing to the furthest hole.

He looked at her quizzically, laying his club across his shoulders and arching his back in a lazy stretch. "Ye really don't understand golf at all, love, do ye?"

"Nae, and one day ye can tell me all about it." She eyed the approaching crowd. "But today ye've got to be on your way."

She leaned across the counter and pushed at his chest, which only served to amuse him.

"If I didn't know better, lass, I'd say ye were plannin' some kind o' clandestine engagement."

His words startled her. 'Twas precisely what she was planning. Philipe had scrawled this location and date on the note he'd given her, the one that the Highlander had intercepted. Was that why Drew was here at this exact time and place? He'd claimed he couldn't read, but what if that weren't true? Had Josselin's mission been compromised?

His next words put her fears to rest.

"But a tryst with the queen's secretary himself!" he said, whistling. "What high aspirations ye have. Don't worry, lass. I won't get in the way o' your courtin'." Leaning toward her, he confided, "Though I suspect ye'll discover I'm a far better kisser than that mincin' twit."

She opened her mouth to rebuke him, then heard Philipe drawing dangerously close as he extolled the virtues of the course at Musselburgh.

"Aye, that's it," she shot back, her voice thick with sarcasm. "I've an impendin' tryst with Philipe. So if ye'll leave us alone..."

He flashed her a sly grin and made a deep, submissive bow to her before turning to wave brazenly at the approaching entourage.

At her gasp of horror, he clasped his club to his chest and silently mouthed the words, "Far better." Then, blessedly, he turned away and trekked back to his ball.

Josselin blushed at the reminder, nervously tucking a stray lock of hair behind her ear. Thankfully, Philipe seemed to be engaged in conversation with a small group of noblemen and probably hadn't spotted Drew.

'Twasn't until the entourage arrived at her beer wagon that Josselin realized with disappointment that the queen was not among them. As usual, they were all men—some nobles, some soldiers, some servants, some commoners— and everyone was thirsty.

She filled cup after cup until one of the youths caught her eye. He looked strangely familiar. He was short and fair of face, and his hands seemed small on the tankard he handed her to fill. When he glanced up in thanks, Josselin took a second look at his wide brown eyes and glanced quickly away before the lad's secret could get out.

The youth was one of the Four Maries. She was sure of it. In fact, after careful inspection, she spotted all four of the queen's ladies in masculine garb, scattered among the men.

Philipe had told her that the queen liked Josselin's

attire. Had Josselin inspired the women to disguise themselves?

She smiled in wonder. Most of the group of golfers and gamblers had no idea that their ranks had been infiltrated by women, and none of them knew they stood among royalty.

Then she noticed the tall, handsome, gangly youth in the scuffed black doublet, baggy brown trews, and feathered cap, and her smile grew even wider.

Chapter 16

Drew couldn't stop grinning as he strode across the green. 'Twas mad, he knew, but matching wits with the wee blonde with the reckless temper, flashing eyes, and wicked tongue was almost as exciting as matching strokes with opponents in golf. The beautiful spitfire gave as good as she got, and 'twas a pleasure to tangle with a woman who was so bright and full of fire.

He'd been right about the rendezvous at Musselburgh. Standing in the midst of the crowd, right on schedule, was Philipe de la Fontaine. But why was he meeting Jossy at the links? Certainly not for a tryst.

Retrieving his ball and clubs, Drew made his way to the start of the course, where the contestants and spectators were gathering.

Today Drew would face off against the champion of Carnoustie. The purse was sizable, and there were sure to be scores of enthusiasts gambling on the outcome. Already the green teemed with a motley crowd—noblemen, servants, soldiers, apprentices, merchants, men young and old, rich and not so rich—all eager to increase their wealth.

'Twasn't difficult to discern which man was his rival. Dressed in a dapper green doublet with slashed sleeves in the German style, his shock of white hair tucked under a black cap with a white feather, the man held court at the tee, regaling his slack-jawed admirers with legendary tales of his triumphs on the links. The man was a born storyteller, reenacting some of his swings with such enthusiasm that he nearly whacked several bystanders who wandered too close.

Indeed, 'twas one of those near misses that alerted Drew to the scrawny youth who gave a peculiar squeak as he dodged out of the club's way.

Drew studied the young man as the fellow moved through the crowd, then stopped to talk to another youth. Something wasn't quite right about him. In fact, neither of the lads looked right. Despite being full-grown, they had not a hint of a beard between them, and their faces were as pink and sweet as peaches. Their behavior was strange, too. Their glances were secretive and suspicious, as if they were up to mischief.

The truth finally smacked him in the forehead. They weren't lads. They were lasses disguised as lads.

Marry, 'twas like a contagion!

Was there a shortage of proper gowns in Scotland? Were females infiltrating the men's ranks to spy on them? Or was this a backlash to John Knox's fashionable denigration of women? Maybe 'twas true what Drew's uncles claimed—that the Scots sent lasses into battle—because they didn't realize they were lasses.

Whatever the reason, Drew found it curious that no other men seemed to notice there were females among them.

Drew waited politely until his opponent finished demonstrating his dramatic final putt from yesterday's game to approach and offer his hand. "Drew MacAdam."

"Ronald Metz."

The man had a firm handshake, a wide smile, and a gleam in his eye that said, I'd be delighted to pummel you.

Drew nodded in greeting, fairly confident he was not going to be pummeled today.

He was right. Metz was good. He was obviously a seasoned golfer. But Drew was better. He had youth on his side—a smooth, powerful swing that allowed him to place the ball precisely where he wanted it.

He also had a secret incentive. As childish as 'twas, Drew intended to make Jossy eat her words. She'd discounted him as a cheat. He'd prove otherwise. There was nothing like the prospect of gloating to inspire one's performance. So he saved his most impressive shots for the green in front of the beer wagon, where Jossy would be sure to hear the gasps of disbelief and congratulatory cheers from the crowd.

At the seventh hole, the contestants took a break, and servants were sent to fetch beer for the thirsty spectators.

Meanwhile, Drew kept a watch on Philipe, who remained behind with the nobles. The secretary hadn't yet openly acknowledged Jossy. Drew wondered what the man was up to, why he'd ordered this mysterious rendezvous if he was bent on ignoring the lass.

By the last hole, the game was close enough to generate a continuous cacophony of threats, bets, and cursing from gamblers, detractors, supporters, and drunks. Drew didn't care. He'd learned from his training with a sword to block outside distractions, to go in for the kill.

When he gently nudged the ball into the hole with his putting cleek, half the crowd erupted in cheers, and half of them turned the air hot with their swearing.

He grinned. He'd won by a stroke.

And now Jossy owed him an apology.

"Victory for the Highlander!" somebody crowed.

"Brilliant, MacAdam!"

"Fine game, lad."

Metz dispiritedly extended his hand. "Well played, MacAdam," he grumbled.

Drew shook his hand and beamed with Highland charm. "'Twas an honor to play ye, Metz. Your golfin' exploits are legendary." 'Twasn't entirely true, but Drew *had* been listening to them all morn, and his praise seemed to take the edge off of Metz's disappointment.

"Sir, Ambrose Scott," a tall lad in the crowd said by way of introduction, offering his hand to Drew. "I'd like to buy the champion a pint, if ye'll allow me."

If Drew was rattled by the youth's offer, he wasn't about to show it. And he knew better than to turn it down. After all, one didn't refuse beer from the Queen of Scotland.

Chapter 17

Nae," Josselin whispered in horror. Her heart thudded like a mallet on an empty beer cask as the crowd swarmed toward her. "Nae."

That was *not* the Highlander approaching with a smug, I-just-won-the-championship grin on his face. And that was *not* Queen Mary walking beside him.

"Bloody hell."

Curse Drew MacAdam! He was going to ruin everything. She'd told Philipe that the Highlander meant nothing to her. If Drew started flapping his jaws about his acquaintance with Josselin, Philipe would think she'd violated his trust. And if the lout said anything unseemly to the queen...

Ballocks. Drew probably didn't even know she was the queen. Nobody seemed to recognize her. There was no telling what secrets he'd let slip.

This was going to be disastrous.

Wiping her palms anxiously on her apron, she searched for Philipe. Perhaps she should tell him the truth about her acquaintance with the Highlander and warn Philipe before Drew could do any harm.

But the secretary was walking in the opposite direction, highly distracted, conversing with another nobleman.

She was on her own.

It took a great deal of her willpower not to address the queen as Your Majesty, not to reveal that she knew Mary's secret, to treat her simply as one of the townfolk. It took the rest of her willpower not to wallop Drew MacAdam as he came smiling up to the beer wagon, clearly basking in his victory.

Josselin did her best to ignore Drew, but 'twas nearly impossible, especially when the queen issued a startling request.

In a throaty voice with a flawless Scots accent, Mary told her, "I'd like to buy a pint for the champion." She held out a hand to Drew for his tankard.

Josselin felt like all the air had been sucked from her lungs. The queen wished to buy Drew a beer?

Appalled, she glanced at Drew, who grinned as he surrendered his cup.

Josselin knew very well who that gloating grin was for, and she longed to smack it right off his face. But she didn't dare deny the queen, who held out Drew's tankard to be filled.

"O' course," she said between clenched teeth, taking the cup.

As she filled it, Josselin forced herself to take several calming breaths. 'Twould not do for the queen to see how upset she was. But she had to think of some way to get Drew away from her before he said something foolish.

"So, Ambrose, are ye a golfer?" Drew asked Mary.

Like that.

Josselin stiffened. The queen, a golfer? 'Twas a stupid

question, like asking King Henry VIII if he'd ever been married.

"I've been known to toddle about a course now and then," the queen said.

'Twas an understatement. Everyone knew Mary was an avid sportswoman. She played tennis, hunted, rode, golfed. Faith, she could probably best the Highlander in a caber toss.

"Indeed?" Drew asked.

Josselin didn't like the speculative tone of his voice.

"Aye," Mary replied. "But I've never played such a marvelous course."

"Playin' Musselburgh is like wooin' a fair maid," he confided. "It requires a firm hand, but a gentle touch."

"Wooin' a maid? Then I should do quite well," Mary asserted, which sent her disguised ladies into fits of suppressed giggling. "In fact, sir, I wager I could conquer just about any hole with my great club," she boasted suggestively, "and in fewer strokes than ye."

Josselin nearly dropped Drew's tankard as laughter erupted over Ambrose's ribald remark.

"Could ye now?" Drew replied with a chuckle.

"Aye, and if ye're willin', I'd like the chance to prove it, here and now. Let's play the Hollow Hole, ye and me."

"Now?" Drew asked in surprise. "But 'twould hardly be fair. Ye've never played here, and—"

"No matter. We'll make it a gentleman's bet, a penny to the winner. What say ye?"

The crowd was already chattering in excitement, placing their own wagers on the spontaneous match.

"I don't know," he said doubtfully, shaking his head. "I really can't..."

Josselin turned on him with wordless fury. Was he going to refuse? Refuse the queen? How dared he?

She shoved his beer at his chest and shot him a glare as fierce, pointed, and powerful as lightning.

Drew frowned, disconcerted. When he tried to take the tankard from Jossy, she wouldn't let go. He watched her, trying to discern the ferocious message she was sending with her gaze.

He deepened his frown until she finally gave him an infinitesimal nod. She obviously wanted him to agree to the challenge.

"Can't? Or won't?" the queen asked slyly, setting off a deluge of taunts and dares from the spectators, who were already neck-deep in wagering.

Drew looked quizzically at Jossy. Didn't she realize the young man was Queen Mary? Surely she didn't want an uncouth Highlander tangling with her beloved sovereign.

But the determined glint in Jossy's eyes told him 'twas exactly what she wanted.

'Twas mad, he knew, but he let Jossy win. He smirked in surrender, and she let him have the tankard.

He raised his cup to the crowd. "I meant to say I really can't," he amended, "*turn down* such a temptin' offer."

The crowd cheered, and Jossy sighed in relief.

Drew shook his head and set his beer down on the counter.

"Save this for me, lass, and remember," he said under his breath, "this was *your* idea."

"Aye, fine," she muttered, "but listen. I expect ye to lose."

"Do ye now?" She had so little faith in his talents.

While Mary and her cohorts moved away from the beer wagon to negotiate with Metz for the use of his clubs, Jossy leaned in close.

"There's somethin' ye should know," she confided, briefly scanning the area for witnesses. "That's not a man."

He looked at her.

At his lack of response, she repeated, "That's not a man."

"I know."

"Ye do?"

He smiled, amused. "Aye. Even a sheep-swivin' Highlander can tell the difference between a—"

"Shh." She spoke even more softly. "Ye've got to let her win."

"Why?"

"Why? Because she's...she's..."

"Because she's a woman?" He shook his head. 'Twas the harsh lesson he'd learned from his father's suicide. "Nae," he murmured. "The lass knows full well what she's gettin' into. If she's got the ballocks to enter the field o' battle, then she'd better have the ballocks to face the fact she may lose."

Chapter 18

Josselin watched the Highlander walk away, surprised into silence by his words, which were hauntingly familiar to her ears.

'Twas exactly what she'd always said of her mother and the battle at Ancrum—that Lilliard hadn't been naïve, as everyone claimed, that she'd known very well what she risked.

But Josselin couldn't afford to dwell on the past now. The Highlander was already on his way to the tee, about to best the queen at golf. She couldn't let that happen. Mary needed allies now, not challengers. God knew she already had enough enemies in Scotland.

Josselin's beer wagon driver had gone off to watch the game, and she knew she shouldn't abandon her cart. 'Twas full of beer, after all, and there was nothing more tempting to a Scot than the prospect of a free pint. But something had to be done. The honor of the queen was at stake.

Fortunately, nobody was interested in drinking at the moment. The crowd had rushed back to the green to watch and wager on the new contest.

So Josselin stowed away her earnings, took off her apron, and left the beer wagon, hurrying across the field to catch Drew before he could make a terrible mistake.

At least Drew had had the courtesy to allow Mary to make the first drive. When Josselin arrived at the tee, the queen was settling into a comfortable stance, surrounded by shouting spectators. Josselin tugged surreptitiously at the Highlander's sleeve.

He frowned, surprised at the interruption.

She pulled him close to whisper into his ear. "Ye can't win."

He shrugged, murmuring back, "If that's what ye believe, then bet against me."

"Nae. I mean ye *mustn't* win."

A smile touched the corner of his lip. "And ye mustn't tell me what to do, darlin'."

She only had a limited time to make him understand. "Damn it, Highlander," she bit out, "I'm serious."

"And so am I, lass," he whispered back. "I've never thrown a game in my life. I'll not start now."

Anger and urgency made her reckless. She hissed, "Even if ye're playin' against... against the Queen o' Scotland?"

He sighed and lifted a brow. "Ye don't think I know that?"

She gave a tiny gasp.

"MacAdam!" the Queen interjected. "Are ye goin' to tee up, or do ye intend to dally with the beer wagon wench all day?"

Josselin's face flushed with heat as laughter circled around her. But when she tried to protest, Drew intervened to make matters worse.

He gave the queen a wide grin. "Ye must admit she's a toothsome lass and a sore temptation."

As if that weren't bad enough, he crooked his elbow around Josselin's neck, drew her close, and planted a brazen kiss on her mouth.

Despite her outrage and against her will, Josselin's heart leaped into her throat. Drew's lips were hot and commanding, calling to some primitive yearning within her. She felt his damp chest through the thin layer of his shirt and breathed his male scent, instantly intoxicated by his earthy essence. And God help her, her head grew dizzy and her knees weak.

When he released her, 'twas all she could do to stand upright.

But the hooting crowd soon sobered her, and rage flared in her like dry tinder put to flame. She heaved an angry breath, ready to rake the Highlander over the coals for his insolence.

Then she caught a glimpse of Mary, who was watching her with a knowing smile, and Josselin realized she must carry out this pretense, no matter how distasteful. A royal spy dared not create a spectacle.

So she summoned up a sugary smile and fluttered her lashes at Drew.

"Go on then, love," she managed to purr between clenched teeth. "Play your match. I'll be waitin' at the beer wagon when ye're done."

She didn't wait for his reaction. She didn't dare. She'd already drawn enough attention to herself.

Picking up her skirts, she skipped back across the green, thanking the Saints that Philipe hadn't seen the Highlander kissing her.

But as she came within sight of the beer wagon, her breath caught, and she stumbled to a halt. Standing beside the cart, a scowl of condemnation creasing his brow, was the queen's secretary.

He cursed her in French, upbraided her for deserting her post, and threatened to relieve her of her position, all of which she listened to with silent forbearance. At least he hadn't witnessed that kiss. But when he accused her of endangering Mary, she took offense.

"I would never do anything to endanger the queen," she proclaimed, straightening proudly. "In fact," she said pointedly, crafting an outright lie that she'd have to seek absolution for later, "I only left to take a pint to the tall, dark, handsome lad in the black doublet and the feathered cap. He looked terribly thirsty."

Josselin prayed that Philipe would be satisfied, both that Josselin had seen through Mary's disguise and that she'd catered to the queen's needs without prompting. Hopefully, he wouldn't bother to confirm her story. As she'd discovered with Kate Campbell, sometimes 'twas easier to lie than try to explain an uncomfortable truth.

Philipe seemed to believe her and was suitably impressed. After a spate of requisite grousing and muttering, he finally agreed to entrust her with the information he'd learned earlier from the nobleman.

Apparently, at the first news of Mary's return to her throne, Queen Elizabeth's man, Lord Walsingham, had sent spies to Scotland. An uneasy truce existed between the two queens, since no one was quite certain who would rightly inherit the English throne should Elizabeth die without issue. Walsingham posed an enormous threat to Mary. As master of Elizabeth's spy network, he'd devised cunning tactics that were difficult to discern, as well as brilliant encryptions that were nearly impossible to decipher.

Worse, there were those in Scotland, among them John Knox and his followers, who would be glad to ally with the English to overthrow Mary.

Philipe had therefore increased the ranks of Mary's agents over the last several days in order to root out enemy spies. Josselin's services would be even more vital now. Since messages would come to her in greater numbers, she was to report to the links at Musselburgh on a daily basis.

Most thrilling was Philipe's warning that Josselin might be called upon to do more than just deliver messages. She would also be charged with keeping her eyes and ears open for suspicious persons who could be counterspies. They might come in the form of trusted individuals—priests or midwives or sweet-faced maids. But she was to trust no one who didn't bring her a triple-notched tankard.

Josselin gave Philipe her solemn promise to uphold his orders. She even managed to wait until he was gone before allowing a glimmer of excitement to enter her eyes. This was what she'd trained for—to serve the Scots queen, to fight against the English, and to get revenge on the brutes who'd murdered her mother.

Leaning dreamily back against a cask of beer, she imagined rooting out a counterspy and engaging him in mortal combat. He'd underestimate her abilities, and she'd surprise him with a few painful slashes of her sword. He'd thrust. She'd parry. He'd advance. She'd retreat. They'd battle back and forth for several moments. She'd let him think he was winning. Then, just as he was about to deal the killing blow...

"MacAdam! MacAdam!" came a rhythmic chant from across the field. "MacAdam! MacAdam!"

Ballocks!

She pushed away from the cask with a frown.

The insufferable cad had done it. He'd knowingly bested the queen.

'Twas bad enough that John Knox had verbally attacked Mary only a few weeks after her arrival, challenging her faith and, rumor had it, reducing her to tears. Now the Highlander had made a fool of her on the golf course in front of everyone.

But when the mob came trooping across the green, Josselin was astonished to see Mary marching at the fore beside Drew, a huge grin wreathing her face. And when she came up to the beer wagon for refreshment, the queen saluted the Highlander with her tankard.

"Well done, sir, well done," she said. "Thank ye for your indulgence. 'Tis a long time since I wooed such a fine Scots course. I can see I'm goin' to have to learn to court the lady properly."

"Patience and persistence," Drew advised. "A lady too easily won is not worth the winnin'," he said, giving Josselin a knowing wink.

Josselin clenched her teeth. It took every ounce of her restraint not to pour his beer over his head.

Chapter 19

Drew didn't think he could have gotten himself into a bigger mess if he'd tried. God's wounds, an Englishman playing golf with the Queen of Scotland? His uncles would never believe it. Even *he* was having trouble believing it, and he was standing beside the young royal.

He was using as much Highland charm as he could muster to keep up appearances, but 'twasn't easy under the hostile watch of the Selkirk lass.

Jossy had no cause to be vexed with him. He'd done as she wished. Against his better judgment, he'd accepted the queen's challenge.

He may have refused to let Mary win, but that was a matter of honor. No golfer worth his clubs would intentionally throw a match.

And if he'd been forced to take certain liberties with Jossy, 'twas only in the interest of maintaining a believable pretense. 'Twas only a kiss. 'Twasn't his fault if her heart may have quickened or her breath caught or a strong wave of desire washed over her, and the world seemed to disappear around them.

Not that it had affected *him*. He was accustomed to

ignoring distractions. Aye, his pulse raced, but surely not because of that kiss. His pulse raced because he was in the presence of his most powerful foe. He might as well have placed his English neck on the executioner's block.

'Twas still a mystery to him, what role Jossy had been asked to play for the royals. If she was merely the beer-wagon wench, then why the need for such secrecy? There was something suspect about this arrangement.

Jossy's fierce glare told him 'twas no concern of his. But he still felt responsible for the Selkirk lass, who was completely out of her element in Edinburgh. Drew had seen what had happened to those close to King Henry. Royals might be dangerous enemies, but they could be even more dangerous allies. And if Drew had to play Jossy's lover to find out what was going on, he was more than willing to make that sacrifice.

She'd certainly need instruction, however, if they were to carry out the ruse. At the moment, the lass looked nothing like an adoring mistress. She looked ready to carve him up like a Sunday roast.

The queen finished off her beer and secured her empty tankard to her belt, then dug in her coin pouch and pulled out a penny.

"Here's what I owe ye, sir." She flipped the coin up, and Drew caught it. "Ye can buy that pretty wench o' yours a trinket."

Drew reached across the counter and snagged Jossy by the waist, pulling her near. "What do ye fancy, dar-lin'? A ribbon for your hair? A bit o' gingerbread? A kerchief?"

Jossy's body went as rigid as a golf club, and the smile

she gave him could have cracked glass. But she managed to answer him sweetly for the queen's sake.

"Ach, I'd dearly love a new thimble," she said, "so I can guard against pricks."

He pretended not to notice her choice of words. "'Tis yours, love," he promised, leaning in to give her a hearty smack on the lips.

The queen bid them farewell then, joining the crowd headed for Edinburgh. The taverns would be filled with Drew's supporters tonight, who'd spend their winnings on drink and spin tales about the great match between Metz and the Highlander.

Jossy's smile stayed fixed to her face until Mary was out of sight. Then she wrenched out of his grasp, giving him a great shove and a glare that would pierce armor.

"Why did ye do that?" she demanded.

"Do what?"

She wiped her mouth with the back of her hand. "Kiss me."

He laughed. "What would ye have me do? Ye're the one who came skippin' out to the green after me like some lovesick calf."

Her jaw dropped. "Lovesick…" Then, at a loss for proper words, she growled and tore off her apron.

"If ye're goin' to make a habit o' deceivin' the queen, darlin', ye'd best learn to do a better job of it."

"I'm not…deceivin' the queen," she told him, though she wouldn't look him in the eye to say the words.

"She thinks ye're just the beer-wagon wench," he said. "But there's more to it than that, isn't there?"

Her blush was confirmation, even if she denied his claim. "Ye don't know what ye're jabberin' about."

"What contract did ye make with that secretary?" he pressed. "Has he indentured ye? Blackmailed ye? Made ye sign away your life?"

She threw her apron down on the counter. "'Tis no bloody business o' yours."

He grabbed her hand, and she gasped. "'Tis, if ye come to harm because of it."

She tugged back in protest, but not hard enough, he noticed, to pull free.

"Ye needn't worry about me," she said sulkily. "I can manage on my own."

"In Selkirk ye could manage on your own. But this is Edinburgh. Ye're dealin' with powerful, dangerous folk— folk who could have ye imprisoned for life or burned at the stake or torn, limb from limb, as a traitor."

Damn! His assertion made *him* shudder. He should heed his own warning. If a wee lass from Selkirk was in danger, how much more at risk was an Englishman?

"I'm no traitor," she assured him.

Her misplaced confidence was frustrating. "'Tisn't the point. Royals are always negotiatin' loyalty on a whim and inventin' treason where there is none."

"Not Mary."

"Mary isn't a power unto herself. She's beholden to lairds and clerics and kings in faraway lands. She's likely not even privy to the details o' your arrangement with Philipe."

Philipe might be working for the queen, but he probably wouldn't hesitate to manipulate any negotiations to his own benefit.

"We have no arrangement," she insisted, pulling her hand free, "other than his offer of employment."

He didn't believe her for a moment. Nobody coerced a tavern wench to sign a document for work.

"Employment," she continued, "I'm grateful to have. Not many can say they've served beer to a queen."

"Neither can ye," he pointed out, "not without revealin' her identity. Is that what ye signed? An oath o' secrecy?"

"'Tisn't your affair what I signed," she snapped, though she seemed more anxious than angry. "We have no further business, ye and me. I'm goin' to keep hawkin' beer, and ye can run along and do your golfin' elsewhere."

Lord, she was a tyrant. "I'll do my golfin' where I please, darlin'," he said with a laugh.

"Well, ye'd better stay clear o' my beer wagon."

He shook his head in amused disbelief. "Ye're a bossy minx. And an ungrateful wench."

"And just what should I be grateful for, knave? That ye grabbed me and had your way with me?"

"Had my way with ye?" He chuckled, which made her blush. "If I'd had my way with ye, love," he murmured ruefully, pinning her with a smoky gaze, "ye'd be flat on your back beside that last hole."

Chapter 20

Josselin never wanted to see Drew MacAdam again. Not after what he'd said to her yesterday. He was a nasty-mouthed, heavy-handed, swaggering cad, sticking his nose—and his lips—where they didn't belong.

She should have slapped him for his ribald remark, and she told herself if she hadn't been so overwrought by the events of the day, she would have.

But he'd bid her a swift, mocking farewell before she could gather her wits, and she'd only been able to stare after him in open-mouthed outrage.

She kicked a wooden block under the wheel of the beer wagon, then whipped out a rag, angrily scrubbing the plank of her makeshift counter and shooing a fly that was buzzing around the tap.

Then she forced herself to take a deep, settling breath. This morn she had to focus on the task at hand and forget about that wayward Highlander. With any luck, he'd moved on to Cockenzie or Leith or St. Andrews, miles from Musselburgh, and she'd be free of his brain-muddling distraction.

Taking Philipe's instructions to heart and keen to distinguish herself by identifying and capturing a spy for the queen, Josselin had arrived before the players this morn, and as the first group approached, she scoured their ranks for suspicious characters.

'Twas only an hour before she received a tankard with three notches along the lip. Without blinking an eye, she filled the cup and pried loose the note affixed underneath. But when she turned to hand the brimming cup back to its owner, her gaze drifted past his head to the man grinning behind him, and she almost spilled the beer.

Collecting herself, she managed to successfully pass the tankard to her target. Then she faced the troublemaking Highlander, crossed her arms over her madly pounding heart, and gave him her fiercest scowl.

They spoke simultaneously.

"What the hell are *ye* doin' here?" she demanded.

"Are ye stalkin' me, lass?" he asked.

Her arms fell out of their fold. "Stalkin' ye!" she spat, brusquely snatching away the next customer's tankard. "Don't be a swollen-headed arse."

" 'Tis the thimble I promised ye, isn't it?" His eyes twinkled with mischief. "Ye didn't have to come after me for it, darlin'. I'd have found a way to—"

"Please!" she scoffed, waving the tankard at him. "Do ye think I'd drive a beer wagon all the way from Edinburgh to Musselburgh for a paltry thimble?"

"Well, if ye didn't come for the thimble, then ye must have come to see me," he concluded with a grin.

The curious bystanders, who'd been watching their discourse with interest, murmured in agreement and turned to see her response.

Giving the smug cad a long, withering glare, she silently counted to three.

The man whose tankard she held broke the silence. "Pardon me, but could I have my—"

"Look. Highlander," she bit out, punctuating her words with jabs of the tankard. "I'm runnin' a beer wagon. I didn't come for the bloody thimble. And I certainly didn't come for ye. Just because we shared a kiss or two—"

"Three," he corrected.

"Fine. Three."

"Ye shared three kisses?" one of the crowd asked.

She lowered the tankard. "It doesn't matter how many kisses—"

"In some parts o' the Highlands," another onlooker said, "a kiss is as good as a betrothal, and three kisses—"

"Ach, for the love o' Saint Peter!" she said, throwing up her hands and glaring at the crowd. "Can ye not mind your own affairs? This isn't the Highlands, and I'm not his damned betrothed. Aye, I kissed him thrice. But I'll bloody well ne'er do it again."

There was a long silence, and Josselin lifted her chin, satisfied her point had been made.

Then someone from the back of the crowd said, "Five shillin's says he gets a fourth kiss," and the air was suddenly filled with counter wagers.

Josselin's jaw dropped in utter amazement. She'd never seen a mob so eager to gamble as the men who attended golf matches. And they seemed willing to wager on almost anything.

A fourth kiss? Were they mad? Couldn't they see how she despised Drew MacAdam? Marry, she found the man so despicable that she could hardly breathe properly in his presence.

He caught her eye then, and to her surprise he gave her a sheepish smile, as if apologizing for the crowd's behavior. Flustered, she turned away to fill the empty tankard.

By the time she finished the task and gave the man his beer, most of the horde had become distracted by an arriving golfer and had wandered off, already wagering on the outcome of the game.

But Drew was still standing at the counter. He was frowning down at an unfolded scrap of paper in his hands.

Suddenly, Josselin's heart slammed against her ribs. She slipped her thumb into the hidden pocket of her skirt. The spy's missive wasn't there. Hell, she'd never tucked it away. She hadn't had a chance. She'd gotten distracted by . . .

The Highlander looked up and caught her eye.

She couldn't be sure, but she thought she detected a grim cast to his normally mocking gaze.

Panicked, she snatched the note from him.

"What the devil do ye think ye're doin'?" she demanded, so mortified that her hands were shaking as she folded the missive and tucked it into the top of her bodice.

"Just returnin' your note."

"Ye weren't returnin' it. Ye were readin' it."

He snorted. "Ye know Highlanders can't read."

"Then how did ye know 'twas mine?"

He shrugged. "I saw ye drop it."

Flustered by her own carelessness, she blurted out, "Well, maybe ye shouldn't be watchin' my every move."

"And maybe ye should hold more tightly to your love letters."

She stiffened. If he couldn't read, how did he know 'twas a love letter? She glanced up, meeting his eyes.

In an instant, his grin returned. "'Tis the second one ye've dropped at my feet," he teased.

But Josselin was almost certain that in that split second before he smiled, she'd seen something entirely different in his gaze.

Something all too perceptive.

Chapter 21

Disappointment.

That was what Drew felt as he turned his back on Jossy and walked across the green to meet his opponent.

'Twas foolish. How could he be disappointed when he had no right to expect anything of the lass? She didn't belong to him. She didn't owe him anything. In fact, she didn't particularly care for him. At least that was what her words said. Her lips, however...

Curse the Fates, he thought, kicking at a loose chunk of sod. He was bewitched by the wee willful wench. And, according to the letter she'd just tucked into that lovely crevice betwixt her breasts, so was someone else.

He'd only skimmed the thing. But it had begun with "My dearest Josselin" and ended with "Your worshipful Duncan." Scattered between were words like "kisses," "heaven," "yearning," and "quench."

'Twas sickening, such flowery, sugar-sweet language. Indeed, it surprised him that a woman as forthright as Jossy would lap up such honey. But he'd seen her place the sappy declaration next to her heart.

He told himself 'twas no matter. If the lass was so shallow she'd succumb to such empty flattery and overwrought promises, then perhaps the fawning Duncan deserved her.

But that wasn't how he felt. He felt disappointed.

He'd never met anyone quite like Jossy.

She seemed, in a word, genuine.

She had a wild spirit and a startling frankness, an unwavering loyalty and audacious ambition. He liked her strength—the way she'd stood up to the drunk on The Royal Mile, scolded the gossips in the alley, and challenged *him*.

Even her weaknesses were honest—blushing when he touched her, gasping when he said something to shock her, melting in his arms when he kissed her.

Jossy's every response—whether 'twas anger or pride, fear or satisfaction, shame or desire—was genuine.

The fact that she had a secret lover was contrary to everything he'd believed about her.

Drew crouched to scoop sand into a tee and placed his ball on the small mound. As he lined up the shot, the crowd waved their arms and shouted, but he neither saw nor heard them. His thoughts were still on the lass from Selkirk who'd betrayed him.

Betrayed him?

The word had popped into his mind unbidden just as he swung his longnose club, and the ball hooked, going completely off target.

The crowd let him know in no uncertain terms just how bad his shot was, and he grumbled a curse under his breath.

Betrayed? Where the hell had that come from? There was nothing between them to betray. He had offered Jossy an escort to a tavern. She had accepted. That was all.

Everything else had happened because Drew hadn't been able to keep his nose out of her affairs and his mind out of the bedchamber.

He scowled. His ball had landed in the rough. The match had only started, and already he was falling behind young Colin Barrie, the novice from Dunbar.

He slogged through the thick marram and flattened the grass as best he could for the difficult shot, choosing a niblick from among his clubs for the task.

Who was this Duncan anyway? Drew had expected the note Josselin had dropped to come from Philipe. Was Duncan a golfer? Someone from The White Hart? One of Philipe's friends?

He placed the head of the club behind the ball and swung back.

'Twasn't that he was jealous, but...

When he swung forward, his club jammed into the sod just behind the ball, chipping it almost straight up. When it landed, it rolled meekly onto the green, a few inches from the edge of the rough and no nearer the hole.

"Shite."

The crowd concurred.

Jealous? Had he actually thought that? Whatever Drew was feeling, 'twasn't jealousy. How could he be jealous of someone he'd never met?

Or had he?

While young Barrie was busy eyeing up his shot, Drew scanned the men jostling each other for a good vantage point. One of them might be Jossy's sly suitor. One of them might have slipped the love letter to her at the beer wagon this morn. But which one?

There were half a dozen nobles among the onlookers,

a number of the merchant class, and a few students. 'Twas unlikely the rest of the bunch could read or write. He sized up the possible candidates, one by one.

The nobleman with the fur-trimmed collar was old enough to be Jossy's grandfather.

The scowling merchant with the black beard looked too cynical to write a love letter.

Students were impulsive and romantic. Could one of them be Duncan? Perhaps the tall one with the broad shoulders? Or the one with the laughing eyes and the straight white teeth? Or the fellow with the head full of golden curls?

Drew ground his teeth. 'Twas probably that golden-headed one. Women adored blond curls.

Somebody jostled him.

"Are ye goin' to play or not?" the scowling merchant asked.

"Aye. Aye."

Faith, he had to get his mind back on the game. There were men counting on him to win.

He chose his fairway club and settled it behind the ball, eyeing the distant hole. He wondered if the silver-tongued Duncan had bet for or against him.

Silently cursing his stupid jealousy of a man he didn't know over a woman he didn't possess, Drew cocked his arm and swung forward with surprising force. The club hit the ball with a loud crack, and it shot like an arrow across the green, bypassing the hole completely and eventually rolling to a stop in the middle of the marshy spot on the far side of the course.

"Oh, that's bloody brilliant," he muttered, shaking his head.

A shoving match broke out then between Barrie's cocky supporters and Drew's disappointed ones. By the time they reached the seventh hole, the violence had escalated into a full-scale brawl, Barrie was winning by five strokes, and Drew was no closer to identifying the elusive Duncan.

Chapter 22

Josselin's hands were still shaking as she surreptitiously retrieved the note from her bosom. She never read the missives. The less she knew, the safer she was.

But the Highlander had taken a good, long look at this one. If he'd been able to decipher anything...

"My dearest Josselin," it began. She quickly skimmed the contents. 'Twas the sort of sugary prose a lover might write to his mistress, and 'twas signed, "your worshipful Duncan," which was, of course, a fictitious name.

Josselin knew there was some type of code encrypted into the letter. She didn't know what 'twas. She didn't want to know. But she certainly didn't want anyone else to find out. 'Twas her responsibility to make sure the missive didn't fall into the wrong hands.

She studied the note a moment more. Then, satisfied 'twas a convincing love letter, no more, she put it away.

If only she could put away her thoughts so easily.

They kept straying to Drew MacAdam, and the more she thought about him, the more uneasy she became.

This time, 'twas more than his sky blue eyes and sly

grin that worried her, more than his startling embraces and troubling kisses that set her heart to pounding.

This time, she began to think deeply about her relationship with the Highlander.

Was it mere coincidence that they kept showing up at the same places? Or could it be he was following her?

He'd seemed very concerned about the document she'd signed with Philipe. Was it possible he wasn't interested in her welfare so much as her activities?

He'd intercepted two of her missives now and had ample time to look them over. He insisted he couldn't read, but what if he was lying? What if he'd known exactly what he was looking at?

It suddenly seemed very plausible that the Highlander might be a spy for Walsingham.

The thought sent a sobering shiver up her spine. The man had stood within a blade's reach of the queen yesterday, knowing full well who she was. He could have assassinated her.

Worse, Josselin herself had led him to her. She'd insisted he play against the queen, practically shoving him onto the green. And when he'd used Josselin for cover, she'd gone along with his ruse, pretending she was his mistress. Bloody hell, she'd *kissed* the traitor.

She brought trembling fingers to her lips. How could she have allowed him, allowed an enemy *spy*, to get so close to her?

Philipe had warned her that agents were usually those who aroused the least suspicion—tavern wenches, stable lads, even monks. She supposed a golfer from the Highlands was as unlikely a spy as there could be.

She wiped sweaty palms on her apron. What should she do now?

Josselin was accustomed to fighting duels, where one faced one's enemy openly with a sword. Subterfuge was not in her nature. Perhaps she should stay out of this particular fight. Perhaps she should alert Philipe to the peril and let him do what he thought best.

Then she smiled ruefully. Walk away from a fight? 'Twas unthinkable.

Josselin was her mother's daughter. She'd no more refuse a challenge than she'd refuse a thirsty patron with a purse full of silver.

Besides, going to Philipe and admitting her error in judgment would be unwise. How would she explain that she'd let Drew see those two missives? How would she assure Philipe that she was a competent agent when she'd been seen consorting with the enemy? And did she even have enough solid evidence to prove beyond the shadow of a doubt that Drew MacAdam was a spy?

Nae, she couldn't say anything to Philipe, not until she had more proof.

As distasteful as the prospect was, if she wanted to unmask him, Josselin had to get closer to the Highlander, persuade him to trust her, compel him to expose his secrets.

'Twas the same cat-and-mouse game her Da Angus had taught her in swordfighting. By drawing the enemy in and feigning helplessness, she'd lull him into complacency. Then, when he least expected it, she'd strike at his heart.

Her own heart quivered at the thought. 'Twas a dangerous game. If she became impatient and lost her self-control, she might strike too soon. If she misjudged the distance and drew too close, she'd leave herself vulnerable to attack. Worst of all, she might finally strike at him with all her might, only to discover that she was the unwitting victim in *his* game of cat-and-mouse.

She shivered, then mentally scolded herself for such nonsense. She wasn't talking about a swordfight, after all, though she was sure she could best the golfer in a duel with one hand bound behind her back. 'Twas only a harmless flirtation she planned, nothing that might leave a scar.

Still, when she thought about intentionally ingratiating herself to the Highlander, courting his affections, encouraging his intimacy...

Marry, her belly didn't flutter half as much when she was preparing to do battle with a blade.

Josselin took a determined breath and tossed her apron down on the counter. She was no coward. She was fully prepared in mind and body to put herself in harm's way for her country, for her queen, for the memory of her mother. If only her racing heart would believe that...

Drew was disgusted with himself. He'd let emotion get in the way of his game. As a consequence, he'd lost. Badly. 'Twas a good thing he'd been battling with a golf club and not a sword, for such inattention might have cost him an arm or a leg instead of only his pride.

Long after the victorious Barrie had left the field on the shoulders of his cheering companions, Drew was still sulking at the last hole, sitting on the sod with his chin in his fist, staring pensively out toward the shifting sea.

"Hey! Highlander!"

He turned to see Jossy heading toward him, carrying two tankards in her hand. The sunlight burnished her hair to a gleaming gold, and the soft breeze ruffled the linen across her breasts, reminding him of what would never belong to him, of what belonged to the insidious Duncan.

"Here's the pint I owe ye," she said, offering him one of the tankards, then plopping artlessly down onto the grass beside him with the other.

He shook his head, amused. The lass was certainly unpredictable. He raised his tankard in thanks, and she clanked her cup to his. They both took a sip, then resumed gazing silently at the sea.

"I lost," he finally admitted, taking another consoling swig.

"I'd say 'twas more like slaughter."

He nearly choked on his beer. "Well, don't be waterin' it down, lass. Give it to me straight."

"'Tis true," she said with a shrug. "At least 'tis what they were sayin' at the beer wagon."

He clucked his tongue. "And ye came all the way o'er here to tell me so?"

She acted hurt. "O' course not."

"Then why *did* ye come?"

"I told ye, I owed ye a beer."

"A beer," he said doubtfully. "And that's it?"

She frowned guiltily into her cup. "And perhaps an apology."

"An apology. For what?"

"For snappin' at ye, after ye helped me and all. My da says I've got a temper as short as a lamb's tail."

He smiled. He rather liked her temper. 'Twas so easy to ruffle her feathers, to set her off balance, and once she was off balance...

His smile faded. He dared not go down that road. "'Tis

perfectly understandable. Ye didn't want me perusin' your private note."

"Aye, but ye *did* say ye couldn't read."

"I did," he said carefully.

"So I suppose there was no harm done. Indeed, I owe ye thanks for its return."

His smile was forced this time. He wondered if the mawkish note was still tucked between her lovely breasts.

Then he furrowed his brow. Where was her elusive suitor anyway? Everyone had left the links. Where had he gone? Surely Jossy wouldn't dally on the course with Drew when "your worshipful Duncan" was waiting.

"Well, ye've thanked me," he assured her. "There's no need to tarry."

"Are ye sendin' me away?"

He chuckled. "Perhaps." Then he cocked his head at her. "I'm guessin' that letter might be another invitation from your French friend?"

"Philipe? Oh, nae. The letter? 'Twas nothin', really, just a wee note from an admirer."

He was surprised she was telling him the truth. "An admirer?"

"Aye," she said shyly.

Drew cast his glance around the course. "And won't this admirer be displeased to see ye sittin' here with me?"

"What?" She froze for an instant, like a startled deer, then licked her lips and said, "Oh, nae. 'Tisn't the way of it at all."

"Indeed?" He took a long pull of his beer, contemplating her cagey manner. The lass might be telling the truth, but she was definitely hiding part of it. "Well, I'd be jealous if ye were *my* lover."

"Lover? Oh, nae, he's not my lover," she said in a rush. "Nae, nae, not at all. He's only...He's..." She paused to collect herself. "Duncan..."

"Duncan?" Faith, she really *was* telling him the truth. He was impressed.

"Duncan is more of a...a devotee than a suitor."

"Hm."

Drew took another long drink to conceal his pleasure at hearing this news. Perhaps he'd delay his departure from Edinburgh after all.

Chapter 23

Josselin suddenly realized it was going to be hard to woo Drew's affections while she was constantly receiving love letters from Duncan. She supposed she should have thought things out more carefully.

She feigned a casual shrug. "He's really nobody," she said, which was oddly the truth.

For once Drew didn't reply, but sat quietly, sipping his beer and watching a flock of gulls circling over the distant waves.

'Twas obvious she'd have to take stronger measures if she wanted to loosen the Highlander's tongue.

"Do ye know The Sheep Heid Inn?" she asked.

"'Tis where I'm stayin'."

"Indeed?" She supposed 'twas no surprise. The Sheep Heid was the nearest inn to the Musselburgh course. But that bit of information might be useful. "Well, I've got an hour or so before the next golfers arrive, and the wagon will be safe enough with Davey, the driver. Come sup with me. I owe ye supper."

He looked over at her, one eye squinting against the sun. "I can't have ye payin' for my supper, lass."

"Why not? I'm earnin' wages now, and 'tis the least I can do to thank ye. If 'tweren't for ye, I'd have no work at all."

"But 'tis only a tavern wench's wages," he pointed out.

"Hmph!" she scoffed. "I wager I earned more silver today than ye did."

He winced. "True." He shook his head. "Ach, ye drive the dagger deep, lass."

She scrambled to her feet and waited while he gathered his clubs and balls and slung the bag over his shoulder. Then she walked with him to the inn.

Entering under the sign of the ram's head, they were welcomed by the smells of mutton stew bubbling over the fire and free-flowing ale. Unfortunately, half a dozen of the Musselburgh regulars had commandeered the largest table, and they recognized Drew, so their progress was delayed by greetings and condolences on his game. But Josselin managed to secure a small spot in a dark corner where they could converse in private. She ordered two trenchers of stew and two pints of the tavern's best ale. A couple of the strong brews and she was sure to have the spy singing like a sparrow.

Drew pushed back his empty trencher and gazed in amusement at the adorable lass across the table. She was breathtaking. She was relentless. And she was drunk off her arse.

Of course, she wasn't aware of that. Nor was he about to enlighten her to the fact. He continued to chat with her as if nothing was awry, patiently answering her slurred interrogation, satisfying his appetite, and enjoying the view.

"Where'd ye say ye're from?" she asked him for the second time.

"Tintclachan."

"Tint. Clach. An." She said it slowly, as if to memorize it. "An' how long've ye been travelin' the Lowlands?"

"Three years or so."

"Three years." She paused to take another incautious swig of her third ale. "An' ye're stayin' here at this inn?"

"At the moment," he told her, adding in a whisper, "up the stairs, third door on the right."

She nodded as if digesting all this. Then she raised a skeptical brow. "Are ye certain all ye do t'earn your keep's golfin'?"

He laughed. "I assure ye I usually play better than I did today." He studied her face, lingering on her enchanting eyes and her enticing lips. "My attention wasn't on the game."

"Huh." She leaned forward, like a barrister gravely questioning a convict. "An' what *was* your attention on then?"

Drew flashed her a lazy grin. He might be able to hold his ale better than the lass, but there was still a pleasant buzzing in his head that made him speak impulsively. "I had my eye on a short-tempered blond lass."

She frowned.

He added, "One with fiery green eyes?"

She continued to frown.

"And a honey-sweet mouth?" he suggested.

She looked puzzled for a moment. Then she gasped. "'S'me."

He saluted her with his tankard.

"But I'm nobody," she argued. "'M jus' a lass from

Selk—, Selkirk. Why would ye want to spy—" She stopped suddenly, biting her lip as if she'd said too much.

His gaze was drawn to those succulent lips. He might be feeling the effects of the ale, but 'twasn't the ale that made him want to taste her again. Nor was it intoxication that awakened the beast slumbering below his belt.

"Oh," she breathed, finally understanding. Then a glint of interest flashed in her eyes, and she leaned forward to rest her chin in the cup of her hand. "Ohhh."

Drew clenched his jaw. At this angle, mere inches apart, he could see the sweet shadow between her lovely breasts, could too easily imagine how silky her flesh was there, too vividly envision resting his head upon her soft, warm...

He grabbed his tankard and took a large gulp of ale, a gulp he definitely didn't need and shouldn't have taken.

She arched her brow seductively above smoldering green eyes. "An' am I distractin' ye now?"

He smiled in self-mockery. "Ye know ye are."

The lass might be half-drunk, but she knew damned well what she was doing. The wee minx was riling him up like a lad poking at a hornet's nest. Shite, another ale, and she'd have him by the ballocks.

Josselin returned his smile, then hiccoughed. Things were going quite well, she thought, even if she had drunk a wee bit more than she'd intended. So far in her inquisition of Drew MacAdam she'd learned he'd been in the field for three years, he was staying at this inn—up the stairs, third door on the right, and he was born in...what was it again? Tint. Clach. An.

She creased her brow. What an odd word. Sometimes

she wondered if Highlanders named their burghs by clearing their throats. Tintclachan. She'd have to write that down as soon as she had pen and parchment.

Meanwhile, Drew had definitely taken an interest in her. Her plan to get closer to him was working. Soon she'd have the besotted Highlander eating out of her fingers and spilling all his secrets.

Marry, she must have some talent as a spy after all. 'Twasn't as difficult as she'd imagined, nor as unpleasant. Indeed, sitting in the cozy tavern with a full belly by the warm fire, watching the way the light danced over his hair and flickered in his smoky blue eyes and kissed his curving lips...

Her chin slipped suddenly off her palm.

She blinked. Perhaps she shouldn't have ordered that last ale. She'd meant to get the Highlander drunk, but at the moment he didn't look half as addled as she felt.

In fact, he looked amazing.

In the firelight, his skin was golden, and his eyes were the deep color of the sea. Where his hair hung in jagged locks, shadows played across his cheek, flirting with the upturned corners of his lips and sweeping over his angular jaw, already shaded by a day's growth of dark beard.

She remembered how it felt—that short stubble— rough against her cheek, in contrast to the gentle pressure of his mouth, and the memory sent a delicious shiver through her bones.

'Twasn't that she wanted to kiss him again. God knew 'twas not a sensation she cared to repeat—that blood-simmering dizziness that left her speechless and breathless and witless and weak.

On the other hand, if 'twould further her progress

toward uncovering his secrets, she supposed 'twas a wee sacrifice she must make for queen and country.

Of course, she'd keep the tightest rein on her affections. She didn't intend to bed the man, after all. 'Twas only a kiss. And they'd kissed before. Thrice.

Aye, she resolved, she'd do it.

No sooner did she make that decision than, moving her tankard out of the way, she rose from her chair and bent toward him. She captured the back of his shaggy head with one hand, clasped his suddenly slack jaw with the other, and molded her lips to his.

Chapter 24

Drew was so astonished by the lass's attack that he actually flinched.

In the next instant, of course, he moved from astonishment to baffled pleasure.

Finally his male instincts took over. He seized the opportunity . . . and the lass . . . and returned her enthusiastic kiss, ignoring the clatter of upset tankards and spoons as they grappled across the table.

She tasted of ale and woman and desire, the last flavor more intoxicating than anything he'd ever drunk before. His head whirled as she came after him with a vengeance, pressing her lips to his with delicious determination.

What had come over the lass, he didn't know. Nor did he much feel like asking. He only wanted her to keep on.

As she continued her impulsive caress, the world somehow gradually dropped away. Suddenly there was no tavern, no ale, no crackling fire, only this beautiful woman and her irresistible kiss. Her touch was as real as anything he'd ever felt, and he longed to embrace her more fully. But he was half afraid to move, lest he burst the fragile bubble of the moment.

So while she clung to him, he slowly tangled his fingers through her tresses, angling her face so he might delve between her eager lips. She responded with a soft mewl of pleasure and let her mouth fall open, granting him leave to explore. Ever so gently, he swept his tongue across her soft lips, and she sighed, shivering, into his mouth.

But when he would have made patient forays with the tip of his tongue into the sweet recesses there, gradually earning her trust, tempting her to greater intimacies, all at once Jossy made it abundantly clear she was having none of that.

She grabbed his face between forceful hands and, with a groan of feminine need, opened her mouth wide and utterly devoured him.

The lusty growl he returned must have come from some animal lodged in a deep, dark corner of his chest. The wild creature charged to the surface, shoving aside Drew's noble intentions and ravenously slaking its thirst on the willing maiden.

And still she didn't recoil. Instead, she demanded more, clawing at his neck, gasping against his mouth, thrusting and parrying with her tongue as if they were engaged in a duel to the death.

His blood boiled, his heart pounded, and his cock strained at his trews, as hard as the oak table over which they tussled. Faith, if he'd been the coarse-mannered Highlander he pretended to be instead of an English gentleman, he'd have cleared the table with a sweep of his arm, tossed up her skirts, and taken her then and there.

What the Highlander had done to her, Josselin didn't know.

She couldn't think.

She couldn't breathe.

And she couldn't stop.

He was scattering her focus and shattering her restraint, stripping away her inhibitions and destroying her self-control. Yet she'd never felt more vibrant and alive.

Her lips tingled as his mouth moved restlessly over hers with a nameless hunger. Her heart raced, her bones melted, and she could hear the blood singing in her ears. She knew only that she desired, she needed, she craved, and that some sensual reward kept eluding her, dancing just out of reach.

A moment more, and she might have lost herself completely to desire. But with the last remaining dregs of reason, she managed to hold on long enough to sense the change in the room.

Applause.

The men in the tavern were clapping. And whistling. And cheering.

She opened her eyes.

He heard it, too. He grunted and frowned like a groggy child, then lifted his lids a quarter of an inch.

Recognition struck them simultaneously, and they drew apart. Josselin stumbled back, plopping down onto her chair while Drew scrutinized the applauding audience with a stormy scowl.

"That's it, MacAdam!" someone crowed. "I knew ye wouldn't disappoint."

"Four kisses! Pay up, Cullen!" another man shouted. "That's two pounds ye owe me."

"Oh, fine," Cullen grumbled. "Anyone want to gamble on five then?"

"Five!" someone yelled back.

"Those Highlanders are a lusty lot," the tavern wench declared, giving Drew a wink. "If I were ye gentlemen, I'd wager on six."

Hoots and cries went up, and for a few moments, Drew looked disoriented, as if he'd been roughly wakened from a deep sleep. Then, bemused, he shook his head as he settled back down onto his chair.

But Josselin felt the blood rise in her cheeks. She was humiliated and confused and, aye, a wee bit tipsy, and she longed to skewer a few of the leering spectators. Lucky for them she couldn't summon up the coordination to draw her dagger.

What had happened? What had Drew done to her? She'd meant to give him one kiss, that was all, a kiss to incur his trust and loosen his tongue.

Loosen his tongue. Aye, she'd certainly done that, she thought as an unwelcome wave of desire washed over her. But then he'd done...whatever 'twas he'd done, and he'd ruined everything. He'd made her forget all about her objectives, her progress, her service to the queen. Not only that, but he'd drawn attention to her, which was the last thing she wanted.

Yet there he sat, looking not a bit sorry.

'Twas ungentlemanly, uncouth, and unforgivable. With an angry pout, she reached across the table and gave him a good shove.

"What was that for?" His brow furrowed in genuine confusion.

"Ye know what."

She huffed out an annoyed breath, then shot to her feet. Unfortunately, she didn't quite have her balance, and she listed a bit to the left. Drew caught her arm to steady her, and she slapped his hand away.

But at her next step, her knee buckled, and she would have fallen if he hadn't caught her waist.

"Easy, lass."

She sighed. Bloody hell. This assignment was not going well at all. Her legs had turned to custard. Everyone was staring at her. And curse it all, she couldn't even remember the unpronounceable name of the Highland spy's hometown.

"Let's get out o' here," he murmured.

She glared at him, making a halfhearted effort to wrench herself out of his grasp. But his gaze softened, and the curious vulnerability she saw in his eyes took the edge off of her ire. Still, nothing save leaving would ease the sting of her shame.

They departed to the bawdy jeers of the tavern patrons, and if it weren't for the Highlander whisking her quickly out the door, she might have hurled a few choice oaths their way.

Drew was glad of the sobering sea breeze that slapped his face as they left the tavern. It cooled his fevered brain, even if it couldn't quench the fire burning in his loins.

Only one thing could do that.

And that wasn't going to happen. Not today.

Perhaps if he'd truly been a ruthless Highland laird, accustomed to seizing what he wanted and damn the consequences, he might have taken advantage of her innocence. 'Twould have been easy to seduce the wanton maid, given she was in her cups and over her head.

But his uncles had raised him to be an honorable

man. Never in his life had he violated an unwilling lass or seduced an unwitting one, and he wasn't about to start now, even if that lass was an enemy Scot.

While they weaved their way back to the beer wagon, Jossy remained silent, which was a blessing. He didn't think he could endure discussing what had happened at the tavern, and he certainly didn't want to dwell on what wasn't going to happen now.

Instead, he did what he'd always done when he suffered from excessive sexual frustration.

When they arrived at the links, he took out his fairway club, stood at one end of the course with a dozen balls, and hit the bloody hell out of them.

Chapter 25

Two ales. That was Josselin's new limit. Faith, she'd almost exposed herself and endangered her mission by imbibing too freely yesterday. True, a bit of the ale's fortification had expedited her progress somewhat. But from now on, she'd avoid walking that narrow precipice between tipsy and sloshed.

If the Highlander came to the links today—and the odds were in favor of it, seeing as how a number of his supporters were demanding to win their coin back and knew he could prevail against the visiting golfer—she wouldn't make the same mistake again.

So she believed, until Drew arrived on the course at dawn, gazing at her with his seductive blue eyes, tempting her with his sweet, wicked grin. Then she suddenly longed for a cold pint in which to douse her lust.

She told herself over and over that he was only a target. There was no true affection between them. 'Twas all a ruse. If he was a spy, as she suspected, they were probably playing at the same game. Any romantic overtures were cool, calculated manipulations on both their parts.

That was what she told herself.

Her heart, however, told her something entirely different. It leapt as he came toward the beer wagon. It fluttered as he flashed her a contrite smile. It pounded as she recalled the warmth of his lips pressed to hers.

"Good mornin'," he said.

"Mornin'." Marry, was she blushing? She tucked her hair behind her ear. "Ye're here early."

"I've got somethin' for ye." He dug in his pouch, enclosing something in his palm. "Hold out your hand."

She did. He slowly uncurled his fingers on her palm, sending an uninvited shiver up her arm and leaving behind a tiny metal bauble.

She smiled. "A thimble."

"To guard against pricks," he told her with a wink.

"Ye didn't have to."

"Oh, aye, lass." He leaned in closer, confiding, "'Twas at the queen's command, after all."

She placed it on her finger, admiring it as if 'twere a priceless ring of gold, which made Drew chuckle. Then she tucked the thimble into her pocket and casually asked, "So...do ye think she'll ever challenge ye again—the queen?"

Drew's reply could be important. If he *was* a spy, and he'd scheduled a match with Mary, Philipe would surely want to know about it so he could make certain the queen was well-defended.

But Drew only grinned. "Not unless she's lookin' to drain the royal coffers."

"Faugh!" Josselin bristled at the slight to her queen. "Mary's said to be an exceptional golfer. She was likely only havin' a bad day. Ye said yourself 'twasn't fair to challenge her when she'd ne'er played the course before."

"Oh, I'm sure she's a fine player," he said with a cocky tilt of his brow. "'Tis only that I'm better."

"Hmph. How much skill can it take to knock a ball about on the grass?"

His jaw dropped at her insult, and he shook his head.

"That's it, lass," he said with a grim smile, glaring at her in feigned threat and grabbing her wrist. "I've heard enough out o' ye about the dubious merits o' my sport."

He tugged her out from behind the counter.

"What are ye..." she stuttered. "Where are ye tak— I can't leave the beer wa—"

"Davey!" he called, startling the driver, who was napping atop his perch. "Keep an eye on the wagon. Jossy will be back in half an hour."

Davey gave him a vague wave.

She pulled back, panicked. "But what are ye—"

"Ye're goin' to learn to golf."

"But I can't just... I'm supposed to stay at—"

"Don't fret, love," he said, tugging her forward again. "Ye'll get no business at this hour."

She went along reluctantly. She hated to leave her post, but what he said was true. 'Twould be an hour before the crowd would even arrive. Besides, she was supposed to be forming a closer bond with the spy, wasn't she? And what better way to bond with him than to share his passion?

Those words hadn't come out quite right in her mind, but 'twas too late now. The Highlander was already dragging her across the green and lecturing her on the finer points of his silly game.

"The club's too long for ye," he said, sizing it up against her as he bent to scoop a handful of sand out of the first hole to form a mound. "But ye can slide your hands down the shaft a bit."

She clenched her fists around the club.

He laughed, rising to stand behind her. "Ye don't want to throttle the thing, darlin'. Here."

When he suddenly enveloped her, folding his arms over hers, she jerked reflexively.

He immediately let go. "Wait," he said, spinning her around to face him. "Let's get rid o' this." He unbuckled her belt, lowering it—and more significantly, her dagger—to the ground. "There."

He turned her back around and resumed his intimate position, which was so unnerving that she actually glanced about the course to check for witnesses. Thankfully, they were alone.

"Place your hands so," he said, guiding her hands with his own, "and hold it like ye would your dagger—not too tight, not too loose. Aye, that's it. Now spread your legs and bend your knees a wee bit, centerin' yourself. Good balance is the key."

Josselin was having a hard time listening. His body practically surrounded hers. His arms were warm and sure, his chest felt like a wall of muscle at her back, and below that...

"Most importantly, keep your head down. There's no need to be watchin' where the ball goes. 'Twill take care of itself. Ye need to focus on gettin' your swing right, and the rest will follow. Do ye want to try then?"

She nodded.

With his hands over hers, he slowly swung the club back and up behind her head, then forward and up again in a great arc. 'Twas not unlike the exercises she did with a sword.

"That's it. Now try again. Keep your leadin' arm straight, and just tickle the blades o' grass with the club."

They swung together a second time, a third, a fourth.

She closed her eyes. Every inch of her skin felt charged, and swinging their limbs together created a pleasing sensual friction. His voice was low and seductive against her ear, and the way he was pressed against her backside made her feel faint.

"Ye're a bit stiff," he said.

She had to bite her lip at that, for she wasn't the only one who was a bit stiff.

"Keep your knees bent and your head down. Aye, better."

She swallowed hard and tried to focus. She could learn this. If Queen Mary could do it, she could do it.

"That's it," he said, easing back away from her. "Now try it on your own."

Relieved of his proximity, she relaxed and tried several more swings. Soon the movement began to feel natural.

"'Tis like wieldin' a sword," she remarked.

"Aye," he said with a laugh, "though I'm not goin' to ask how ye know that."

She made a dozen more swings. "Are ye goin' to let me hit the ball, or am I supposed to swing at empty air all day?"

"That depends."

"On what?"

"Are ye plannin' to hit it true?" he said with mock gravity. "Because I don't have that many balls, and I can't afford to lose one in the firth."

She glared at him.

He broke into a grin. "Come here then," he said,

motioning to her. "Watch me. Ye address the ball like so."
He spread his legs slightly to form an uneven triangle with
the ball, which perched on the mound of sand. He moved
aside then, inviting her to stand in his place.

She imitated his stance and placed the head of the club
behind the ball.

"That's right," he said. "Now look down the green
until ye see the hole."

"Where?"

He placed his head beside hers and pointed it out. "Do
ye see it?"

His hair was soft against her cheek, and his breath was
warm and stirring. She couldn't see the air in front of her,
much less the hole.

"Aye," she lied.

"Your feet should line up with the hole, but after that,
ye don't want to look at it. Ye want to keep your eye on the
ball."

She nodded, and he took a large step backward for
safety's sake. Keeping her gaze locked on the elm ball,
she reared back and slashed forward with all her might,
finishing the swing above her head.

The ball hadn't budged. She frowned.

He snickered. "Well, that's one way to make sure ye
don't lose the ball."

"What did I do?"

"Ye tried too hard. Don't chop at the thing. Swing
through it."

She squared up to the ball again.

"Bend your knees."

She did.

"Find your balance."

She did.

"Keep your eye on the target, and take a smooth, even swing."

Josselin realized his instructions sounded very familiar. 'Twas the same advice her da's gave her for sword-fighting. Maybe golfing wasn't that different from dueling. Perhaps if she imagined the wooden ball was the head of an Englishman...

She hit the target this time with a crack, and she felt the shiver of the club all the way up her arm. When she looked up, the ball was rolling gently across the green.

"Well done!" Drew said, applauding.

She shrugged, though she had to admit there *was* something satisfying about knocking a ball about with a stick. "Now what?"

"Ye go find it and hit it again."

She did. It took her nearly twenty strokes and a few different clubs, but she finally got the ball within close range of the hole.

"Now ye're ready for the puttin' cleek," he said. "Ye just need a light tap. Some like to kneel to putt, but I prefer to stand."

She smiled. Of course the proud Highlander preferred to stand. Then so would she. "I'll stand."

He nodded. With amazing dexterity, he hooked his boot under the grip of his putting cleek as it lay on the ground, flipped the club up smartly into his hand, gave it a twirl, and handed it to her with a cocky flourish. Then he came behind her again to guide her swing.

Perhaps 'twas the exertion of the game or the heat of the sun, which was fully above the sea now, or just her proximity to a man who might be a dangerous spy, but

Josselin felt suddenly warm as Drew placed his arms around hers once more and whispered against her hair.

"We'll try a few swings without the ball. Line your feet up with the hole, find your balance, and keep your head down."

He'd pushed up his sleeves now, and the touch of his bare flesh on hers was heavenly.

"Here's the secret," he confided. "Take a few deep breaths."

They breathed together.

"Now let out all your air, give one smooth swing, and push the ball into the hole."

They practiced three more times, then Drew backed away and pronounced her ready to address the ball.

She took three breaths and let out the third, easing the club forward, and swept the ball straight into the hole.

Then she let out a whoop and turned to grin at Drew.

"I did it!"

His eyes sparkled, his teeth flashed in the morning sun, and before Josselin even knew what she was doing, she rushed forward to give him a hug of victory.

Laughing, he picked her up and swung her around. She squealed, clinging to him, and for a moment she felt like a child again.

Then his circling slowed, and his grin faded, and she grew aware that they were *not* children, not at all. His body felt powerful and masculine against hers. His mouth looked delicious and inviting. The spice of his damp skin was heady. And the smoldering lust in his gaze...

"MacAdam!"

Ballocks.

She staggered back, stunned, and Drew steadied her,

then scowled, nodding to acknowledge the interloper on the course, his opponent, Michael Cochrane.

"I thought that was ye!" the man shouted, trotting over to greet him. He was a burly fellow with bushy brows and a long beard, and there was a satchel of golf clubs slung over his broad shoulder.

"Cochrane," Drew called out. "Ye're early."

Cochrane shook his head. "Nae. There's already a line at the beer wagon. So how've ye been, MacAdam? I hear ye beat the trews off o' Metz. And ye've been makin' a name for..."

Josselin didn't hear anything else. A line at the beer wagon? Faith, where had the time gone? She had to get back. What if she missed her contact?

With her heart in her throat, she picked up her skirts and fairly flew across the green.

Chapter 26

Josselin decided she must be the worst spy ever. Not only had she misplaced missives, abandoned her post, drunk herself into a stupor, and grown dangerously fond of a man who might be an enemy of the queen, but she didn't have anything to show for all her efforts.

Fortunately, she hadn't missed her contact. He came midway through the afternoon, and his note was now safe with her.

But what was she going to do about the Highlander?

He'd done something to her this morn. Playing golf with him had made her feel alive, the way she did when she perfected a new move with her sword. The two of them seemed to be kindred spirits, delighting in the same small triumphs and cursing over the same disappointments. But kindred spirits didn't begin to describe the closeness she felt to Drew when he wrapped his arms about her or whispered against her cheek or pressed his warm, full staff against her backside...

She fanned herself with a rag.

This was insufferable. Drew MacAdam was an enigma. She didn't know whether to kiss him or kill him.

She had to find out whether he was a spy, here and now. If he was, she'd know for certain that his flirtation was only a ruse to get information from her. But if he wasn't...

Her heart flipped over at the possibilities, but she put her head firmly in charge.

If he wasn't a spy, she could move on to another target, knowing Drew was harmless.

Drew and Cochrane were back on the far side of the course, battling it out for the second time today after tying their first match and taking a break for the crowd to visit the beer wagon. All their tankards were full now. They wouldn't return for a while. Josselin could leave Davey in charge and steal away to The Sheep Heid.

'Twould take half an hour at most. Josselin could make her way to the inn, sneak into Drew's room, rifle through his things, and be back at the beer wagon before the Highlander was done for the day.

Then she'd know for sure where they stood.

Aye, she decided, untying her apron and leaving it on the counter. By sunset, she'd know if Drew was friend or foe.

The tavern wench at The Sheep Heid gave her a curious perusal when she walked in, but Josselin recalled her Da Will's advice about hiding a weak defense with a strong offense. She gave the maid an arrogant scowl, holding her head high as she made her way up the stairs.

Fortunately, nobody locked doors in a small village like Musselburgh. She pushed her way through the third door and closed it quickly behind her.

The room was dim. The shutters were closed, and the fire was banked. Pausing a moment to let her eyes adjust to the darkness, she spotted a candle. She took it to the hearth and stirred the coals just enough to light the wick.

These were definitely his quarters. An array of golf clubs leaned against one wall, and two saffron shirts were hung on a cupboard near the fire to dry. A pitcher and basin sat on a small table in the corner, and beside them were his personal items.

She walked around the bed, giving it an anxious glance. She could too easily imagine the handsome Highlander stretched out naked upon it.

Setting the candle down, she inspected his belongings. There was a razor, tooth powder, and a mirror case, nothing suspicious. She picked up the chunk of wool-fat soap and sniffed it. It smelled like Drew—clean and manly, with a suble hint of clove. There was also a wooden comb that probably didn't get much use.

Next she searched the cupboard. The top shelf was filled with hose and linen rags, a few belts and leather gloves, and other odds and ends of clothing.

Cutlery and tools occupied the second shelf, along with small bottles of what seemed to be either spices or medicines.

The bottom shelf held a small wooden chest, and Josselin's heart raced at the sight. If any evidence existed to prove Drew was a spy, 'twould probably be in that chest.

She carefully slid it from the shelf. 'Twas surprisingly heavy for its size, and she swiftly set it on the bed.

Gazing down at the simply carved box, she hesitated. Truthfully, she didn't want to find proof that Drew was a spy. As uncomfortable as 'twas to confess, she...

She...liked...the Highlander.

There was absolutely no good reason for it. He was

rude and crude and cocky. He teased her and smirked at her and kissed her without leave. He was everything Lowlanders despised about Highlanders.

But there was something in his eyes and his smile that told her there was sunken treasure to be found beneath his turbulent sea, and Josselin was curious enough to want to delve under those waves.

Still, she dared not let her heart have its way until her head was satisfied with the man's innocence and all suspicions were put to rest.

So, taking a deep breath, she carefully lifted the lid of the chest and brought the candle near. To her surprise, bright coins gleamed up at her in the candlelight—a veritable fortune. She'd never seen so much silver in one place. 'Twas true what he'd said then—one *could* make a living, knocking a ball around in the grass.

She let a few coins trickle through her fingers, making sure there were no secret documents hidden in their midst. Then she closed the lid and returned the chest to the cupboard.

He seemed to have no other possessions. Still, a good spy would cache incriminating evidence in the least conspicuous places. So she searched the cracks in the walls, the stones of the hearth, beneath his pillow, under his bed. There was nothing.

One spot remained. Behind the door, a heavy woolen plaid hung from a peg on the wall, draped over a pair of tall boots. She ran her fingers over the folds of the plaid and found something rigid. Moving the cloth out of the way, she exposed a finely tooled leather scabbard. One end of it rested in one of the boots, and propped against the wall was the silver hilt of the sword within it.

Biting her lip, she tipped the weapon toward herself and ran her fingers over the wrapped leather grip. 'Twas of excellent craftsmanship, the kind of blade a swordmaster might own. What was a golfer doing with it?

She angled her head to examine the graceful arcs of the swept hilt. Where had Drew gotten such a fine sword? Had he stolen it? Taken it in payment of a golfing debt? Killed someone for it?

Unable to resist taking a peek at such a beautiful weapon, she began to slide the sword gently from its sheath. She smiled. The blade was of fine steel, probably Spanish. 'Twas brilliant, flawless, and sharp enough to split a hair. What she wouldn't give to own a sword like...

A thump on the stair startled her. Someone was coming. She blew out the candle, dropped the sword back into its scabbard, scrambled behind the plaid, and froze.

Chapter 27

Despite the lack of light, Drew knew the instant he walked into the room that he wasn't alone. 'Twas almost impossible to see into the shadows, but the waxy scent of a freshly extinguished candle hung in the air, and he could sense...a presence.

For once, he wished he'd worn his sword. With a blade in his hand, he always felt invincible.

He supposed he could back out of the room and save himself the trouble of an altercation. But he had valuable golf clubs inside, not to mention his earnings, and he wasn't about to let a common thief get the better of him.

Closing the door behind him as if nothing was wrong, he slipped the satchel of clubs off his shoulder, sliding out the jagged-edged niblick he'd just broken on a sand shot.

Reason told him that the intruder had probably slithered under his bed. 'Twas the only place in the room to hide. If so, the man was essentially trapped and helpless. Still, Drew would feel more comfortable facing the rascal with his sword in hand.

Listening in the direction of the bed for sudden movement and firmly gripping the niblick in his left hand, he sidled casually toward the plaid hung on the wall and fumbled beneath the fabric for his scabbard.

The instant his fingers contacted flesh, his instincts took over, and he reacted with lightning speed. He might not have his blade at hand, but any weapon would do in a pinch.

He gripped the niblick in both hands, planning to trap the intruder against the wall.

But the scoundrel slipped out from beneath his plaid and skittered along the wall like a startled cricket.

Drew pursued, following the sound of panicked breathing. Twice his fingers contacted cloth, but each time, the slippery villain managed to skip out of his grasp.

Finally he cornered the intruder. With a growl of victory, Drew advanced slowly forward, raising his niblick horizontally to force the fellow back. Then he slammed him against the wall, pinning him there with his body and pressing the shaft of the niblick across the man's scrawny throat.

One moment more, and Josselin might have been able to unsheathe that magnificent sword and defend herself against her assailant. But he'd entered too quickly, found her too soon, and cornered her with the speed of a hunting hound.

Whoever had sneaked into Drew's room knew what he was doing. Maybe he was a master thief. Or a Reformer contact. Or an assassin. Whoever he was, he'd been trained in mortal combat. And whatever weapon he pressed against her throat was threatening to close her windpipe. If she didn't act now, within a few heartbeats she'd run out of air.

Fortunately, she always carried her dagger. Wincing

against the bruising pressure at her throat, she drew her knife and drove her hand forward toward the man's belly.

Which suddenly wasn't there.

He'd dodged out of the way.

She tried again, but her dagger swished through empty air. Somehow his weapon pushed tighter against her neck, and the dark room began to fill with bright spots of light.

She clawed at his forearm with her left hand and slashed once more, this time aiming for his left arm. At the last instant, as if he'd read her intent, he pulled that arm out of reach, which made him loosen his stranglehold on her slightly.

Thank God Angus had taught her a few dirty fighting tricks. Forgetting about her dagger, she cocked her leg and brought it up hard to drive her knee into his crotch.

And missed.

He'd apparently guessed 'twould be her next move.

Luckily, his dodge had made him drop whatever he'd been holding against her throat, and it clattered to the floor.

She sucked in a welcome breath and swung her knife forward in a wide circular arc, hoping to find a target. But the blade whistled through the air. Stepping forward, she tried again. And again.

Where had he gone? She squinted into the shadows and listened for sounds of movement.

Without warning, she was seized low about the knees and upended. She gasped, expecting to hit the floor and crack her skull.

But she didn't. She fell headlong onto the bed, and before she could recover from the shock of her soft landing, she was crushed into the bedding by the weight of her assailant.

He pried the dagger from her fingers, then seized her

wrists, securing them with one fist above her head and trapping her beneath him.

She struggled against him to no avail, and for several moments there was only the sound of their labored breathing.

"Well, now," her attacker finally grunted, his Highland brogue unmistakable, "let's see what we have here."

Josselin stiffened. 'Twas Drew. But how could that be? He was a golfer, not a fighter. Wasn't he?

A dozen questions fired through her brain in the span of an instant.

What was he doing back so soon from the course?

Did he not realize 'twas her? Or had he followed her here?

Where had he learned to fight like that?

Was he a spy? Or wasn't he?

She'd found nothing incriminating in his room. But that didn't necessarily mean Drew *wasn't* a spy. Maybe he wasn't the kind of spy who gathered information or passed encrypted missives. Maybe he was the kind of spy who killed those who got in the way.

With his free hand, Drew used a golf club to reach the hearth, stirring the coals. They flared enough to afford a small bit of light, enough for Drew to see who she was and for Josselin to glimpse the horrified look on his face when he *saw* who she was.

"Jossy?"

He immediately released her wrists and levered himself off of her chest, still straddling her.

So that answered one of her questions. He hadn't known 'twas she when he attacked. But several other questions remained.

If Drew was only a golfer, why did he have that sword?

How had he known someone was in the room?

And where the bloody hell had he learned to fight like that?

Now that she was discovered and he'd released her, should she feign innocence? Did he mean her no harm? Or was she still in danger?

"Jossy?" he repeated, blinking in disbelief.

Josselin compressed her lips. Her da's had taught her to err on the side of caution. Self-protection was paramount.

So, searching the mattress with the flat of her hand, she located her dagger, closed her fingers around the grip, and swept it up to the point of his chin.

His eyes widened. "What the...? Jossy, 'tis me."

She hesitated, uncertain of how to proceed, but unwilling to let down her guard.

"Jossy, lass," he said, raising his palms in surrender, "I didn't mean to hurt ye. If I'd known 'twas ye..."

He shifted his weight as if to climb off of her. She stopped him with a poke of her blade.

He flinched. "Whoa, lass, I was only goin' to move off o' ye."

"Why are ye back so early from the links?"

He narrowed his eyes, surprised by her question. She jabbed again at his chin to hurry his answer.

He sucked a sharp breath between his teeth. "I broke my niblick."

"And?"

His soft blue eyes were growing darker by the moment. "I came to fetch another," he bit out. "Now I have a question o' my own, lass."

Josselin held her breath.

"What the devil are ye doin' in my room?"

Chapter 28

Josselin's mind went blank. What could she tell him? That she suspected he was a spy? That she'd rifled through his things to see for herself?

At her hesitation, Drew acted swiftly. Before she could squeak out a reply, he easily batted away her dagger hand, pried the blade from her grip, and set the point at her throat. The sudden shift in power was breathtaking.

"I said it before," he smugly reminded her. "If ye've got the cods to enter the field o' battle, then ye'd better have the cods to lose."

Breathtaking and infuriating.

"Now, lass, I'll repeat my question. What are ye doin' in my room?"

Her brain worked furiously, trying to come up with a plausible excuse, which wasn't easy, considering there was a blade at her throat and a Highlander straddling her.

"Let me take a wild guess," he said. "Did ye come to rob me?"

"Nae!"

He clucked his tongue. "The wages I've earned in the

last week alone would make a handsome prize for a tavern wench from Selkirk."

"I'm not a thief!" she retorted so vehemently she
almost impaled herself on her own dagger.

"Nae?"

"Nae!" Suddenly inspired, she challenged him with a
steely glare. "But what about *ye*? Maybe *ye're* a thief."

He smirked. "Me?"

She arched a sly brow. "If ye're not a thief, then what's
a golfer doin' with a sword?"

Drew's stomach plummeted. Damn! The meddlesome
lass had found his sword. How was he going to explain
that?

He frowned. He had to do something fast, and he'd
learned from battling with a blade that a strong offense
could hide a weak defense.

"What!" he barked, shaking his head in disgust. "Ye
went snoopin' through my things? Marry, lass, didn't your
da's teach ye 'tisn't right to go pokin' your nose where
it doesn't belong?" He muttered an oath. "Here I was
thinkin' ye were a forthright lass. But ye're not, are ye?
Once my back is turned—"

"I *am* forthright," she insisted.

"Ye couldn't wait to rob me blind," he said, sadly realizing that he might be right. "Ye knew where my room
was. Ye waited till I was in the middle of a match. Then
ye sneaked past the innkeeper. Didn't ye?"

She caught her lying lip under her teeth. Drew could
tell he was hitting the ball square off the tee, and it
depressed him, probably more than it should have, for
he'd spent a merry morn with Jossy on the links, and he'd

begun not only to desire the lass, but also to genuinely adore her.

He let out an unhappy sigh, wishing he'd left the room while he had the chance. He might have found himself short a few coins, but at least he'd not have been so miserably disappointed.

"I...I wasn't goin' to take anythin', I swear."

"O' course ye weren't. Ye were only takin' a wee promenade about my room."

"Maybe."

He snorted. "Ye expect me to believe that?"

"'Tis the truth."

He leaned in close enough to brush her cheek with his whisper. "Then why, darlin', didn't ye wait for me to give ye the tour?"

"I..." She faltered. "I wanted to surprise ye."

He lifted a brow. "Well, that ye did."

"Nae. I mean...I wanted to..." She reached up one tentative hand and touched his throat. She swallowed hard, and her fingers trembled as they slipped lower to his chest, edging beneath the fabric of his shirt to contact his skin. "Surprise ye," she breathed.

He stiffened and cocked his head, suspicious. "Surprise me?" But already his body was responding to her feminine overtures. Already he was prepared to believe her.

She nodded. She lifted her left hand as well and caught the open edges of his doublet.

The dagger wavered in his grip. Could it be true? Could she have come for...him?

She curled her fists in his doublet and pulled him toward her. She was staring at his mouth, her lips parted in anticipation.

He shouldn't trust her. A woman with a knife at her throat would do or say anything. And a Scotswoman was about as trustworthy as the North Sea.

But he didn't want to believe Jossy was a thief. And he didn't want to believe she'd lie to him. What she was doing to him now—pulling him close for a kiss to show him how much she desired him—*that* he wanted to believe.

Against his better judgment and cursing himself for a lusty fool, he succumbed to her wishes, withdrawing the blade and lowering his head to hers.

Of course, he wasn't a complete simpleton. He tossed the dagger well out of her reach. But 'twasn't the only weapon in her arsenal, and he left himself dangerously vulnerable to the most powerful weapon a woman could wield.

"Well, darlin'," he murmured, "what kind o' surprise did ye have in—"

Josselin shut him up with a kiss, pulling him close and grinding her mouth against his with artless abandon.

She had no idea what she was doing. In one moment she'd been at the mercy of a possible thief-spy-assassin, and in the next she'd managed to disarm him with the impulsive promise of…

Hell, she wasn't quite sure what she'd promised.

His lips were warm, and she could taste the enticing sweat of battle upon him. She had to admit 'twas not an unpleasant flavor.

The smell of his skin—clean and slightly scented with the lingering spice of his soap—was agreeable. The heat of his body against hers was rather welcome—indeed, 'twas strangely arousing.

God's bones! She was definitely in over her head now.

She wasn't a seasoned spy. She didn't know how to lie and cheat and sneak around. She was accustomed to direct confrontation, not deception. She'd acted on pure instinct. He'd cornered her mentally and physically, and she'd responded with the first thing that had popped into her mind.

Now she was trapped in her own ruse, forced to kiss him, forced to pretend she'd come here, not to spy upon him, but to seduce him.

Marry, what she knew about seducing men would fit in that thimble he'd given her.

But she'd always been taught to have a strong offense. Trying to remember what they'd done before, she deepened the kiss, coaxing him on with soft mews. Then she pitched her mouth across his, teasing it open with bold sweeps of her tongue.

He answered with unexpected zeal, seizing her face between his hands and tipping her head to access her more fully. He threaded his fingers through her hair, anchoring her, then parted her lips with his tongue to invade the recesses within.

She should be frightened. This was a skirmish for which she was completely unprepared. But every brush of his lips soothed her fears and excited her, and soon she yearned for more spirited combat.

Beneath his palms, she could feel her pulse racing. Her heart pounded, and the blood rushed through her veins, as intoxicating as any ale. Her head swam in a hazy sea of need and turmoil and longing, and she had no desire to be pulled from the perilous waves.

He growled against her mouth, and the sound sent a curious sizzle along her spine, waking her senses and making her dare more.

She let go of his doublet and slipped her hands inside, letting them roam over his broad shoulders and the smooth contours of his chest. Through the thin saffron shirt, she felt the sultry warmth of his body. And as mad as it seemed, the sensation triggered a pleasing twinge between her legs.

Meanwhile, his hands forged their own seductive path across her flesh. He skimmed her throat with the back of his knuckles, and his fingertips drifted across her collarbone to slip beneath her chemise, caressing the skin there.

She shivered at the delicious, forbidden contact and rose to meet it, longing to feel his hands delve further beneath her clothing.

As if sensing her desires, he loosened the laces of her bodice and slipped the chemise from her shoulder, baring the top of her bosom. Her breasts thrust upward, aching for his touch, daring him to trespass there. She moaned as waves of delicious torment filled her head.

When she thought she'd drown in the lusty current, he broke off the kiss, nuzzling her ear to whisper, "Is this what ye came for, love?"

His breath spiraled into her ear, awakening something deep within her brain, and she shivered, answering him with a sigh.

"Is this what ye want?"

He pressed his lips in a sweet trail down the side of her neck, and she turned her head aside to give him access. Anticipation curled her toes and made her clench her fists in his shirt.

"Aye," she breathed.

He bestowed gentle kisses along the upper curve of her

bosom, moving lower and lower until her nipples stung with yearning. She arched up, wishing he would free her breasts and feast upon her.

He chuckled softly. "Oh, Jossy, ye're a wanton wench."

Maybe she *did* know what she was doing, after all, she thought, before rational thought deserted her and she surrendered to instinct.

He did as she willed then, pulled down her bodice to expose her breasts, then lowered his head to capture a nipple in his warm, wet mouth.

She gasped, arching reflexively and twisting her fists tighter in his shirt, wanting...

She didn't know what she wanted. More. Closer. Deeper.

He began to suckle at her, and she felt the exquisite tug of his lips all the way to the core of her being. The tingling between her thighs became a burning need, and she thrust her hips up as well, seeking some unnamed relief for the fiery torment there.

He moved to her other breast and lavished the same satisfying attention on her straining nipple. But instead of quenching her thirst, his bold efforts only aggravated her need.

She pulsed up against him again, and this time she felt all too vividly the evidence of his arousal. Even through the layers of his shirt and trews, she could tell his cock had grown as hard as steel. Which sent a heady tremor through her bones.

She was doing it, she realized. She was seducing him. And that knowledge gave her a sense of power. Even while she languished at his mercy, she had him wrapped around her finger, just where she...

He slipped his hand down between her legs and, with remarkable precision, found the very spot that hungered the most. 'Twas as if lightning had struck her. Sweet fire blazed through every nerve. And for the first time in her life, Josselin felt in danger of losing control.

"Do ye like that, lass?" he murmured. "Do ye like it when—"

She surged upward with the last ounce of her will and bowled the Highlander over onto his back. A strong offense, she repeated to herself. Now she had him right where she wanted him.

Josselin's response was more forceful than Drew had expected. But he wasn't about to complain. Only a fool would complain when a beautiful half-naked blonde sat astride him.

She was breathtaking. Tendrils of her hair dripped like honey over her bare shoulders and flirted with her heaving breasts, still wet from his suckling. Her lips, swollen with kisses, parted in invitation. Her eyes smoldered with passion.

Lord, he wanted her more than he'd ever wanted any woman. His blood was hot, his appetite was whetted, and his cock was primed for trysting.

She tore open his doublet, wrenching it off of his shoulders, and pulled up the shirt underneath, baring his chest. Then she caught his wrists and held him down, asserting her superiority with a rough kiss of claiming.

He didn't mind. Not at all. Her breasts were soft and warm upon him. Her lips were sweet and supple. That she wanted him enough to take command of his body only sharpened his desire.

He let her have her way with him, pinning him to the bed, plundering his mouth, taunting him by brushing her tempting breasts against his chest.

But the wild hound in his trews was not so patient. It languished in the heat of her onslaught, beneath the welcome weight of her buttocks, begging to be unleashed.

She mirrored his lovemaking, leaving a trail of kisses down his neck, then pushing his shirt up to bathe his chest with her tongue. She gradually found her way to his nipples, and as she gently lapped at him, he closed his eyes at the divine sensation.

All the while she gently rocked back and forth upon his lap, probably unaware of her actions. But the effect upon him was like flint on steel. Soon his need would burst into flame.

He adjusted his hips beneath her, lifting his thigh slightly between hers to give her the friction she craved. She pressed against him, rocking harder, seeking relief.

"I know what ye want, darlin'," he breathed. "I can—"

She never gave him the chance. All at once, she thrust her hand down and seized his restless cock.

He gasped, and his hips instinctively thrust upward.

As she began to stroke and squeeze him, driving him to new heights of desire, the little minx actually smiled faintly, as smug as a cat slurping cream.

"Jossy, love," he breathlessly warned her, "ye're playin' with fire."

"Am I?"

He smiled back and reached down to return the favor, rubbing purposefully between her legs and eliciting a ragged gasp from her.

But instead of retreating shyly, the lass actually

attacked him with more aggression. She loosened the laces of his trews and boldly shoved her hand inside, grasping his cock as if 'twere a rare prize.

Current flooded every nerve, and he groaned with the pleasure-pain of her assault. Only sheer willpower kept him from spilling his seed into her hand.

But two could play her game.

He tugged up her skirts, slipping his hand underneath to seek out the hot core of her need. He glided his fingers through her soft hair and over her warm, moist folds. Lord, she was already drenched with the dew of desire. He parted her swollen lips and found and fondled the precious nub within. She moaned deeply, and the primal sound fueled his passion.

Supporting herself on one arm and still holding his cock in her tantalizing grip, Josselin planted her knees on either side of him, positioning herself strategically above him.

Amazed and thrilled by her unashamed aggression, he mustered his last ounce of nobility to stop her.

Holding her back with a hand upon her chest, he gasped out, "Wait, lass. Have ye done this before?"

Her eyes were glazed with determined passion.

"Ye can't..." he explained, "ye can't just... If ye've never... Let me..."

"I've never golfed either," she panted, "but that didn't stop me."

Then, before he could prevent her, she sank down onto his hips, sheathing his cock in her welcoming warmth, and the deed was done.

Chapter 29

Satan's claws!

Josselin bit her lip against crying out. For an instant she couldn't move, couldn't breathe. 'Twas like impaling herself on a great jagged knife.

Beneath her, Drew stiffened. "Oh, lass!" he whispered.

She refused to let him see her weakness. He'd warned her, after all. Aye, 'twas painful, but it had been her idea, and she wasn't about to back down. Besides, she could no more undo what had been done than she could recall a careless slash of the sword.

So she blinked back the tears of pain starting in her eyes, clenched her teeth against the size of him inside her, and tried to move.

"Nae, love," Drew murmured, stopping her. "Let me."

She didn't want to let him take the offensive, and she didn't want his pity. 'Twould show she was weak. But he gave her no choice. For a man who didn't have the bulging muscles of a caber-tosser, he was damned strong. Holding her against him with one hand on her buttocks, he gently rolled with her until he was once again on top.

Humiliated, she refused to meet his gaze. She'd felt so victorious a moment ago, and now...

"The pain will pass in a moment," he told her, tenderly brushing the hair back from her brow, "I promise."

"'Tis nothin'," she lied. "I've had worse from a blade."

He cupped her cheek and kissed the corner of her lip. "Breathe through the pain, and try to let it go. I won't move a muscle till ye give the word."

He kissed her again, this time full on the mouth, and she answered instinctively. Considering his bold invasion below, his trespass upon her lips was surprisingly delicate.

He stroked her with a feather-light touch, murmuring against her ear, "I'm sorry if I hurt ye."

But already her muscles were relaxing around him, adjusting to his fullness, and she could feel the delicious erotic glow gradually returning to her skin.

The frantic need she'd experienced a moment before was gone. In its place was a slow-building, tender craving that was soothing her hurt and taking her to a sweeter place, a place to which they were journeying together.

"That's it, love," he said. "There's no hurry. 'Tis a dance, not a race."

His soft touch—along her jaw, over her shoulders, upon her breasts—began to bring her to life again. Soon, floating in a haze of arousal, she started to respond, returning his kisses, clutching at his shirt, weaving her fingers through his wild hair. Caught up in bliss, she almost forgot about her discomfort.

"If ye'll allow me," he whispered, "I can make it better."

She couldn't imagine anything better, but she wasn't about to argue with him. She nodded.

He slipped his hand down to the place where they were joined, massaging her gently as he pulsed inside her. She sucked in a sharp breath, not of pain, but of pleasure, as his fingers found her most vulnerable spot.

Like a swordsman with a blade at her heart, he held her hostage. With the slightest movement of his fingertip, he controlled her passion. He could send her lust spiraling out of bounds or withhold his touch to leave her begging for more.

It shocked her to know how easily he'd usurped her dominance.

Thankfully, he was merciful. He stroked and circled and caressed her flesh with expert care, returning to claim her mouth with sweet persuasion. He played her with the same finesse he used on the course, keeping his eye on the target and nudging her gently toward the goal.

A strange yearning grew deep in her belly, and her breath came in rapid gulps as, of their own will, her hips rocked up, eager to mate with him. Lust mixed with despair as she realized he was going to win. In another moment, she'd surrender to the demands of her own body, and he'd emerge victorious.

Then a curious thing happened.

"Oh, Jossy," he said tightly, withdrawing his hand, "please say ye're ready."

She peered up into his face. His eyes were dark with desire. His nostrils flared, and his lips were compressed with restraint. His brow was deeply furrowed, as if he suffered some terrible agony. Faith, he was as vulnerable to her as she was to him.

That knowledge sent a thrill of power through her veins. They were equals in this arena.

"Aye!" she cried, wrapping her arms around his neck.

He moved within her, and this time there was no pain, only a satisfying fullness that made her arousal more complex. She strained upward, pressing against him, and he answered, delving more deeply. She drove against him to hasten his thrusts, and he complied, pumping to a faster rhythm. She curled her legs over his, claiming him, and he responded with a groan of delight, enfolding her in his arms.

Together they strove with increasing desperation until lust began to bubble up inside her like beer left overlong in the cask. She arched up, and in one frozen instant of time, every impulse centered on that one vulnerable pinpoint where their bodies connected. Then the world shattered into a thousand pieces, exploding outward like shards of a burst bottle.

Drew had managed to restrain himself, despite Jossy's wanton gazes and welcoming arms and enthusiastic kisses and enticing moans and mouthwatering breasts and thrusting hips. But when she contracted around him in the throes of ecstasy, 'twas all he could do to keep from hammering the poor lass into the mattress.

His release came upon him like the powerful drive of a longnose club, striking hard and catapulting him high into the heavens. He shuddered with the strength of it, and when he finally fell to earth, his satisfaction was so complete and so perfect, 'twas as if he'd sunk his ball in one stroke.

Utterly drained, he used the last of his energy to ease off of the lass so he'd not suffocate her. He gathered her to him, holding her close and kissing her hair. And for the first time in his life, he felt like he was exactly where he belonged.

"Are ye all right?" he whispered.

"Mm."

He smiled and snuggled closer.

She mumbled against his throat. "Are *ye*?"

His smile widened into a grin. "Oh, aye, lass."

She breathed a contented sigh that tickled his chest and warmed him down to his toes, and he closed his eyes, utterly fulfilled.

He must have dozed off then. When he awoke, the fire had gone out, and he could hear Jossy breathing in the dark beside him.

Worried she might get chilled, he carefully dragged the coverlet over her shoulders, but his movement woke her.

She stirred groggily for a moment, then sat up with a gasp. "Shite!"

His heart knifed in his chest. "What?" Damn, he should have known she'd blame him for...

"The beer wagon!"

She threw back the coverlet and scrambled off the bed.

Relief flooded him. He sat up, raking his hands through his hair, which was probably a tangled mess. "Don't worry, lass. I'm sure Davey's... Shite!"

"What?"

"I left Cochrane on the course."

Later that night, Josselin tried to maintain a stern expression as she pushed Drew back against the tavern wall, poking him in the chest. She knew she was failing miserably.

"I told ye ne'er to come to my place o' work."

She looked nervously over at the innkeeper of The White Hart, hoping he was too busy with patrons to notice her.

Drew only grinned and coiled a lock of her hair around his finger. "Ye're done workin'."

Damn him! When he looked at her with those irresistible laughing eyes and arched that seductive brow, she couldn't stay vexed with him for long.

"Shite."

An unwilling smile tugged at her lips, and she shook her head at her own folly. He wasn't going to leave, and in truth, she didn't want him to. She didn't know what enchantment he'd worked on her today, but she could hardly bear the thought of separation.

"Come on then," she told him in mock disgust, untying her apron. "At least order me supper so we've a reason to sit at the table."

Josselin watched him walk to the counter, her gaze dropping to his handsome arse, and a lusty shiver went through her. She wanted him again.

'Twas absurd. Only this morn she'd been a maid, pure as snow, and already she was a wanton, ready to crawl into bed with the next man who wagged his handsome arse at her.

Nae, she corrected, not any man. 'Twas only Drew who left her hot and troubled.

She'd never imagined that making love could be so divine.

She'd seen the hasty, furtive coupling of animals. For Josselin, it had always seemed like a ruthless duel in which the male always won.

She'd even glimpsed the occasional harlot in an alley, and that had appeared to be a transaction in which the female was largely detached.

This had been something altogether different, like swimming together in a wild sea or fighting side by side in battle. She'd felt helpless and powerful all at once, both worshipper and goddess. And for the first time in her life, she hadn't wished she was a lad, but exalted in the fact that she was a woman.

She smiled as she watched him return with a pair of ales. How she could have doubted Drew, she didn't know. Aye, she'd wondered about that magnificent sword, but he'd explained that the weapon had belonged to his father. He'd learned to use it, but the only combat he ever engaged in took place on the golf course.

He certainly wasn't a spy. He could never be a follower of that woman-hating John Knox. Drew was kind and gentle and sweet and charming and luscious and...

"Ye'd better stop lookin' at me like that, darlin'," he murmured with a smoky glance, setting down the tankards, "or I'm apt to bed ye right here in front o' the whole tavern."

She blushed with wicked delight. "And I'm apt to let ye."

He laughed. 'Twas a wonderful sound, and it warmed her like a winter fire. Oh, aye, she planned to bed him again—tonight, if he'd have her. After all, her lodgings were just upstairs. She raised her tankard in a toast, and he gave her a smile that promised a long night of hot trysting. Indeed, with the Highlander for company, she expected she'd never be cold again.

Chapter 30

Simon Armstrong, Andrew's uncle, pulled the cap lower over his brow as he limped down Edinburgh's Royal Mile, resisting the impulse to glance up at the imposing gray stones that frowned down at him as if to say he didn't belong here.

'Twas the truth, he supposed. He was English. He didn't belong here. But neither did Queen Mary. She'd shunned King Henry's son, after all, and fled to Paris. In Simon's opinion, she should have stayed there and left Scotland to Queen Elizabeth. And if Simon had anything to say about it, the self-professed Scottish queen would go back to France—the sooner, the better.

Of course, Simon didn't have anything to say about it. He was only a pawn in Elizabeth's chess match with Mary. But even pawns could distinguish themselves, and that was his hope.

Unlike his brothers, Robert and Thomas, he was no longer fit enough to go to war. His last skirmish with the Scots five years ago had left his only son dead and Simon crippled, and his old eyes weren't what they used to be. But he'd be damned if he'd let his injuries keep him from serving the English crown. His brothers' sons served in Elizabeth's army. Even Andrew—the son of their dead brother Edward and a swordsman beyond compare—fought in tournaments throughout England, honing his skills for the coming war with Scotland. Simon might be crippled, but he could still serve his country.

So a month ago, when Queen Elizabeth's secretary, Sir Francis Walsingham, approached the loyal Armstrong brothers—Simon, Robert, and Thomas—with this unique opportunity to serve the queen, they were honored beyond words.

For two weeks now, the three of them had shared a remote cottage in Scotland, a few miles south of Edinburgh. 'Twas all they shared. Their service was a matter of great secrecy, and they never disclosed their assignments, even to each other.

Simon turned off the Royal Mile and down a narrow lane. A pair of unruly university students ending their day of studies jostled him as they passed, but Simon kept his eyes trained on the cobblestones. Above all, Walsingham had told him, a spy must be invisible.

In a place as crowded and active as Edinburgh, 'twasn't a difficult task. He usually ventured out at twilight, when nobody paid heed to a gray-bearded old cripple in a tattered coat and worn leather boots.

Simon leaned heavily on his walking staff as his old wound throbbed. He squinted down the curving road from beneath the brim of his cap. 'Twasn't much farther to The White Hart. Once inside, he could settle into his dark corner and order a pint, keeping alert for any snippets of relevant conversation, and give his leg a much-needed rest.

'Twas rumored the tavern was a favorite haunt of

Mary's secretary, Philipe de la Fontaine. Walsingham had sent Simon there to be his eyes and ears. He was to report any unusual activity or suspicious characters and note everything that de la Fontaine said.

He'd been coming every evening for two weeks now, and he had to admit 'twas a rather dull assignment for a man trained for combat. He'd sat for hours, sipping at his beer, which he'd quickly learned was much stronger here than in England. No one had mentioned the name of Mary.

The only day that Philipe de la Fontaine showed up, he chatted with the innkeeper for a few moments, asking how his son Duncan was faring and inquiring after the French wine he had on order, which the innkeeper said hadn't yet arrived. He then joined a table of three merchants, played a single game of dice, which he lost, and, after less than a quarter hour, he left the tavern.

Simon had been tempted to follow the secretary, but Walsingham's admonition about remaining inconspicuous rang in his ears. There would be other opportunities, he told himself.

Perhaps this evening he'd learn something valuable, he thought as he pushed open the door of The White Hart.

When his feeble eyes grew accustomed to the dim interior, he was disappointed to discover his usual table was taken. A man sat there with a lass who frequented the tavern. They were conversing over trenchers of leek pottage.

He squinted at the other tables around the room. There was an empty spot near the counter. 'Twasn't quite as secluded, but as long as he sat quietly and made no trouble, he'd blend into his surroundings, as innocuous as a stick of furniture.

Easing onto the stool and propping his walking staff against the wall, he huddled over his beer and surveyed the occupants of the room.

De la Fontaine wasn't here, but that wasn't surprising. Mary probably kept him busy looking for English spies under her bed. Two lads chatted with the tavern wench, but 'twas nothing unusual—the same two lads came by every evening to flirt with the lass. A trio of men played at dice, and their conversation was mostly quarreling over whose turn 'twas or who owed whom how much.

Simon took a sip of foamy beer.

Two gentlemen at one of the tables were studying a piece of parchment. One of them shook his head gravely. The other's shoulders slumped, and he gave the first a disgruntled frown. Then the first pointed at something on the page, and the second cocked his head, as if considering it.

Could they be planning something? A rendezvous? An ambush? A plot to assassinate Elizabeth?

He couldn't hear them, so he had to rely on what he could guess from their gestures.

They were arguing over whatever was on the parchment. The first man obviously wasn't happy with it, and the second kept offering changes, albeit reluctantly. The first frowned over the document and finally dismissed the thing with a wave of his hand, which sent the second one scrambling in panic to please the first.

Simon had to find out what they were discussing. They might well be putting the polish on a conspiracy to overthrow the English crown.

Leaving his beer and his cap conspicuously on the table so no one else would usurp his place, he slowly hobbled past the pair toward the hearth, ostensibly to warm his hands at the fire.

As he passed, he squinted down at the parchment. 'Twas a drawing of a cupboard with leaves and flowers carved into the doors. The man was obviously a craftsman then, presenting plans to an exacting patron.

Whatever their differences were, they didn't seem to be engaged in a dangerous plot, so Simon moved on to the hearth.

As he stretched his fingers toward the fire, he glanced at the couple occupying his usual table. As he'd remarked on previous nights, the lass was quite lovely . . . for a Scotswoman. She was fair of face with golden locks and looked to have all of her teeth. Her companion . . .

Simon frowned.

There was something familiar about the man. 'Twas hard to tell in the shadows of the tavern, especially with his weak eyes, but Simon thought he might have seen him before.

'Twas possible, he supposed, even in a place as big as Edinburgh, to see the same person twice. But this was something more than simple recognition. There was something hauntingly, eerily familiar about him.

Then the man laughed at whatever the lass said, baring his teeth in a grin that was unmistakable, and Simon staggered, catching himself on the hearthstones to keep from collapsing.

Invisible. He had to remain invisible. He turned his back on the couple and fought to breathe steadily, trying to make sense of what he'd just seen.

There was no mistaking the young man. Aye, two years had passed—his hair had grown shaggy and there was a day's growth of beard on him—but he was the same bright-eyed lad Simon and his brothers had raised from the age of six.

What the hell was Andrew Armstrong doing *here*?

Simon stared into the flames, his eyes mirroring their fierce heat. The lad was supposed to be in England, fighting in tournaments. What the devil was he doing in a Scots tavern?

Simon balled his fists against a mad urge to grab the lad by the scruff of the neck and march him out of The White Hart all the way back to England, where he belonged. Of course, he didn't dare. 'Twas just the sort of irresponsible action that would earn him Sir Walsingham's disapproval and subsequent dismissal.

But seeing Andrew here had thrown a loose cog into the machinery of Simon's mission, and he knew he'd be of no use as a spy until he solved the mystery of what his nephew was doing in Edinburgh.

He racked his brain for an explanation. Was it possible the lad had been recruited by Walsingham as well? Could he be an agent of the queen? It seemed too improbable, and yet 'twas the only thing that made any sense.

He heard the scrape of a chair behind him, and he froze, wondering if Andrew had recognized him after all. But no tap on his shoulder followed, and when Simon dared peek again, Andrew was on his way up the stairs with a hand around the lass's waist. To his further disgust, he saw that the lad was dressed in a saffron shirt and tartan trews, like a bloody Highlander, and he carried a satchel of golfing clubs over his shoulder.

Simon glowered in revulsion and disappointment. Andrew wasn't a spy, and he wasn't a swordsman on the tournament circuit. He was apparently enjoying a life of leisure, consorting with the enemy, playing Scots golf and swiving Scots whores.

He was dishonoring the memory of his father, who had died at the hands of these despicable people. 'Twas an unforgivable affront. It broke Simon's heart to know his nephew had lied about everything, and he wouldn't rest until he discovered the reason why.

But first he had to get the lad out of this godforsaken country. Andrew was family, and Simon had sworn on Edward Armstrong's grave to protect his son. Walsingham's men were thick here. If any of them discovered the lad was consorting with the enemy, he might well be viewed as a traitor to England.

His heart heavy, Simon limped back to his table, slugged down the beer, jammed his cap down over his head, snatched up his walking staff, and headed home. Kidnapping was an undertaking that would require all three Armstrong brothers.

Chapter 31

For once, Josselin had no trouble ignoring the man who came to her with the notched tankard. In fact, she almost forgot to retrieve the note cached beneath his cup. This morn, she only had eyes for Drew MacAdam, who was teeing off in the distance. Her gaze lingered on his broad shoulders, his strong arms, his fine arse. The memory of how he'd used them in her bed the last three nights made her fan her face with her coif.

She understood now why the bards wrote sonnets to love, why troubadours sang of little else. 'Twas a proper obsession—a sport as addictive as swordplay, a passion as moving as a prayer.

And yet 'twas more than that. In the forging of their bodies, she'd felt a forging of their hearts. There was something deeper betwixt them—shared laughter, shared loyalty, shared . . . love.

Love?

The word brought a flash of heat to her cheeks. Surely she didn't know the Highlander well enough to love him. She was only confusing love with lust.

But that didn't ring true. As Kate had oft told her, the

heart knew better than the head in matters of love. She'd assured Josselin that when her time came to choose a husband, 'twould be best to listen to her instincts.

At the time, Josselin had only rolled her eyes. She'd had no intention of choosing a husband. 'Twas her ambition to follow in her mother's footsteps and devote herself to battle.

But that was before she'd met Drew. And 'twas before she'd tasted the glorious rewards of bedding a man who lavished her with adoration.

She shivered at the memory, then glanced crossly at the sun, which was moving as slow as treacle across the sky today. Drew had promised to buy her a midday meal at The Sheep Heid. She smiled to herself. 'Twas more than pottage she hungered for.

After what seemed an eternity, Drew finally came loping up to the beer wagon. As usual, her heart leaped at the sight of him, until she saw that he wore a frown.

"I can't sup with ye today," he sighed.

Her heart sank.

He reached out and took her hand. "'Tisn't that I don't want to, darlin'." He pulled her close, whispering, "Shite, I'm as hard as a niblick for ye and hungrier than a wolf."

His lusty words sent a thrill through her.

He glanced over his shoulder and waved to a young lad across the green.

"'Tis a messenger from some high and mighty clan chieftain," he explained with a grimace. "He wants to meet me in the woods."

"In the woods?" There was a prickling along the back of her neck. "Why?"

He shrugged. "Maybe he wants a second for a foursome.

Or maybe he's just lookin' to place a wager. Some nobles are secretive about their vices. They'd rather not have it bandied about that they're gamblin' on such a . . . a vulgar game."

"God's cods," she said with a pout.

"Anyway, I've got to go." He hurriedly patted her hand, adjusted the clubs on his shoulder, and turned to leave. "I'll make it up to ye at supper," he called back, giving her a wink, "I swear."

What compelled Josselin to follow him, she didn't know. Maybe she'd simply gotten into the habit of spying. Maybe she worried he might come to mischief, meeting with some conniving clan chief. Or maybe she feared he'd already tired of her and might be off for a tryst in the woods with some new lass.

Of course, she didn't dare nip at his heels. She watched him carefully to see where he went, then had Davey tend to the wagon while she followed Drew at a distance, keeping a cautious hand on her dagger.

By the time she reached the forest, he was nowhere to be seen. But Will had taught her how to track and how to look for signs of passage. A path of freshly flattened grass led through the trees, and she took it, disappearing into the soft-shadowed green. From Angus, she'd learned how to move silently through the woods, and she did so now. Her progress was slow and stealthy, and though she listened for the sound of Drew's passage, all she heard were twittering sparrows and the occasional scuffling of a lizard.

Hell. Where had he gone?

She stopped in the shade of a sycamore, scanning the brilliant green leaves and ferns and moss around her for signs of movement. A single squirrel scampered up an oak, but that was all.

Just as she was about to continue along the path, she heard a distant shout. She froze, listening intently. There was another shout, and another. The shouts were too far away to distinguish, but it sounded like a pack of men.

She took a tentative step forward.

A loud bellow rang through the woods, and she knew at once 'twas Drew.

"Jesu."

Her heart plummeted. She unsheathed, her fist clamped tight around her dagger, and charged forward.

It must be thieves, she thought. The woods were crawling with them. She only prayed 'twas thieves and not murderers.

She tore down the path now, not caring that she kicked up leaves and startled a bevy of quail. She was too alarmed to use stealth, too desperate to consider she might be outnumbered. Drew was in danger, and she had to save him.

She followed the sounds of shouting. As she ran, her heart felt like a sharp stick poking her in the side, prodding her to hurry, hurry before 'twas too late. The yelling quickly subsided, but she could still hear a scuffling further ahead, off the path.

Finally she managed to locate the culprits. She broke through a thick grove of aspens beside the path into a clearing. There she found Drew lying facedown on the ground, his clubs scattered amid the leaves.

There were three men holding him down. They whipped around when she burst upon them, their eyes wide with surprise.

She quickly calculated her fighting odds. They looked as old as her da's, so she had youth on her side. One of the men, who seemed vaguely familiar, was leaning on a walking staff, but he and his two accomplices—one burly, the other tall and broad-shouldered—wore swords.

She was at a disadvantage. But she wasn't about to let them know that. 'Twas time for a strong offense.

"Unhand him, ye villains!" she barked, snapping her skirts out of the way and wielding her dagger before her in threat.

"What the—"

"Ye heard me! Let him go!" She tossed her head and flared her nostrils, searing the ruffians with a glare. "Now!"

Her bravado wasn't working. They only frowned up at her.

"Jossy!" Drew's cry was muffled in the leaf fall.

"'Tis his Scots mistress," the man with the staff explained to the others.

"With a blade." The burly man shook his head. "Of course."

"Come, my lady," coaxed the tall man, in the foreign accent she knew all too well. "Put down your weapon. We won't hurt you if you'll—"

"Bloody hell. Ye're English!" she spat. All at once, the old rage she felt about her mother's murder and the new-found protectiveness she felt for Drew surged to the surface like lava in a volcano, and she exploded.

She charged the men, careless of the fact they had swords, with no other thought but to slash their despicable throats.

To her amazement, they didn't draw their weapons, but stood to face her barehanded.

She froze, her dagger raised.

Ballocks! Now what was she supposed to do? She

couldn't slay them in cold blood. Aye, they were English, but chivalry was chivalry.

Frustrated, she lowered her dagger. Then she realized she could still use their error to her benefit. They'd had to let go of Drew to deal with her.

"Run, Drew!" she shouted. "Run!"

He pushed up from the ground and flopped onto his back, then rose up on his elbows. But he didn't even try to escape.

Maybe he couldn't, she thought. Maybe he was hurt.

"Bastards!" she yelled at the men. "English cowards!"

They winced, likely fearful her cries might draw others.

"Lass!" Drew said in warning.

"Are ye afraid to fight me, ye pig-swivin' poltroons?" she challenged. "Are your English ballocks so shriveled ye can't even stand up to a wee Scots lass?" She waved her dagger in menace, but none of them would answer her. "God's bones, ye're nothin' but a bunch o' bloody lobcocks."

"*She's* got a mouth on her," the burly one finally said in wonder.

"Lass," Drew said.

"Come on!" she taunted, brandishing her blade. "Who's to know? What's to stop ye? Ye attacked an unarmed Highlander. Why not me?"

"What? *Him*?" The burly man jerked a thumb over his shoulder.

To her astonishment, the three men laughed grimly and shook their heads.

"He's no Highlander," the man with the staff growled. "He's as English as we are."

Chapter 32

What?" Jossy snapped. "Don't be ridiculous! Tell them, Drew. Tell them where ye're..."

Drew gazed up at her, his heart heavy with guilt. A whole range of emotions played across Jossy's face—disbelief, realization, horror, rage, and finally a cold hatred—and there wasn't a damned thing he could do or say to make her hate him less.

He wasn't sure what pained him more, that his uncles believed he'd betrayed his father's memory or that Jossy believed he'd betrayed her trust.

Somehow he'd deluded himself into thinking he had a hope of happiness with Jossy. Maybe he'd lived so long as a Highlander that he'd begun to believe his own fiction.

How could he have thought she'd never discover he was English? Or that if she did, she'd somehow forgive him?

He was a bloody fool.

"Jossy," he tried, scrambling to his feet, "I never meant to hurt you."

She flinched.

"You have to believe me," he said. "I...I love you."

Drew knew 'twas the truth the moment he said it. It

didn't matter that she was Scots and he was English. Their hearts beat to the same rhythm. Their spirits soared in the same dance. They were meant to be together...even if theirs had been an ill-fated love.

"Let her go," Robert said.

"You'll find another mistress," Thomas chimed in.

"One who isn't a bloody Scot," Simon bit out.

Drew turned on them. "She's not..."

He cursed under his breath. She *was* a Scot. But he'd been blind to that fact. He'd never once thought of her as his enemy. She was Jossy. Sweet, beautiful, spirited Jossy.

He raised apologetic eyes to hers. But he couldn't do anything to ease the pain of betrayal he saw there, the hurt that lay naked underneath the fiery fury of her glare.

"'Tis time to come home, lad," Robert said.

Drew clenched his jaw, his gaze still fixed on Jossy. "This *is* my—"

"She cannot love you," Thomas said gently. "You're her enemy."

He looked into Jossy's stormy eyes and glimpsed the awful truth. Thomas was right. She loathed him. Not only for being English, but also for deceiving her.

He couldn't blame her. Everything he'd told her was a lie. Everything except...

"I love you, Jossy," he breathed.

Her chin quivered, and he saw her eyes fill with tears, but the brave lass refused to shed them. Instead, she shoved her dagger back in its sheath, jerked her chin up proudly, and marched away.

"Jossy!"

Simon grabbed his forearm. "Let her go. You know it yourself. She's better off this way."

Drew hesitated, wondering if 'twas true. Could Jossy ever forgive him? Did her hatred for the English outweigh her affection for him? Was she better off forgetting him and finding some lucky, loyal Scotsman to love?

The thought crushed him.

But as he thought about her leaving—walking swiftly out of his life—an even more unsavory thought wormed its way into his brain.

Bloody hell, he had to stop her.

"Jossy!" he called, weaving through the trees. She was already well down the path. "Jossy, wait!"

His words had the expected effect. She began walking faster.

"Damn," he said under his breath, taking long strides to catch her.

Behind him, his uncles shouted at him to let her go, but he paid them no mind. Did they truly believe that way-laying Drew and forcing him to return home with them would somehow show him the error of his ways? He was a grown man, for God's sake. If he'd sneaked off to Scotland, 'twas because he wished to be there.

He should have ordered them home when he'd first laid eyes on them. If he had, the old fools might have made it safely to the border.

But now they'd done damage. They'd revealed themselves to a fiercely loyal Scot.

"Jossy, wait! I only want to talk to you."

'Twas an outright lie. But he'd already told her so many lies. What was one more?

She increased her pace, never looking back. Her skirts snapped in the air, and her hair streamed out behind her.

He began to run then. He had to catch her before she got out of the woods.

The unfortunate truth was he couldn't afford to let Jossy go. He still didn't know what her relationship with Philipe de la Fontaine was, but he knew Jossy was devoted to Queen Mary. And the way she was feeling now, there was probably nothing she'd like more than to turn four Englishmen over to the authorities. If he let her leave, she'd go immediately to the queen.

She heard him coming and cast a startled look over her shoulder. Picking up her skirts, she began to run in earnest.

Cursing the desperation that forced him to such measures, he bolted down the path, gaining quickly on her, and tackled her to the ground, turning so his back would take the brunt of the impact when they fell.

'Twas like capturing a thrashing wildcat. He swiftly confiscated her dagger and tossed it out of reach, but she fought him with her heels and elbows, landing a number of painful blows.

He put up with her struggles, holding her patiently, his arms wrapped around her waist, until she wearied herself. Even then, she lay stiff against him as her breasts heaved with every rasping breath.

"Jossy," he said, "I can't let you go."

"But I hate ye," she said bitterly.

He swallowed hard. "I know."

Faith, 'twas like a knife in his heart to hear those words, but no worse, he supposed, than the wound he was about to inflict.

"I mean I can't let you go," he explained regretfully, "because you'll run straight to the queen."

She stopped breathing.

"'Tisn't that I blame you," he said. "But I know where your loyalties lie. I can't let you go."

She was quiet a long time. When she finally spoke, her voice was low and solemn. "If that's the way of it, at least let me die with my dagger in my hand."

"What?"

"If ye're goin' to kill me—"

"Kill you! What? How could you..." He hugged her closer to him, though she'd gone stiff as a club. "After all we've...Do you really think I'd..."

Of course she did. She probably thought Englishmen were monsters. He'd thought as much of Scots...until he'd lived among them. Now 'twas hard to dredge up a healthy grudge against the lot.

"Nay," he said. "I meant what I said. I love you, Jossy. The Fates curse me for a star-crossed fool, but I do."

Then the Fates must curse her, too, Josselin thought, because some tiny piece of her heart still beat for this man who was supposed to be her worst foe.

But the rest of her was filled with loathing—for him and for herself, rage, and a thirst for revenge.

How could she have been so blind and so gullible?

Bloody hell! She'd been beguiled by an Englishman. She'd supped with him, flirted with him, kissed him.... She squeezed her eyes shut in horror as she remembered what else she'd done with him.

"I never meant any harm, to you or your country," he told her sadly. "I only came to golf. But now...You have to understand, Jossy, I can't leave you behind. I'm going to have to take you with me."

He was right. He'd be a fool to let her go. She *would* rush to Queen Mary with news of English spies in the forest. 'Twas her duty as a Scotswoman. 'Twas her duty as Lilliard's daughter. He had to abscond with her. If he didn't, he'd be signing his own death warrant.

But she wouldn't make her abduction easy. She'd fight him at every step. He might have disarmed her, but at the first opportunity, she'd find a way to escape. And God help whoever stood in her way.

The three men were coming down the path now, the one with the staff hobbling behind. She knew now where she'd seen him. He came regularly to The White Hart.

What she didn't understand was why, if they were Drew's countrymen, they'd lured him into the woods and wrestled him to the ground.

"God's blood, Andrew, let the wench go," the tall man in front grumbled.

"She's better off without you," said the man with the staff.

"Unless, of course," sneered the burly one, "you've put a babe in her."

Josselin felt the world go still. She hadn't thought of that. What if 'twas true? What if he'd gotten her with child? A chill slithered up her spine. She couldn't give birth to the child of an Englishman. 'Twas too horrible to contemplate.

"We have to take her with us. She has connections," Drew said, holding tight to her waist and hauling her to her feet, "to Mary."

"The queen?" the three men asked in unison.

Lucifer's ballocks! His words stunned Josselin. Why had he told them that? Now they'd never let her go. Even more motivated to make her kidnapping as difficult as possible, she began thrashing against Drew, who somehow held her fast with one arm. She started screaming at the top of her lungs and managed to get out three long shrieks before Drew silenced her with a wad of linen.

"God's teeth!" the man with the staff said. "She could summon the dead with that caterwauling."

If only 'twere true, Josselin thought. She'd summon her mother to make minced meat out of these English bastards.

"Connections to the queen, you say?" the burly man asked, rubbing his grizzled chin in speculation.

Drew nodded. "If we don't bring her along, she could very well set the Scots army on us."

The man with the staff gave her a disparaging glare and suggested, "We might lose her somewhere in the forest."

"Nay," the burly man said. "If she has connections to the queen, maybe we can learn something from her. A few well-placed clouts might loosen her tongue."

Drew's free arm shot out like a snake striking. He grabbed the man by the front of his shirt, hauled him close, and snarled. "You touch one hair on her head, old man, and you'll answer to me."

When he let go, the man staggered back, blinking in surprise.

"Have you gone soft, lad?" the man with the staff asked gruffly. "Have you lived here so long you've forgotten about your father?"

Josselin felt Drew stiffen, but he didn't answer the question.

"We do this my way," Drew said, "or I stay in Edinburgh."

The men seemed utterly bewildered by the idea and began arguing among themselves. Finally the tall man conceded on behalf of all of them.

"Fine. We'll take her with us."

Drew gave them a curt nod. "Now," he said, "where are the shackles you brought along?"

The men feigned ignorance.

"Don't try to tell me you thought you could single-handedly drag me all the way back to England without shackles."

The tall man cleared his throat and produced a pair of black iron manacles.

Josselin kicked and bucked against Drew. He was nonetheless able to clap one iron around her right wrist. Then, to her consternation, he fastened the other to his own left wrist.

"Are you mad, lad?" the man with the staff asked.

The burly man shook his head. "I wouldn't even shackle myself to a *willing* wench."

"Faith, Andrew, I hope you know what you're doing," the tall man sighed.

It appeared she and Drew's three English friends had at least one thing in common. They all thought he was daft.

Chapter 33

She just ... vanished," the beer-wagon driver said with a shrug, tipping his chair back against the wood-paneled wall of The White Hart Inn.

The three old comrades-in-arms—Will, Angus, and Alasdair—as primed for a fight as they'd been on the Ancrum battlefield years ago—scowled ferociously at the man.

"What do ye mean, she vanished?" Will ground out.

Angus brought his boot down on the rung of the man's chair, bringing it upright with jarring force.

The man's eyes went wide, and he glanced nervously at the three men. "She was there all morn," he said, gulping, "and then suddenly she wasn't."

"Poof?" Alasdair narrowed his eyes in threat. "Into thin air?"

"I mean," the man amended, "I saw her go off ..."

"Go off?" Will said. "Where?"

"Toward the woods. After that golfer."

"Golfer?" Alasdair frowned.

The beer-wagon driver smirked. "She was always chasin' after him."

Will clenched his teeth. "Go on."

"Then it got dark. The way I figure it, she must have caught him." He grinned at his own jest, but one glance at Will's scowl and his smile faded. He scratched his arm defensively. "I couldn't stay. Like I said, it was gettin' dark. I had to come back to the inn."

Angus growled. "Ye son of a—"

Will stopped Angus with a shake of his head. They were in a crowded inn. Starting a brawl would only delay their progress, and they'd already lost a day.

"Look," Will said, crouching down to speak to the man in a reasonable voice. "What's your name?"

"Davey."

"Look, Davey. We need to find the lass. Ye were the last one to see her. So ye're goin' to show us the place she disappeared."

" 'Tis all the way in Musselburgh," he whined.

Will fought the urge to backhand the puling dolt, instead muttering, "Then we'd best be leavin' now."

Deciding 'twas in his best interests to cooperate, considering he was outnumbered, Davey gave a sulking nod and shuffled to his feet. He nodded to the innkeeper. "They want to look for the beer-wagon wench."

The innkeeper scowled. "Everyone's lookin' for the beer-wagon wench."

Will scowled back at him, and the innkeeper motioned him toward the counter to confide, "The queen's secretary was sniffin' around last night, askin' after the lass."

"The queen's secretary?"

Will hadn't expected that. When he'd discovered Josselin wasn't in the royal army, but was working as a beer-wagon wench, he'd assumed she'd exaggerated her connection to the queen.

Maybe she hadn't exaggerated after all.

"Did he say anythin' else?" Will asked.

"He seemed a bit out o' sorts, though 'tis hard to tell with the man. He said I was to send word to Holyrood at once if she turned up. Then he muttered somethin' about her bein' a dead woman."

Will's heart turned to ice. A dead woman? What the devil was Josselin involved in? Had her bold tongue gotten her into trouble with the royals?

"A dead woman?" he repeated. "Are ye sure?"

The innkeeper grimaced. "I think that's what he said. 'Twas hard to tell with his funny way o' talkin', but a dead woman, aye."

"Nae, nae," the tavern wench chimed in, "not dead *woman*. Dead *wrong*."

"Dead *wrong*?" The innkeeper shook his head doubtfully. "Dead wrong about what?"

The tavern wench shrugged. "How would I know?"

"Bedwoman," said a man at the counter. "The Frenchman said she was his bedwoman."

"Bedwoman?" the tavern wench said with a laugh. "What the hell is a bedwoman?"

"Probably French for a lady o' questionable virtue," the man replied.

"Besides," the tavern wench said, "she wasn't *his* bedwoman. She was swivin' the Highlander."

Will felt ill. He never should have let Jossy go to Edinburgh alone. With a shudder of dread, he grabbed Davey by the arm and growled to the others, "Let's go."

"If ye find her," the innkeeper called as the three headed out the door, "she owes me a day's wages."

'Twas early afternoon when they arrived at the Musselburgh links. There was a commotion on the course, wagerers complaining because there had been a forfeit of a match. One of the players, a Highlander, hadn't shown up, and he was nowhere to be found, not even at the inn where he was supposed to be staying.

'Twas too much of a coincidence, Will decided. Could he be Josselin's golfer? Had they run off together?

Will ground his teeth. 'Twas too distasteful to think about. Jossy was only a child. At least in his mind she was.

Nonetheless, 'twas a distinct possibility that she'd gone willingly with the man, and that troubled the three of them only a wee bit less than thinking she'd been abducted. Still, whether she'd gone willingly or not, they'd go after Josselin and exert their fatherly influence to persuade her to leave the filthy, cradle-thieving bastard and come home.

Thankfully, there was a clear path into the woods at the place where Davey said she'd disappeared.

Will had always been the best tracker of the three da's, though he hadn't used his skills since the time they'd served together in the Scots army, tracking the enemy. He put his rusty talents to work now as they entered the forest.

'Twasn't long before they discovered signs that there were more than just two travelers. It appeared one of the men had a walking staff. At one point, deep footprints in the mud indicated someone had been running at high speed. And at the spot where the tracks abruptly left the path, there were numerous broken branches, torn leaves, and ruts in the earth, evidence of some sort of scuffle.

This, more than anything, convinced the three that

they needed to make haste. Josselin was outnumbered and in danger.

They didn't eat. They didn't sleep. They marched through the woods with the same cold-blooded determination they'd had years ago marching to war. They'd already lost one maid of Ancrum. They weren't going to lose another.

And thanks to Will's still keen eyes and their relentless pace, on the second night, they managed to catch up with her.

Chapter 34

For two frustrating days, Josselin endured the company of the Englishmen, who she finally learned were Drew's uncles, as they traveled south through the thick Scottish woods, avoiding the main roads. They supped on oatcakes, hard cheese, and berries they found in the forest and never crossed paths with a single Scot. She was beginning to despair of ever getting an opportunity to escape.

Drew kept her shackled to him almost constantly. On the first day, he'd gagged her as well. But the linen had sucked all the moisture from her mouth and left her insufferably thirsty. So she promised she wouldn't cry out, and though the others chided Drew for trusting a Scotswoman, he took her at her word and removed the gag.

Of course, she would have broken her word and screamed her bloody head off if they'd ever run into another single soul.

But on the third day, they crossed the border, and with each mile farther from Scotland they traveled, Josselin grew more ill at ease.

All she knew of England was that 'twas filled with bloodthirsty villains who burned and pillaged the homes and churches of good Scots, stole cattle, razed crops, and cut down women in battle.

Even if she somehow managed to escape, she wouldn't live long without Drew's protection. This was the land of her enemy. Once 'twas discovered she was Scots, the English would no doubt descend upon her like wolves cornering a lamb.

They'd probably take turns on her first.

Then they'd rough her up, blacken her eye, break a few bones.

Maybe they'd beat her to death. Or maybe they'd make an example of her, burning her at the stake or hanging her in a public square.

She shuddered.

She'd never been afraid of death. But then she'd always imagined death would come in glorious battle. After all, 'twas how her mother had died. She had no intention of leaving herself at the mercy of her enemy to be raped, tortured, and executed.

Of course, the answer crouched like a patient hound in the darkest corner of her mind, waiting for her to summon it from the shadows.

For a while she pretended to have forgotten 'twas there. But occasionally throughout the day, it reared its ugly head, reminding Josselin that it waited for her. And the farther into enemy land she traveled, the more restless it grew. Finally, when the lengthening shade of evening stretched over a landscape that was becoming increasingly foreign and menacing, she called the animal forth.

She'd signed that oath to Philipe de la Fontaine and to the queen, vowing that if she fell into enemy hands, she'd kill herself before she'd surrender any information. 'Twas her duty to honor that promise. And she might not have as clear a chance later.

How she'd do it, she wasn't certain. She was shackled to Drew, and he'd confiscated her only weapon. But after three days together, he wasn't as watchful as he'd once been. She probably couldn't overpower him, but she might be able to steal his dagger and inflict a mortal wound upon herself before he could stop her.

'Twas nightfall when her opportunity came. She lay awake beneath the full moon, waiting, her heart pounding, while the men drifted off to deep sleep. After a long while, Drew at last rolled away from her, leaving the dagger he wore on his hip within her reach. She took a breath to steady her nerves and mouthed a silent prayer.

Then, in one swift, bold move, she jostled him forcefully with her shackled hand. Half-awake and distracted by her rough handling, he never noticed that she simultaneously slipped the dagger from his sheath with her free hand.

"What is it?" he mumbled, rolling toward her.

"I need to use the bushes," she whispered.

He sighed, then struggled up to his elbows and gave his head a vigorous shake to clear it. "All right."

She tried to avoid looking at him, reminding herself that he was her foe. But 'twas nearly impossible. When he raked back his tousled hair, she remembered how soft it had been upon her bosom. When he yawned, she remembered his hungry mouth claiming hers. When he stretched his arms, she remembered how sweetly he'd held her in the aftermath of their passion.

Tears started in her eyes, and she blinked them back. For what she was about to do, she needed courage, not mawkish reminiscing.

He unearthed the shackle key and helped her to her feet, then swept up Simon's sword, and they left the clearing.

She dared not risk waking the others, so, concealing the dagger in the folds of her skirts, she led Drew a considerable distance before she finally stopped beside a large shrub.

Drew gave her that sleepy one-sided grin she'd once loved. "Faith, Jossy, I've spent less time shopping for a golf club," he teased. "Are you sure this will do?"

A knot jammed in her throat, and it took all her will not to—damn her vow and damn their past—rush into his arms.

Tucking the sword under his arm, he lifted her shackled wrist. She hoped he couldn't see how her hand trembled as he unlocked the manacle.

Then she was free.

Swallowing hard, she stepped away from him and pretended to rummage beneath her skirts. She peered at him from beneath her lashes, watching till he politely averted his gaze.

She stared at the naked dagger in her damp palm. The blade looked so cold and gray and forbidding in the moonlight. She turned the weapon in her hand until it pointed toward her and placed the sharp tip under her ribs, praying she had the strength to plunge it into her heart.

The cold reality of death made the blood drain from her face, and she broke out into an icy sweat. Her stomach clenched, and her mouth watered with nausea. If she waited much longer, she thought she might be sick.

So she closed her eyes, held her breath, and counted silently.

One...

Two...

Chapter 35

While he waited, Drew whistled softly and absently twirled the point of Simon's sword in the dirt. He hoped this wouldn't take too long. After their inconvenient trek through the wilds of north England, he could use a good night's rest. Impatient, he stole a fleeting glance at Jossy.

He froze mid-whistle. Even under the pale light of the moon, he could see she'd turned as white as parchment. Her lips were compressed into a thin line, and her chest rose and fell with rapid, shallow breaths. Sweat popped out at her brow, and she looked as though she was about to lose her supper.

Then she squeezed her eyes shut, swaying ever so slightly, and he turned to watch her, frowning in concern. Misgiving suddenly pricked the back of his neck. What the...?

He clapped a hand to his sheath.

'Twas empty.

His heart in his throat, he dropped his sword and lunged forward, knocking the dagger from her hand with his fist, using such force that the weapon sailed across the clearing.

She went limp, and he caught her awkwardly with his left arm and half of his body, staggering under her dead weight. At first he thought she'd fainted, but she was conscious, just half-aware, as if she'd just awakened from a strange dream.

His heart stabbed at his ribs as a maelstrom of emotions coursed through him—despair, panic, hurt, and then brutal, inexplicable rage.

"Nay!" he bellowed, shaking her roughly. "Nay!"

She had no reaction to his violence, just looked at him quizzically. "Am I...dead?"

"Nay!" he snarled. "Nay, you're not dead! And you're not going to die. Do you hear me?" He shook her again, his anger rapidly growing out of control. "I won't let you die! I won't let you die like my..."

He stumbled back a step.

God's blood. 'Twasn't Josselin he was yelling at, he realized. 'Twas his father.

That long-buried pain had risen to the surface. He suddenly recalled in vivid detail the anguish of seeing his father's body swaying from the rafters, the hollow grief of watching his uncles bury him, his devastation as he realized his father had left him...forever.

He never spoke of his father's death. His uncles had forbidden it. When anyone asked, they were simply told that Edward Armstrong died in battle. All these years, Drew had had to live with a lie and suffer in silence.

No more.

For years he'd blamed himself. He'd been the last one to see his father alive, and he'd agonized over that. Was there something he could have said, something he could have done, to prevent his death? As young as he'd been, he'd still felt like he could have stopped his father if he'd only known.

And if Josselin thought for one moment he'd allow her to snuff out her life the way his father had, to have another death on his conscience...

"I'm supposed to be dead," she whispered. Her face crumpled in despair. "Damn you!" she wailed, beating on his chest with her fists. "Damn you! I'm supposed to be dead! I'm supposed to be—"

"Nay! Nay. You're not," he said firmly, gripping her by the shoulders and forcing her to look at him. "Listen to me. You're young and beautiful. You have your whole life in front of you. You'll marry. And you'll have children. And you'll be there for those children. You'll *be* there, do you hear me?"

Tears filled Josselin's eyes. She couldn't stop trembling. Indeed, if 'tweren't for Drew holding her up, she'd likely have collapsed. But if he thought she was grateful he'd saved her life, if he thought his passionate words would convince her to live, he was wrong.

She'd been mentally prepared to die. She was *supposed* to die. Drew had dragged her from the grave. And ruined everything.

Now she was condemned to die at the hands of her enemy—a wretched, ghastly, dishonorable death.

She attempted to wrench herself out of his arms, to no avail, then hissed, "Why couldn't ye have just let me die in peace? 'Tis what I wanted."

He flinched, incredulous. "In peace?" he snarled. "Oh, aye, 'twould have been peaceful for you. But you intended to kill yourself on *my* blade! God's blood, did you never think of what that might have done to me?"

Truthfully, she hadn't. She guiltily lowered her gaze. "'Twas the only way."

"The only way to what? Take the craven way out?" He shook his head. "And ye told me ye were no coward."

His insult stung. "Ye don't understand," she said bitterly. "I'm dead already. Ye killed me when ye brought me to England."

"I had to bring you here. You know that. I couldn't let you turn my uncles in."

"And now they'll turn me in." She didn't add that even if they didn't, she was obligated by her service to the queen to take her own life.

He cupped her jaw in his hand. "Jossy, I won't let harm come to you. I love you. I don't care whether you're Scots or English or . . . or from the moon. No matter what else you believe of me, believe this. I love you."

She gave him a brittle smile. He didn't understand. "If ye truly loved me, ye would have let me die. Don't you see? They'll torture me. Once they find out I have connections to Mary, they'll break every bone in my body to—"

"I won't let them have you," he said, holding her face in his hands. "I swear."

He seemed so sure. He spoke with such intensity. 'Twas so tempting to believe him. She wanted to believe him. She wanted to forget that he was English, that she was a spy, that her mother's murder demanded vengeance. She wanted to escape to that heavenly place the two of them had gone, when their bodies were joined and the rest of the world disappeared.

His eyes lowered to her lips, and for one suspenseful

moment, she feared he might kiss her, hoped he might kiss her.

Then the moment passed.

"Listen, Jossy. I had to get my uncles out of Scotland for their own sake, and they wouldn't have come without me. I'll see them home safe, but I don't mean to stay in England." He let out a rueful chuckle. "How could I live in a country without golf?"

He took her hand. "I promise I'll keep you out of harm's way. I won't let anyone take you from me. And if they try..." Using the same trick he'd shown her on the golf course, he flipped up the haft of the dropped sword with his foot, caught it, and twirled the blade in his hand. "They'll have to come through me."

After Jossy and the Englishman left, Will remained crouched in the moonlit bushes for a long while, trying to make sense of what he'd just witnessed.

He knew he should report back to Angus and Alasdair, who waited a quarter mile behind the abductors' make-shift encampment. But after what he'd just seen, he wasn't sure what to tell them.

He'd left his companions slumbering there, exhausted after their two-day journey. But Will's worry for Jossy wouldn't let him sleep, and curiosity had gotten the best of him. So sometime near midnight he'd stolen into the enemy camp, as luck would have it, just as Jossy was rising to leave.

He followed her with utmost stealth as she led her captor a great distance away from the others, and he glimpsed the glint of a blade hidden in her skirts. Perhaps she planned to kill the man and make her escape before his accomplices could catch her. Will unsheathed, prepared to lend a hand if she needed it.

Once he learned she'd gone to answer the call of nature, he'd been abashed and did his best to avert his gaze.

But something wasn't right with the lass. He detected it in her pale face as she closed her eyes with a strange expression of defeat. She wasn't going to kill the man, he suddenly realized in horror. She was going to kill herself.

After that, everything happened so fast, Will scarcely knew what transpired.

The man clouted Jossy's hand, sending the dagger across the clearing to land inches from Will's hiding place, and Jossy collapsed into the man's arms.

Will's heart dropped to the pit of his belly, and he would have cried out to her, but his gasp was smothered by the man's furious shouts. And once Will heard the raw and angry concern in the man's voice—a rage that echoed Will's own—he decided Jossy was safe enough in the man's care. Will settled back weakly on his haunches, glad the fellow was strong enough to give her the stern reprimand she deserved, and watched until his heart could return to a reasonable pace.

'Twas immediately obvious from his accent that the man wasn't a Highlander at all, but from England, which made Will's blood boil, particularly since the brute had his filthy English hands all over Jossy.

But Will reined in his rage. The man had saved Jossy's life, after all. Whatever else he was, he was clearly concerned for her welfare.

Once they lowered their voices, Will could no longer hear them. But at one moment as the couple gazed into one another's eyes, they seemed about to kiss, and Will knew that if they did, he couldn't be responsible for what he might do. Fortunately, his restraint wasn't tested. They drew apart, the man clapped a manacle around Jossy's wrist, and they returned to their camp.

Now 'twas up to Will to decide how to explain it all to Jossy's other da's.

Back at their camp, it took him several attempts with numerous interruptions, but he finally got the news across to Angus and Alasdair.

"I say we rush in now with our swords swingin'," Angus ground out, "murder them all, and take Jossy home where she belongs."

"Now, Angus, be reasonable," Will whispered. "I told ye, Jossy tried to kill herself. 'Tis a delicate situation. She's fragile, and as much as it rubs against our grain, she obviously has feelin's for the one man. No matter how it upsets *us*, care has to be taken not to upset *her*."

Alasdair stroked his chin. "What if we were to work out an equitable trade for the lass? Men o' their sort can be bought off with enough silver."

Angus growled, "The English would as soon lop off a Scotsman's head as let him speak. Ye wouldn't get a word out."

Will had to agree. "Our best approach is a cautious, prepared one. But we're in enemy country now. We can't wait till they lead us to a village full of Englishmen. We have to act soon."

"Here," Angus suggested. "At first light."

Will nodded. "We'll wake up the other three with our swords at their necks. Jossy is shackled to the fourth, but I don't think he'll hurt her. We'll let them live if he gives us Jossy. If not . . ."

Angus puffed up his chest, remembering the long-ago bravery of his youth, and the three of them settled back down on their plaids, their swords in hand, dreaming of the heroic rescue to come.

The plan would have worked brilliantly if they'd wakened before dawn. In their younger days, Will thought in disgust, they would have. But by the time the three road-weary Scots finally stirred themselves, the Englishmen had already left with Jossy.

Chapter 36

Though The Red Lion looked much the same as Kate's tavern, or any tavern, for that matter, Josselin found little comfort there as she huddled by the fire. They'd stopped here because Simon's leg was troubling him. She hoped he'd recover soon. The pair of rough Englishmen in the corner giving her hooded, sidelong glances made her feel as if she wore a banner proclaiming she was Scots.

She rubbed her wrist. At least Drew had removed her shackle. In this hostile environment, she wasn't about to leave his side. Nor would she speak, lest she betray her Scots birth, which seemed to satisfy Drew's uncles all too well.

Her silence, however, didn't indicate peace of mind. Raging in her brain was a fierce moral battle, rife with contradiction.

She'd sworn to the queen to take her life if she fell into enemy hands. She'd already made one attempt.

But was Drew the enemy? He'd sworn to protect her from English foes. And he'd all but promised to return her to Scotland.

If he did return her to Scotland, his own life would be in jeopardy.

But why should she care? He was English and therefore a foe.

Lord, the circle of logic made her head spin.

Still, no matter how much she thought about her murdered mother, no matter how vital her mission was to Queen Mary, no matter how long she'd trained to take up the sword against the English, she couldn't summon up enough moral weight to counterbalance the way she felt about Drew.

To Josselin, he wasn't English. Even if he spoke in that hated accent and had traded his saffron shirt for one of sun-bleached linen, his tartan trews for simple brown, she'd fallen in love with Drew the Highlander. 'Twas hard to imagine he could be a different man just because he was born across the border.

Drew wasn't responsible for her mother's death. He wasn't an enemy spy. He owned a blade, but he had no appetite for bloodsport, preferring to wield a golf club. Even then, though he admitted it gave him some satisfaction to relieve Lowlanders of their coin, he mostly won his matches fair and square.

How could she then despise him?

The two leering strangers finally departed, leaving her alone with Drew and his uncles. She sat, staring into the flames, while Drew went to fetch her an ale.

So lost in thought was she that she didn't notice Simon approach. He must have been sitting beside her a long time, for when he suddenly swore under his breath, it took her completely by surprise.

She looked up, and her heart slammed into her ribs.

He had her note.

How she'd forgotten about it, she didn't know. It must

have been on her person from the time she'd left the Musselburgh links. She supposed in all the excitement of chasing after Drew, being abducted, and trying to kill herself, it had slipped her mind.

The thing must have fallen out of her pocket just now. Simon had picked it up and was squinting at it.

She looked away quickly with studied nonchalance. As Philippe had told her, to the untrained eye, the missive would appear to be a harmless love letter.

"What the..." Simon breathed.

Josselin stole a clandestine glance at the missive, which he was holding upside down and which he'd brought close to the flames to peruse. As she watched, her eyes widened in awe, for between the lines of sugary prose, entire new lines seemed to materialize like magic.

Simon frowned, and she hastily returned her attention to the fire, as if nothing was amiss.

"What's this, wench?" he asked.

Her heart was thrumming like a hummingbird's wings. But she couldn't let him put her on the defensive.

She furrowed her brow at the note. "Where did ye get that?" she whispered furiously.

"It came off your person," he said pointedly.

She held her hand out for the missive, hissing, "Well, give it back. 'Tisn't yours."

"Oh, I think it might be of interest to me."

"What—a love note?" She made a grab for it.

He snatched it out of her reach. "'Tisn't a love note." She frowned as he raised his voice so his brothers could hear. "'Tis something else, isn't it?" He held it up to the light. "In fact, I'd say it looks like a hidden message."

All the breath left her lungs. She lunged for the missive.

But Simon pulled back, waving the note smugly in the air, out of her reach. "I think, brothers, we have a spy in our midst."

Josselin might have done something rash and stupid then, perhaps pushed Simon into the fire, note and all, if Drew hadn't intervened at that instant, snatching the missive from Simon's gleeful grasp.

"What's this?" Drew asked, glancing cursorily at the note.

"'Tis a secret missive," Simon said.

Drew looked closer. "'Tisn't a secret missive, Uncle. 'Tis a love letter." He chuckled. "Too bad the poor sot, Duncan, doesn't know his beloved can't read a word of it." He looked at her, saying pointedly, "Where did you get this, lass? Did that lovesick lad at the links give it to you?"

Relief flooded her. As amazing as 'twas, Drew was coming to her rescue, pretending to read the missive while keeping it out of his uncles' grasp. She managed to choke out, "Aye, 'twas Duncan."

Drew shook his head. "There's never a shortage of admirers around the lass."

"But 'tis more than just a love note," Simon argued. "Strange letters appeared when I held it up."

"Strange letters?" Drew asked. "Uncle, with all due respect, how would you know strange letters from not so strange, since you can't read?"

"The words appeared like objects out of mist."

"Out of mist." Drew turned to his other two uncles and raised a skeptical brow.

Simon scowled. "She's a spy, I tell you."

"She's just a beer-wagon wench," Drew scoffed. He started to hand the missive back to Josselin, but Thomas stopped him.

"Wait!"

Josselin froze, resisting the urge to incriminate herself by jumping up to seize the thing. She held her breath for so long she feared she might faint for lack of air.

Thomas stared at Drew, his face grave. "I've heard of this before. The words are written with the juice of a lemon. The letters are invisible until they're held up to flame. Then they appear..." He glanced at Simon. "Like objects out of mist."

Shite. Drew knew he should have thrown the damned thing into the fire.

Simon he could outwit. But Thomas was bright. He was the one who'd taught Drew how to read. And at the moment, both of them knew exactly what the letter was.

In fact, the instant Drew had seen the note in Simon's hand, everything fell into place. He knew now what Philippe had hired Josselin to do for the queen.

"I'm afraid your mistress is a spy," Thomas said.

"I told you!" Simon crowed.

Drew shook his head in disgust. "How can she be a spy when she can't read or write?"

Simon jutted out his chin. "*I* can't read or write, and *I'm* a..."

He silenced at the sharp looks from his brothers.

Drew lifted a brow in surprise. Then he smugly crossed his arms and perused his uncles, who suddenly looked as guilty as monks in a brothel. "Well, well. Is that what you three were doing in Edinburgh? Spying for—"

"Shh," Robert said, glancing nervously over his shoulder, though there was no one in the tavern but the innkeeper, who was rolling a cask noisily across the floor.

"In any case," Drew said in hushed tones as the inn-keeper disappeared into the cellar, "I assure you if she's involved in espionage, 'tis without her knowledge, which is more than I can say for the lot of you."

Robert frowned, whispering, "You said yourself she had ties to the queen."

"She does," he whispered back. "The queen likes to golf, and Josselin brings her beer on occasion."

Thomas eyed the missive, clearly itching to snatch it from Drew. But Drew returned it to Josselin before Thomas could make his move, and she tucked it quickly out of sight.

"Now," Drew murmured, dusting off his hands, "I sug-gest we forget about these intrigues . . . on both sides."

Thomas fumed. "You should give that message to Elizabeth," he bit out.

Simon jabbed his thumb toward Jossy and muttered, "We should turn her in as well."

"You're harboring a spy," Robert said under his breath. "'Tis treason."

"Aye," said Thomas. "What do you think your father would say about that?"

"He'd be ashamed," grumbled Robert.

"Haven't you learned anything about the scurvy Scots?" Simon hissed. "Did your father die for nothing?"

Their words were like blows of a sword. They cut Drew to the quick, dealing him mortal wounds that left him gasping.

But no sooner was he reeling from their attacks than Jossy leapt to her feet to defend him.

"Listen, ye arse-wisps!" she hissed as loud as she dared. "Ye can say what ye like about the Scots. I'd expect no less from a bunch o' pulin' Englishmen. But I've heard enough o' ye belittlin' your own. Ye should be ashamed o' yourselves! Have ye no decency? Lucifer's cods! Ye three might have lost a brother, but Drew's father was taken from him when he was but a wee lad."

While Drew's uncles stared in amazement, she tossed her hair over her shoulder, and her eyes flashed with fire.

"Any man would be bloody proud to call Andrew his son," she scolded. "He's a fine man. He's kind and fair and brave and decent. He's got a strong arm and a good heart." She pierced them with her gaze and stabbed at them with an accusing finger. "Don't ye dare throw your own pitiful failin's at his feet. And don't ye dare rest your bloody vengeance on his shoulders. Ye're cruel bastards to force him into his father's empty boots. He's his own man. And whether that man is someone ye can be proud o' makes not an arse-hair o' difference. I know his *father* would be proud o' him."

She was magnificent, and Drew looked at her with awe and admiration. No one had ever fought so valiantly for him, and he loved her more in that moment than he'd ever loved anyone before.

For an instant there was stunned silence. Drew's uncles stood in shamefaced, open-mouthed shock while Josselin towered before them like an avenging angel, her face glowing with power, her breast heaving with passion. And Drew beamed with grateful pride.

Then the innkeeper, who'd returned from the cellar to catch the last of her tirade, broke the silence. "God's bones! Did you bloody fools bring a Scotswoman into my tavern?"

It took a great deal of persuasion and considerable coin to calm the innkeeper, and Drew had to promise to keep his "wife" behind a closed door the rest of the evening.

Chapter 37

They've been in there for hours. Do ye think they're stayin' the night?" Angus asked as they peered out from the bushes toward The Red Lion.

A thin stream of smoke still rose from the chimney into the starlit sky, and the windows glowed with flickering firelight, but no one had come or gone for at least an hour.

Will nodded to the tracks that led to the inn. "The lame one's been leanin' heavily on his staff. He's grown weary."

"They'll probably get a good night's rest," said Alasdair, "then light out early in the morn."

"I say we go in now," Angus said, clapping a hand on the pommel of his sword, "take them by surprise, rescue Jossy, and make a run for it."

"Nae," Will said.

"Nae?"

"I've no wish to brawl with a tavern full o' drunken Englishmen."

"Then what do ye suggest?"

"I'm goin' in alone." Will unbuckled his sword. "And I'm leavin' this here."

"Are ye barmy?" Angus said. "Ye just said yourself, the place is crawlin' with bloody English."

"All the more reason to go in unarmed."

Alasdair shook his head. "But ye can't take on Jossy's captors by yourself."

"I'm not goin' to take them on," Will said. "We'll confront them when they're sober, in the morn. And this time we'll be ready for them. We'll take turns on watch."

"Then why are ye goin' in now?" Alasdair asked.

Will frowned. "Because I'm half-starved, and I've been smellin' whatever they've got cookin' over the fire for hours now." He got to his feet, dusted off his clothes, and tried to look as English as possible. "Don't worry. I'll bring somethin' back for ye as well."

'Twas partially true. He *was* hungry. But he also wanted to check on Jossy. The other two hadn't seen the way she'd looked at that golfer. Prying her out of the lad's grasp might not be as easy as Angus and Alasdair imagined. If Will made an appearance at the inn tonight, Jossy would know her da's were watching over her, and she'd be mentally prepared to leave with them in the morn.

The instant he pushed through the door, however, and scanned the interior of the tavern from beneath his lowered cap, he realized that once again he'd arrived too late.

The three older Englishmen sat around a table near the fire, frowning into their ale, but Josselin and the golfer were nowhere to be seen.

The men glanced up briefly when Will walked in, then resumed their grumbling.

The innkeeper finished poking at a log on the fire, then looked over. "I hope 'tisn't lodging you want," he said, clapping the ashes from his hands. "We're full up."

"Just supper," Will mumbled.

He cast an uncomfortable glance up the stairs. 'Twas probably best he hadn't brought his sword. He might have done something foolish, like charge up the steps, fling open the door, and murder the bloody English bastard who was up there with Jossy, doing God knew what.

The moment Drew shut the chamber door behind them, Josselin whirled on him.

"I'll have ye know I'm not sorry for what I said," she stiffly informed him, adding under her breath, "though I *am* sorry I said it so loudly."

He grinned as he unbuckled his swordbelt and leaned his sword against the wall. " 'Twas worth every penny. You were brilliant."

"Well, they bloody well deserved it," she decided, though she was cursing herself for losing her temper. If his uncles hadn't intended to turn her in before, they certainly had cause to now.

"Faith, their bark is worse than their bite," Drew said, setting his satchel of clubs against the bed. "As fierce as they seem, they mean well. They always have. God's truth, if 'tweren't for them, I would've had no upbringing at all."

"Are ye defendin' their cruelty?" she asked, incredulous.

"Not their cruelty, but their intent." He sat down on the edge of the bed and began pulling off his boots. "They may blame the Scots for what happened to my father, but they also believe he was weak, that that was why he . . . why he died. So they've always been stern with me, hoping to make me a stronger man than he was."

"Stern?" she said in outrage. "Is that what ye call it?"

She frowned, pacing off her ire. "I think they're vicious. And connivin'. And spiteful. My da's would never have spoken to me about my mother like that."

"You're a lass."

"Ach! My da's paid no mind to that. They raised me like a son." She shook her head in disgust. "But your uncles, they've treated ye worse than a hound."

He chuckled. "Take care, lass. You're coming dangerously close to defending your enemy."

She stopped pacing.

Marry, he was right. Why should she care how Drew's uncles treated him? He was English. The whole lot of them were. Bloody ruthless English bastards.

She sniffed. "I'm not defendin' ye. If I were defendin' ye, I would have run them through."

He smirked. "Then 'tis lucky for them we're foes."

"And what about ye?" she challenged. "Ye lied for me."

"Aye." He shrugged out of his doublet and hung it on the peg beside the bed.

"Ye knew I could read. And now ye know I'm a..." She lowered her voice to a whisper. "A spy."

He lifted a bemused brow.

She repeated, "Yet ye lied for me."

He shrugged. "I swore I'd keep you safe."

"Ye made that vow," she pointed out, "before ye knew what I was."

"True." He loosened the laces of his shirt.

Josselin frowned, perplexed. "We're enemies," she reiterated.

"Are we?" He smiled at her, and his eyes sparkled. "I've no quarrel with you."

Damn it all, when he looked at her like that, she couldn't think straight. "That doesn't matter. Ye can't turn your back on your blood and your breedin'. Our forebears have been foes for far too long to..."

He pulled his shirt over his head, and at the sight of his bare chest, all her thoughts flew straight out of her head.

"Aye?" he asked.

She blinked. Faith, he was half-naked. How had he come to such a state of undress?

"What are ye doin'?" she demanded.

He smirked and reached up to hang his shirt on top of his doublet. "I'm going to bed. What are *you* doing?"

She felt the blood rise in her cheeks. "But ye can't....I won't....I can't share a bed with ye."

"You did before," he pointed out.

"Aye, but that was before I knew ye were my sworn enemy."

He shrugged. "Fine."

"Fine?"

"Aye. Fine. Then you can sleep on the floor."

"What?"

"Look, 'wife,'" he said, "I've been traveling for three days and have yet to get a good night's rest." He grabbed the pillow, punched it a few times, then stretched out on the bed with his hands behind his head. "I'm not about to be robbed of sleep by your prejudices." He closed his eyes.

Her jaw dropped. "I'm not your wife. I don't care what ye told the innkeeper. I'll not share a bed with—"

"Or your offended sensibilities."

Fuming, she scoured the chamber, looking for another place to sleep. There was none.

Without opening his eyes, the cocky varlet patted the mattress beside him in invitation.

With a glower that would melt iron and a string of curses that would have earned her a scolding from her da's, she flounced onto the bed. Her only satisfaction was his grunt of displeasure when she yanked the pillow from beneath his head and appropriated it for herself.

And even that was short-lived. A moment later, he shackled her to his wrist. She couldn't blame him. At the moment, she'd like nothing better than to find her dagger and run him through.

Chapter 38

Jossy!"

Drew's eyes flew open. In the dim light of dawn, it took him a moment to remember where he was. Then the naked leg draped possessively over his thigh brought a river of memories racing back, and he smiled.

Jossy was still asleep. Her lashes lay softly on her cheek. Her hair rested like a golden halo upon the pillow. Her lips looked as sweet as berries. And she was snoring like a mastiff.

He must have been dreaming. He thought he'd heard someone calling for...

"Jossy!"

That time Jossy stirred. "What?" she croaked, still half-asleep.

Drew sat up. His heart pounded.

'Twas a man calling her, and 'twas coming from downstairs. Who could it be? Not his uncles. But who else knew her by name? Who else knew she was here? The innkeeper! Had he pocketed their generous coin and sent for the authorities anyway?

"Jossy!" 'Twas insistent this time.

She sat up abruptly, scrubbing at her eyes, and opened her mouth to answer.

He clapped a hand over her mouth and pushed her back down to the pillow.

She reacted as he expected, twisting and thrashing against him, her eyes wide with outrage.

"Jossy!" the voice bellowed. "Come down!"

"Who is that?" Drew whispered, more to himself than to Jossy.

She answered him with a bite.

He swore and yanked back his injured palm. But when she took a breath to yell, he stuffed the first thing he could find into her mouth, and she got a face full of coverlet.

"Shh, Jossy!" he said. "It might be someone looking to hurt you."

She squirmed under his weight and, as much as she was able, shook her head as if to say nay.

"Do you know who 'tis?"

She nodded.

"Jossy!" came the shout. This time 'twas several men's voices.

He cursed under his breath. God's blood! Was the whole Scots army downstairs?

Jossy began struggling in earnest.

"You know them?" he asked again.

She nodded furiously.

He frowned at her, trying to deduce who could possibly know Jossy was here. Then he realized she was fighting him, not in fear, but in rage. She wasn't afraid of whoever was downstairs.

Nay, it couldn't be, he thought, refusing the first thought that sprang to mind. 'Twas impossible. They couldn't have followed her all the way from Selkirk. Nonetheless, he had to ask. "'Tisn't your da's, is it?"

Her uncertain hesitation gave her away.

"Ah, shite."

He wasn't sure what was worse—one vexed innkeeper with a handful of local authorities or three angry fathers.

Before he could decide, he heard heavy footfalls going past the door and charging down the steps. 'Twas his uncles, he was sure, awakened by the bellows of rage. And they'd probably like nothing better this morn than to spill Scots blood.

Jossy chose that moment to drive her knee up into his belly, and he wheezed in pain. But he wasn't about to let her go. The last thing she needed was to get herself trapped between a bunch of old fools' blades.

"I'm sorry, Jossy," he rasped, "but 'tis for your own good. Don't worry. I won't hurt them. I swear."

Then, as much as he regretted having to do it, he unlocked his manacle and secured her to the bottom leg of the bed, then gagged her with torn bedsheets. 'Twas as challenging as wrestling a wildcat, and he had the scratches and bites to prove it.

The sound of indistinct shouting floated up the stairs. Drew quickly shrugged into his shirt. He had no sword. He'd given it back to Simon. But a fairway club would do in a pinch. He selected his sturdiest from the satchel, tested it against his palm, and sent Jossy one last reassuring look.

She gave him such a scorching glare that he felt the burn of it on his skin. When the ring of steel on steel began belowstairs, she rattled her shackles with unfettered rage and screamed in fury behind the gag.

Drew gently closed the door on her.

'Twasn't quite the bloodbath he was expecting. The six men appeared to be equally matched. And equally rusty. Meanwhile, the enraged innkeeper was hastily stashing his breakables under the counter.

As soon as Drew appeared on the stairs, a burly, bearded Scotsman called him out.

"That one's mine!" the man shouted, heading up the steps.

Drew met him on the stairs and easily deflected the man's first wild slashes with his golf club.

"What have ye done with her?" the man snarled. "What have ye done with my Jossy?"

"She's safe," Drew told him.

The old man jabbed forward, and Drew knocked his blade aside.

"Then let her go," he growled.

"Nay, not now," Drew said, dodging slashes and holding his place on the stairs. "I'm not about to open that door." He glanced around the inn. "Not while...this...is going on."

The man hesitated in his attack and glanced toward the room where Jossy was. Drew was certain if Jossy's da had followed her all the way from Selkirk, he must love her very much. And the man doubtless knew how reckless and impulsive Jossy could be.

"I trust we understand each other?" Drew asked him.

The man pursed angry lips, but gave him a curt nod. "But if ye've touched one hair on the lass's head..."

Drew didn't know how to answer that. He'd touched far more than one hair. "I haven't hurt her. I can promise you that."

The man didn't look pleased, but at least the murderous intent was gone from his eyes.

"Now if we're agreed," Drew said, "I think we should go downstairs before somebody draws blood. My poor lame uncle's getting a fair walloping from your man there, and the innkeeper looks ready to dismember someone."

The man nodded, and they joined the melee, which for Drew was an exercise in strategy as he tried to make sure no one came to harm on either side.

The old men fatigued rapidly, and Drew hoped 'twould not be much longer till they could end the fight and maybe even talk things out like reasonable people.

Josselin narrowed her eyes to cold slits. If that son of an English doxy thought he'd leave her trussed up, helpless, while he did battle with her three da's, he'd sadly underestimated her. He might have sworn not to harm them, but his bloodthirsty uncles had made no such promise. And she'd be damned if she'd sit back and wait for her da's to be slaughtered.

It took patience, persistence, and strength, but she managed to escape. She dropped to the floor and squeezed beneath the heavy oak bed frame, levering it up with her shoulder and lifting the leg of the bed just high enough off the floor to free the shackle.

After that, 'twas quick work to untie her gag and reclaim her weapon from among Drew's things. Wishing that she had a proper sword instead of a dagger, she nonetheless stormed out the door and rushed down the stairs, eager for battle.

The tavern was a mess of overturned tables and broken chairs. Fists flew, blades whistled, and crockery smashed against the wall. The air was thick with grunts and groans, battle cries and vile oaths.

Thankfully her da's were alive and well. Angus was the first one to spot her, and when he saw she had no sword, he tossed his weapon to her.

"Here, lass!" he shouted above the din. "Take my blade! Avenge your mother!"

She tossed her dagger to her shackled hand and caught the sword in her right. All at once, 'twas as if Angus's words had imbued the blade with otherworldly power, a power that seeped from the hilt into her veins, giving her the heart of her warrior mother and firing her blood with a thirst for vengeance.

Pumped full of the rage she was born to, Josselin raised her blade high. "For my mother! For the Maid of Ancrum Moor!"

She brought the sword down with a mighty sweep between Angus and Simon, intending to take over for Angus. But Simon instantly stopped fighting. He looked at her in horror and dropped his weapon to the ground.

"Coward!" she spat, turning in disgust to take on Robert, who had been battling Will. But Robert, too, was only staring at her with his jaw slack, and he tossed away his sword as if 'twere a poisonous snake.

"Come on!" she yelled. "Fight me!"

She looked over at Thomas, who'd been dueling with Alasdair. He stood frozen, his blade lowered. At her glare, he blinked and let the weapon fall.

"Have ye all lost your ballocks?" she cried.

The room fell silent. The English stood with their mouths agape. Her da's frowned in confusion. And Drew, who was gripping his golf club with white knuckles, was staring at her as if he'd never seen her before.

Chapter 39

A hard lump lodged in the pit of Drew's stomach, and he felt sick.

Surely he'd heard wrong. Surely she hadn't said Ancrum.

But the pieces fit. She was the right age. She came from the right place. The history was undeniable.

He longed to stop everything here and now, to silence them all forever, to keep the horrible truth from unraveling. He wanted to whisk Jossy out of the tavern and run away with her, away from his uncles, away from her da's, away from the past.

Instead, he could only watch helplessly, mutely, unable to move, as the inevitable chaos and betrayal unfolded around him.

The bearded Scot scowled. "Bloody hell, what ails the lot o' ye?"

Simon, pale as parchment, answered. "We don't fight...with women."

"Not since..." Robert said, breaking off to glance at Jossy.

Thomas narrowed his eyes at the lass. "Did you say... Ancrum?"

The bearded one pushed his way forward and set the point of his blade under Thomas's chin. "What do ye know about Ancrum?"

"You realize I'm unarmed," Thomas pointed out.

The man muttered into his beard and lowered his weapon. "Well?"

"We fought there, the three of us," Thomas said, "at Ancrum Moor, in '45."

The Scots gasped.

"*Ye* fought there?" the bearded man breathed. "Ye fought at the Battle of Ancrum Moor?"

"Aye."

The bearded man stepped forward until he was nose to nose with Thomas. "So did we."

Simon sneered, "So you're the cowardly bastards who sent women into battle."

The burly Scotsman gestured with his sword. "And ye're the cowardly bastards who slew them."

"I see you're still sending women to fight your battles," Robert said, glaring at Jossy.

"Nobody sent me," Jossy said through her teeth, her eyes fierce, "and nobody sent my mother. But I fight to avenge her, because she was brutally murdered at Ancrum. And ye seem to have her blood on your hands."

"That may be," Thomas said, "but you'll find no combatants here. If you want us dead, you'll have to kill us in cold blood."

"After Ancrum Moor," Simon added, "we took an oath on our brother's grave."

Robert snorted. "We don't fight women."

Drew could see this was going to end badly. Jossy was primed for battle. She'd probably been raised on a thirst for vengeance. She'd probably been looking forward to this moment her entire life. She'd probably dreamed of the day she'd face those who'd left her an orphan.

He knew exactly how she felt. His father may have killed her mother. But in a sense, her mother had killed his father.

Jossy, however, was impetuous and passionate. She might well take Thomas's suggestion and murder them all while they were unarmed.

Blood would be spilled, and nothing would be solved.

If she wanted a fight, he'd give it to her, but not at the risk of her soul and not with innocent men who would never have allowed her mother on a battlefield in the first place.

"I took no such oath," he said quietly, facing her. "Fight me."

She furrowed her brow. "But ye weren't at Ancrum. Ye couldn't have been more than a lad."

"I'm the one you want," he told her. "The one who killed the maid at Ancrum? Who slew your mother?" He leveled her with a grave stare. "'Twas my father."

Josselin felt the world slide sideways as she gaped at Drew. It didn't seem possible.

She'd imagined this confrontation a hundred times—the moment where she'd meet her mother's murderer. He was always brutish and ugly, an evil sneer twisting his face. She'd practiced the curses she'd lay upon his head and envisioned killing him the way he had her mother, with cruel gashes that would make him bleed to death slowly.

'Twasn't supposed to be like this, where death had already claimed the culprit and where the only one on whom she might exact revenge was...a man with whom she'd fallen in love.

She suddenly felt like she'd been kicked in the stomach. 'Twas bad enough that Drew was an Englishman, but the son of her mother's murderer...

God help her, she'd kissed him. She'd touched him. She'd given him her virginity. And he'd utterly betrayed her.

How long had he known? Had he planned this from the beginning? Was it some kind of game to him—seducing and abducting the daughter of the Maid of Ancrum Moor? Was she the prize in his twisted play of vengeance?

She trembled with hurt, with sickness, with rage.

"Andrew!" Simon barked. "Put down your weapon. Have you learned nothing from your father?"

Drew's eyes never left Josselin. "I'm not my father."

"She's a lass, Andrew," Robert scolded. "She doesn't know—"

"She knows what she's doing," Drew said.

"But if you wound her," Thomas said, "if you kill her..."

"If she steps onto this battlefield," Drew said to her, "she'd better know what the stakes are."

Josselin straightened grimly. Now he was speaking a language she understood. It didn't matter what her heart said, what her emotions had been. Her mother's blood demanded retribution. Her da's had trained her for this. 'Twas what they expected, what her mother expected, what she expected of herself. So she turned a blind eye to the handsome Highlander she'd made love to only days before and faced her English enemy with a raised blade and a curt nod.

Simon addressed the Scots. "Andrew's right. This is *their* battle. It should be between the two of them."

Will reluctantly sheathed his blade and nodded to Alasdair to do the same. Drew exchanged his golf club for Simon's sword, and Josselin cast aside her dagger, so they'd be evenly matched. Then everyone moved back to give them room.

Josselin met Drew's eyes and swallowed hard, trying to blot everything from her mind but the duel. She tried to forget his smile, his kiss, his touch. She tried to forget that he was the man who'd saved her life. She tried to think of him as nothing more than her betrayer, the son of the man who'd killed her mother.

'Twas the most difficult thing she'd ever done.

But Alasdair had trained her to shut down distractions, to focus on the fight at hand.

She wasn't afraid. Fear was something she'd conquered long ago. Angus had assured her that even someone of her size always had advantages.

And Will had cautioned her to keep a cool head, for her temper was her greatest failing.

She would win this match. Her opponent was bigger and stronger, but Josselin was quick and clever. She'd spent hours every day honing her talents, and though Drew might be handy with a fairway club, he'd likely let his skills with a sword lapse.

She was about to find out.

She widened her stance and tossed the hair away from her face. "Do your worst," she dared him.

Never losing eye contact, he tested his blade, bringing it whistling down with a flick of his wrist. Then he flexed his knees and lifted the point of the sword, inviting her with a beckoning wave to make the first move.

She frowned. For someone who preferred golf to warfare, he seemed surprisingly comfortable with a sword. But she had the power of vengeance on her side.

Her da's began to yell directives, giving her advice and encouragements. Josselin was deaf to everything but the hot blood of battle rushing in her ears.

With a rage-filled cry, she thrust forward.

He immediately caught her blade with his own, turning it aside.

She attacked again, this time with a diagonal slash.

He blocked the blow with a simple sweep of his arm.

She advanced with a series of quick, short strikes.

Which he glanced aside as if he were swatting flies.

She growled in fury and redoubled her efforts, spinning and slashing and thrusting with her sword, trying to inflict damage anywhere.

But without moving his feet an inch, he managed to deflect every blow.

Damn the cocky rogue! He was toying with her.

Despite her best intentions, she felt her temper rising. She hated Andrew Armstrong. Hated him for being English. Hated him for taunting her. And most of all hated him for making her fall in love with him.

Chapter 40

It had been a long time since Drew had battled with a sword, but he'd trained for so many years that it came as naturally to him as breathing.

Josselin, too, was skilled. But she didn't have his discipline, and she definitely didn't have the coldblooded temperament required to be a master swordfighter.

Instead, he saw burning hatred in her eyes as she struck out wildly at him.

She was quick, but he was quicker. She was clever, but her intent was easy to read. She was agile, but she was wearing herself out.

He needed to keep her attacks at bay just long enough to tire her, to drain her strength and her rage. Then, and only then, could he try to use reason.

He fought defensively at first, blocking her blows, glancing her thrusts aside. But gradually he advanced on her, carefully and strategically backing her into a corner.

Her men shouted out warnings as panic widened her eyes.

He had her now. There was nowhere she could go. She

was tired. She was defenseless. At last maybe he could talk some sense into her.

"I don't want to do this," he told her. "I've no wish to fight you. There's no point in opening an old wound, and—"

He hadn't counted on her swinging her left hand around and knocking him in the side of the head with the manacle.

He staggered back, stunned, and in his moment of disorientation, she managed to slip out of his reach.

He winced as his head began to throb, cursing his own inattention. But he shook off the pain and advanced on her again, charging with aggressive blows to drive her back against the door of the inn. This time he seized the shackle, immobilizing her hand, and came across with his sword hand to knock the blade from her grip.

As her weapon clattered on the floor, there was a loud gasp from the onlookers. But Josselin stood firm as he placed the edge of his sword against her neck.

He was impressed. Most men would cower in her place.

He leaned forward to whisper to her. "Jossy, listen to me. I don't want to hurt you. This isn't our fight. We can't be—"

She drove her knee up between his legs so fast he never saw it coming. All the air left his lungs, and he doubled over as his abused ballocks began to ache. He barely had the presence of mind to withdraw his blade so he wouldn't cut her.

She escaped him again, scooping up her sword as she fled toward the hearth.

He gasped, trying to catch his breath. As he glanced at his audience, he saw they were all wincing in empathy, even the Scots.

Limping in pain, he nevertheless managed to engage her again. He struck her blade with blows heavy enough to jar her bones. She fell back, inch by inch, until her back was to the fire.

Then her heel caught on on uneven plank, and her arms cartwheeled back as she lost her balance.

He seized her around the waist, hauling her forward against him so she wouldn't fall into the flames.

Though she struggled against him, he held her tightly in his grasp and rasped out, "We can't be responsible for the actions of our parents. What your mother did, what my father did, 'twas a lifetime ago."

"He murdered her," she spat.

"Nay," he said. 'Twas time she learned the truth. "'Twas an act of mercy."

She squirmed in frustration against him.

"She was already dying," he murmured, remembering his father's last words, scrawled on the note he'd left behind. "She asked him to slay her. She asked him to end her suffering."

Her da's gasped, and she paused for a moment, taken aback by this information. Then she began pounding on his shoulder with the pommel of her sword. "Why should I believe ye? Ye're nothin' but a bloody English—"

"I told ye my father died in battle," he said, ignoring her blows. "That was a lie. My father took his own life." His uncles started to protest, but he didn't give a damn what they thought. He'd hidden the truth long enough. "When he came home from Ancrum, he sent me off to fetch my uncles. By the time we returned, he'd written out his confession and hanged himself."

"As he deserved," she breathed.

He flinched at her cruelty. But when he looked closer into her eyes, he saw that she was in anguish. What he was telling her was counter to everything she'd ever believed. All her life, she thought her mother had been tortured to death. She didn't know that the one who'd ended her life had done so out of kindness and that he'd paid for his sin with his own life. She'd expended so much energy believing in the injustice of her mother's death that she probably didn't want to hear the real story.

But he was going to make her listen anyway.

"Do you know why he killed himself?" he asked.

She wrenched at his arms, trying to get free.

"Remorse," he said. "Even though he'd killed a woman out of compassion, he was burdened with horrible guilt over it."

Her eyes were filling with moisture, though she still fought him with what remained of her strength.

"You see, my father had no killer instinct," he explained, "and no appetite for war." Then, silently praying he wasn't making a fatal mistake, he dropped his sword to the floor and let her go. "And neither do I."

Set free, Jossy raised her blade, and for one awful instant, Drew feared she meant to behead him then and there. But the sword wavered in her grip, her chin trembled, and a tear spilled down her cheek.

Josselin had the advantage now. Her sword was poised above his head. She could kill him. With one slash she could exact the vengeance she was born to, and be free of the curse of her bloodline.

But what if he was speaking the truth? What if his

father had been the one English soldier at Ancrum with the heart to end her mother's agony?

He stood before her now—unarmed, vulnerable. He'd left his life in her hands. He trusted her. How could she not show him the same trust?

He spoke softly. "My father already paid for your mother's death. There's no more revenge to be had." He held his palms up in surrender. "You can kill me. But if you do, where will the vengeance end? When all our kin are dead?"

He was right. The burden of hate she'd carried for so long was only an empty cask after all. Suddenly, she felt as if a great weight had been lifted off her shoulders.

Tears spilled over her lashes, and she sniffed them back angrily. Bloody hell! She hated to cry, especially in front of her da's. She lowered her sword and swiped brusquely at her eyes with the back of her shackled hand.

There was a collective sigh of relief from the witnesses.

Drew lowered his hands to his sides and asked, "Jossy, can you forgive me?"

She looked at him through tear-blurred eyes. She knew what he meant. He'd lied to her. Kidnapped her. Bedded her. But he'd also lied *for* her. Loved her. And saved her life.

She nodded.

"Can you..." he asked, raising hopeful brows, "love me?"

Will stepped forward with a growl. "Over my dead body."

Simon agreed. "Oh, nay, you don't, lad."

"'Tis time we went home, lass," Angus hastily added.

"Aye," Robert said, " 'tis time we all went home."

Thomas said, " 'Tis settled then."

Alasdair chimed in, "We're all agreed."

Josselin rounded on them with her sword, making them step back a pace. "Nae, we're not agreed," she snapped, glad of an excuse to turn her weeping into ire. "In case ye old fools hadn't noticed, the two of us are full-grown. I think we can bloody well decide our own destiny. It may not be an easy road. But we're strong and brave. The blood o' heroes runs in our veins. Together we have the cods to face whatever fate hands us, and by God's Cross, we'll kick the arses of anyone who stands in our way."

Everyone grumbled at that, everyone except Drew, who grinned proudly, then turned to tip up her chin and plant a sweet kiss on her lips.

There was a unanimous groan from the old men, but Josselin didn't care. She hadn't realized how much she'd missed the taste of Drew. Her bones seemed to melt as he wrapped his arm around her waist, drawing her closer. She sighed into his mouth as he slipped his hand into her hair and kissed her thoroughly. At some point, her sword hit the floor, but she hardly noticed. All she knew was that she was right where she belonged.

Without a word, Drew swept her off her feet and carried her up the stairs. The last she heard of the old men was their disgusted muttering.

"I can't believe you let a lass curse like that."

"I can't believe ye let your nephew golf."

Then Drew slammed the chamber door behind them.

Chapter 41

The heat of battle still raged in Josselin as she attacked Drew, tearing his shirt half off and scrabbling at the laces of his trews.

He countered with just as much passion, heaving her onto the bed and tossing up her skirts.

Their mouths met, and they fed on each other, licking and sucking and feasting like half-starved beasts.

Her hands roamed over his body, delving into the thick mass of his hair, rounding the solid muscle of his shoulder, stroking the sculpted planes of his chest.

He explored her just as thoroughly, stroking her bare arms, ensnaring his hand in her tresses, grazing the flesh over her ribs.

She arched up toward him, breathless with desire, and he pushed her down into the mattress, grinding against her hips.

Impatient, she shoved her hand boldly down the loose top of his trews to find the full treasure within.

He groaned, but his revenge was swift. He nuzzled aside her chemise and suckled at her breast while his fingers searched beneath her skirts and found that hot, hungry spot betwixt her legs.

She moaned in pleasure, squeezing her eyes closed as a wave of lust washed over her. Then she circled her hands around his back, sliding his trews down to knead the solid muscle of his buttocks.

He growled in approval, gently lifting her knee up and out to prepare her for his swollen staff.

Aching with need, wet with desire, she grasped his buttocks and pulled them toward her, impaling herself on his thick cock with a cry of delight.

He dropped his head to her shoulder, overcome with lust, taking a moment to enjoy her warmth. After a moment, he moved against her, initiating the sweet friction that would spark the sensual fire between them.

His flesh was hot against hers, and she burrowed her head against his neck, alternately nipping at his throat and soothing him with her tongue.

She squeezed his buttocks, urging him, guiding him as he plunged into her again and again, ultimately wrapping her legs around him to drive him with her heels. Her head swam in a glorious sea of sensation as she writhed on the pillow.

From deep within, she felt the familiar turbulence begin, a small rumbling at first. She dug her fingers into his shoulders, grounding herself for what was to come. Her heart pounded, and her breath came in gasps as the thunder within her rolled closer and closer to the surface. And then, in one magnificent flash, lightning struck, blinding in its brilliance, and she felt shocked to life.

As she shook with violent tremors, he, too, found his release, roaring with the power of it, thrusting until he could thrust no more, emptied of his seed and drained of his will.

Wary of crushing her, he rolled to the side, taking her with him. Then, with what little strength he had left, he showered the top of her head with grateful kisses.

She laughed in exhausted delight and nestled her face in the hollow of his shoulder. They lay there until their pulses slowed and their breath came in long, contented sighs.

"Do ye think they're gone?" she finally murmured.

"Who—the peevish old men? I hope so."

She smiled and traced a path down his chest with her fingertip. "My da's meant well."

"Oh, aye. So did my uncles. They just don't understand me any more than they understood my father. They expected me to serve in King Henry's army, to use my sword," he said mockingly, "in the glorious war with Scotland." He arched a sardonic brow. "Well, I went to Scotland. But I chose to wage my battles with a golf club."

"'Tis no use fightin' against your nature."

He pulled his head back to gaze down at her. "And what about your nature, my wee warrior?"

"I suppose 'tis what I was born to, bein' the daughter o' the Maid of Ancrum Moor."

He nodded, then grew pensive. "'Twas a tragedy," he breathed, "what happened to her."

She furrowed her brow. "My mother knew what she was doin' the moment she stepped onto that battlefield. I'll always believe that. The real tragedy was what happened to your father."

He smiled ruefully, coiling a lock of her hair around his finger. "If I'd done what my father did—killed an innocent who was suffering—I wouldn't have hanged myself. I don't believe he was weak, but I think he was wrong to feel guilty. My uncles taught me that in war there are no rules." He quirked up the corner of his mouth. "Which is why I prefer golf."

She shook her head in amusement. "Ye truly prefer golf to war?" 'Twas hard to imagine for Josselin, who'd been raised with a blade in her hand and a legacy to her name.

"Oh, aye." He let his fingers drift down her throat and trace a path between her breasts. "'Tis a bloodless battle," he said, "aside from the occasional brawl on the links."

Josselin quivered beneath his touch. "And 'tis profitable," she admitted.

He dragged his knuckles gently beneath her breast, awakening the flesh there. "More profitable to drain an enemy's coffers than his blood."

"No rules," she mused, biting her lip. "I've heard the same thing said about love." She gazed at him with languid eyes. "Do ye prefer golf to that as well?"

He brushed a thumb across her nipple, eliciting a gasp from her, and his irresistible blue eyes twinkled wickedly. "Why don't you get a good grip on my fairway club, and we'll see?"

'Twas late in the day when they fell back on the mattress for the third time, breathless and satiated. Their clothes—what few of them remained—were in a hopeless tangle, as were their limbs and—Josselin feared—their hearts.

"Ye know this is mad," she murmured.

"Aye," he breathed. "We should have chosen a chamber with a quieter bed."

She smiled and halfheartedly punched his arm. "Ye know what I mean. Our queens are enemies." She rested her forearm across her brow. "If this were a battlefield, we'd be at each other's throats."

He rolled lazily toward her. "Is that what you want, lass? You want me at your throat?" With mock ferocity, he lunged at her, playfully biting the side of her neck, making her shiver.

She reluctantly pushed him away, then sat up, pulling up the neck of her chemise in modesty. "I'm serious, Drew. Ye know I have to go back to Edinburgh." She began repairing the damage to her attire and tried to lend some semblance of order to her hair. "If I don't report to Philipe, if I don't deliver the last missive…"

Drew rocked forward, pulling up his trews. "He'll suspect you've either been compromised or you've betrayed the queen."

"Exactly."

He shrugged, as if the answer were simple. "So we'll go back." He ran a finger lightly down her cheek and spoke in his Highland brogue. "Unless ye find ye prefer English swordsmen to Highland golfers."

She was still deciding when they finished dressing and prepared for the journey home.

Fortunately, his uncles had left a small purse of silver at their door, and Josselin's da's had paid for the damages to the inn. Their guardians might not have approved of their consorting with the enemy, but the old fools apparently hadn't killed one another, and the innkeeper reported that they'd departed peacefully in opposite directions.

Chapter 42

Drew had made it sound easy. He and Josselin would return to Edinburgh together, claim to have had a week-long tryst in the woods of Musselburgh, then return to their respective inns to resume their usual activities. She'd return to her beer wagon. He'd return to his golfing. And no one would be the wiser.

Unfortunately, 'twasn't so simple.

Though she'd studiously avoided peeking at the secret writing on that missive, claiming 'twas best she didn't know what it contained, Drew had taken a good look at it, particularly once he noticed to his alarm that the name of "Drew MacAdam" figured prominently in the letter.

Josselin still didn't realize he could read, or she would have taken greater pains to hide the thing. But he'd had time to memorize and decipher the message, and if it meant what he thought it meant, both of them were in great danger.

Of course, he wouldn't tell Josselin that. There was no point in making her worry. Besides, she was a woman who believed trouble was best confronted face to face with a sword in her hand, and this was not the kind of threat that

could be handled that way. 'Twas a matter requiring subterfuge, sleight of hand, and cunning.

If there was anything Drew excelled at, 'twas deception. It only troubled him that, in order to escape peril, he
was going to have to deceive Jossy...again.

The trip back to Edinburgh was thankfully uneventful,
and he was able to deliver Jossy safely to The White Hart
on the evening of the second day. But the kiss he gave her
at her chamber door was bittersweet, for in some ways,
'twas a kiss of farewell.

Josselin had only closed her chamber door a moment
ago, and already she missed Drew. The mere touch of his
lips upon her mouth eased her fears and awakened her
desire. And the press of his body against hers filled her
with such longing, everything else seemed irrelevant.

'Twould be an eternity till tomorrow, when she'd see
him again at Musselburgh. But he was right. They weren't
out of harm's way yet. She needed to get this missing missive delivered to Philipe before he began to suspect she
was a rogue agent.

She sat at the desk and pulled out the note, then
smoothed out the wrinkles with a trembling hand.

Halfway home, she'd realized that she couldn't turn the
missive over to Philipe with the secret writing exposed.
He would know that she'd seen the encoded passages and
could no longer be trusted to carry messages.

There was no way to make the letters invisible again,
so she had to recreate the missive. Thank Alasdair, she
knew how to read and write. But she'd never undertaken
such a thorny task before—trying to deceive a royal secretary with her artless scrawl.

Still, she'd managed to purchase a few quills, ink, and parchment. And she'd procured a lemon at dear cost from the market, squeezing the precious juice into a small vial. She arranged everything carefully on the desk, taking care not to get the parchment too close to the candle.

Swallowing hard and steadying her hand, she began with the original love letter, taking care to copy each loop, line, and flourish meticulously. With each word, she held her breath, making certain she left no blob of ink. So focused was she on creating an exact replica that she paid no heed to the content of the text at all. She already knew 'twas nothing but sentimental drivel.

The candle had burned a quarter of the way down when she finally finished "Duncan's" signature. Carefully replacing the pen, she slid back from the desk and stared at the note, praying 'twould dry before it had the chance to get smudged.

She cocked her head left, then right, stretching out her neck, which had tensed up while she worked.

She was still concerned about Philipe. He'd surely disapprove of her having been absent so long. Though Drew had reassured her that the French were notoriously romantic, that Philipe would accept her story of runaway passion, she wasn't so sure. Mary's secretary was, above all, a suspicious man. Not that that was a bad thing. After all, his suspicious nature was what kept the queen safe.

But as grim as it seemed, if Philipe suspected her cover had been compromised or that the missive had fallen into the wrong hands, he probably wouldn't hesitate to have Josselin hunted down.

She dared not think about that possibility. 'Twas too

horrifying to consider. She had to believe that Philipe would trust in her loyalty to Mary.

More than anything, Josselin didn't want to give the queen cause to doubt her. But though Josselin's intentions were noble, the fact that she was sitting alone in her room, meticulously forging a highly sensitive document that she wasn't even supposed to have seen, made her feel like the worst sort of outlaw.

While the ink dried on the new missive, she picked up the original, looking over the lines of secret writing, which weren't as neat as those done in ink. The lemon juice would be difficult to work with, and the lettering would have to be done quickly, for it went on as an almost clear liquid, and as soon as it dried, it became invisible.

Thus far, she'd studiously avoided looking at the message, for the same reason she always avoided looking at her contacts. The less she knew, the safer she was. Now, however, she couldn't help reading it as she carefully reviewed what she'd have to duplicate.

Even then, she made every effort to read it only as a series of words, letting the meaning slip through her mind like water through a sieve. 'Twasn't too difficult, since some of it was written with cryptic abbreviations. But she'd skimmed only halfway down the page when her eye caught abruptly on two words that stood apart from the rest as vividly as blood on a white rose.

The breath froze in her lungs as she stared at them, unable to tear her gaze away. Surely there was some mistake. There was absolutely no reason for...

She closed her eyes. She was just tired. That was all. She'd focused so long over a quill that now she was imagining things.

Exhaling, she forced her eyes open again. The words were still there, stark and undeniable. Her heart began to pound like the beating of a war tabor.

The missive trembled in her hand, as if 'twere alive, and she dropped it, backing away as it drifted to the floor. Still the words stared back at her.

Drew MacAdam.

'Twas unfathomable. Why should Drew's name appear on a secret document meant for the eyes of the Scots royals? As far as everyone else knew, Drew MacAdam was a Highland golfer. He had no ties to John Knox or the Reformation. Political intrigue was the furthest thing from his mind.

Wasn't it?

Dread dropped like a lump of lead to the pit of her stomach. Drew had deceived her before. Was he doing so again?

She had to find out.

She picked up the missive and began to read.

To Philipe de la Fontaine:
  Have observed W'ham's spy following golfer Drew MacAdam at M'burgh-links for past 2 days. Spy and MacAdam making contact? MacAdam at Sheep Heid. Expect next missive on Friday.
   —D.S.

She had to read it three times before she could understand it completely. D.S. was one of Philipe's contacts. W'ham must stand for Walsingham, Elizabeth's master spy, who would likely have men stationed around Edinburgh. One of them might have been watching Drew at Musselburgh. But why?

Friday was two days ago. If D.S. had been watching Drew, he must have been alarmed when Drew went missing. In fact, Drew's sudden absence would likely confirm D.S.'s suspicions about him being a contact for Walsingham.

But why would Walsingham be interested in a Highland golfer who...

The answer came to her all at once. Drew's Uncle Simon! Drew's uncle had let it slip that he was an English spy, so he must work for Walsingham. It had to be Simon then whom D.S. had seen spying on Drew at Musselburgh.

D.S. had no idea that Drew and Simon were related. He assumed there was some political context for their connection. And he was passing on this information to Philipe.

Of course, it didn't matter that 'twas a purely innocent relationship. Simon *was* an English spy, after all, even if he'd returned to England. And Drew was no Highlander. If Philipe learned Drew's true lineage, and worse, if he found out about Josselin's relationship with him, they could both be in serious danger. Bloody hell, they could be executed for treason.

She gulped and lowered the missive. What was she to do?

Drew packed his things as quickly as he could in the dark. He didn't think he'd been followed, but he couldn't be sure.

He slipped downstairs to settle up with the innkeeper of The Sheep Heid and to leave behind a few important bits of information for the man to remember later.

"So ye're off, are ye?" the innkeeper asked with a yawn, totaling up his charges.

"Aye. Time to go. I've milked the locals dry."

The innkeeper chuckled. "And made some o' them rich—those clever enough to wager in your favor. Sorry to see ye go. Ye know, ye've come to be a hero o' sorts."

Drew arched a cynical brow. "The secret to bein' a hero is leavin' ere ye can muck it up."

The innkeeper nodded. "Wise words." He reversed the account book so Drew could review the charges. "Still, I thought ye might stick around for that wee filly o' yours."

"Nae. A man's got to keep movin'," Drew said with a wink. "Otherwise, a woman is apt to put him in a cage."

"I know just what ye mean." The innkeeper lowered his voice as his wife peered out momentarily from the back room. "That's why ye're leavin' in the dead o' night, eh?"

"No need for hurly-burly," Drew agreed.

"So where are ye headed?"

"Tintclachan," Drew said, counting out coins for the innkeeper, "where I'm from."

"Long journey?"

"A good week."

The innkeeper collected the coins and put them into his coffer. "Will ye be back?"

"Maybe in a year or so."

"Ye do that," the innkeeper promised, "and I'll place a few wagers on ye myself."

Drew bid the man good-bye and set off into the night, keeping a wary eye over his shoulder. If everything went according to plan, all of Edinburgh—including, unfortunately, Jossy—would believe the Highlander had returned home. Only Drew would know differently.

*   *   *

Josselin tapped the feather quill against her lip. What name should she write?

'Twas a travesty, what she was about to do, worse even than simply copying the words of the missive. Changing what was written was tantamount to treason.

But she had to do it. She couldn't leave Drew's name on the note. With any luck, D.S. would never lay eyes on the letter. Hopefully he'd give up his investigation of the Highland golfer and move on to something more useful.

Meanwhile, she had to come up with a name to substitute for Drew's. She didn't want to endanger another innocent soul, but it had to be a recognizable name.

What golfers played at Musselburgh? She remembered Ronald Metz, Michael Cochrane, Campbell Muir, Ian Hay...

All at once, it occurred to her. There was someone who'd played at Musselburgh recently, a memorable character who would be completely above suspicion.

Smiling, she carefully dipped the quill in the lemon juice and scrawled the name across the page.

Chapter 43

As Josselin continued to stare in confusion at the innkeeper behind the counter of The Sheep Heid, her smile grew brittle. "What do ye mean, he's gone?"

He shrugged. "Sorry, lass. He left late last night."

Her heart began hammering in her breast, but she refused to panic. "But his things are still here?"

"Nae. He packed up, settled his account, and set off."

She tried to make sense of what the innkeeper was saying, which wasn't easy when she could scarcely breathe. "Did he say where he was goin'?"

The innkeeper made a strange grimace, as if he knew, but was reluctant to tell her. Which, if he'd known Josselin better, he would never have done.

She seized him by the front of his shirt and jerked him forward across the counter, drawing her dagger to press against his throat.

"Listen, ye hound-swiver! If ye know where he is, ye'd better tell me now, or ye'll be whistlin' out o' your bloody throat for the rest o' your miserable life."

"T-tinkle...Tank..." he stammered. "Tinklake..."

"Tintclachan?"

"Aye, that's it."

She released him, furrowing her brow in thought.

There was no such town. Drew had admitted as much to her. He'd invented it. So where had he really gone?

"Did he say when he'd return?"

The innkeeper swallowed hard, loath to say, but wary of her blade. "In a year."

"A year!"

"Or so."

Josselin blinked. What the devil was going on? Why would Drew leave so suddenly? Had D.S. caught up to him? Had he been forced to flee?

"Did he say anythin' else, anythin' at all?" she demanded. "Did he say why he was leavin'?"

The innkeeper backed away a step, out of her range. "He may have said he wanted to keep movin'."

"Keep movin'?"

"And somethin' about...women...wantin' to put him in a cage."

"Women? What women?"

The innkeeper gave her a fleeting glance and a guilty shrug.

"Me?"

She didn't believe that for an instant. Cage Drew? She'd never given him cause to think that. She'd made no demands of him. She'd never mentioned marriage. In fact, she'd given him her virginity freely, never asking for anything in return. There was no need to cage him—he was bound to her by love and respect and trust.

Only last night Drew had held her in his arms and murmured to her that—for better or worse, no matter their bloodlines, no matter what the future held—their destinies were intertwined. There was no doubt in her mind that he'd meant every word.

Which meant he'd lied to the innkeeper. But why?

He must have had good reason. And if he'd fled Edinburgh, he must have had good cause to do that as well. They were allies now—she and Drew. She might not know his exact intentions, but she must do all she could to uphold the story he'd concocted.

The innkeeper was watching her expectantly, as if he'd never before seen a woman scorned. She supposed she'd better not disappoint him.

With a roar of rage, she stabbed her dagger into the oak counter. "That son of a bitch!"

One by one, she picked up the half-dozen clay flagons lined up along the counter, punctuating her oaths by flinging them to the floor, where they burst with satisfying crashes.

"That cuckoldin' varlet! That miserable cur! That sheep-swivin' dastard! That bloody, good-for-nothin', philanderin' rogue!"

She wrenched her dagger from the counter and shoved it back into its sheath, then skewered the innkeeper with a fierce glare, spitting forcefully into the rushes. "A curse on your sex!"

Whipping around in an angry swirl of skirts, she stalked out of the inn, slamming the door behind her.

Drew huddled over his table in the shadowy corner of The White Hart, pushing the candle away and tugging the hood of his cloak further forward. He adjusted the telltale scarf that swathed the lower half of his face, marking him as a pox victim.

He must truly love Jossy. Why else would he plant himself in an inn thick with Scots spies? Or forego golfing indefinitely? Or take on the guise of a pox-riddled old man with a bent back and a pronounced hobble?

It hadn't been easy, secretly following Jossy for the last several hours. But unbeknownst to the lass, she was in mortal danger. Someone had to keep a close watch on her, and it couldn't be Drew MacAdam.

He hadn't wanted to frighten Jossy by revealing just how much peril she was in. But frankly, the fact that the Highland golfer had been marked as a suspicious character and that Josselin, a spy for the queen, had gone away with him for several days, did not bode well for her.

If she'd disappeared for good, Philipe would have assumed that either her secrecy had been compromised or that she'd double-crossed him. He would have had her hunted down and killed. Indeed, Drew suspected Jossy's suicide attempt might have been part of her spy's oath—a necessary precaution when dealing with the consequences of falling into the hands of the enemy.

There was no question—Jossy needed to return to Edinburgh to prove her loyalty. As for Drew MacAdam, he must appear to have fled to his distant Highland home, far from royal scrutiny. To all concerned, 'twould seem that the tie between Drew and Jossy had been severed. But someone would have to watch over the lass, and it couldn't be Drew.

That someone else was currently staying at The White Hart, in the chamber next to Jossy's. Jossy hardly seemed to notice the hunched old man with the masked face and the gnarled walking staff who'd followed her to Musselburgh this morn. But Drew was content with that. As she'd told him once, the less she knew, the safer she was.

Drew didn't know how long he'd need to protect her. Hopefully, once D.S. learned Drew MacAdam had gone to Tintclachan, he'd give up the hunt, report his fruitless search to Philipe, and Jossy's name would be cleared.

On the other hand, if D.S. had followed them into the woods that day and seen Jossy, a royal spy, abducted by Englishmen, 'twas surely a death sentence for her. After all, Philipe had no way of knowing what traitorous secrets she'd spilled under enemy coercion.

It should be clear in a matter of days where Jossy stood with Philipe. Until then, Drew dared not reveal himself to her. But he'd never be more than a dozen yards away, his sword hidden under his cloak, ready to defend her to the death.

He peered at Jossy over the top of his tankard of beer. 'Twas the worst sort of torture, being so close to her, yet unable to speak to her, to reassure her, to touch her. It crushed him to think she believed he'd forsaken her. He wanted to go to her, tear off his mask, and declare his unwavering love.

He watched as she pushed away her half-eaten pottage and tossed back her beer, then made her way up the stairs. He ached to sweep her off her feet and carry her there, to kiss away her sorrow and make sweet, tender love to her.

He sighed. The poor lass's heart must have broken into a million pieces when she learned he'd left her. Drew hoped when all this was over he could repair the damage he'd done. He prayed she'd forgive him and take him back. Love conquered all, the bards said. He hoped they were right.

Josselin stood in the dark at the top of the stairs, waiting. She knew she wouldn't have to wait long. The hunched man with the masked face and the hooded cloak had been dogging her all day, and once he noticed she'd retired upstairs, he'd no doubt follow at her heels. When he did, she'd be ready for him.

There was a telltale squeak on the stair. The instant he stepped into the shadows of the landing, she pushed him up against the wall, intending to silence any protest with a forceful kiss. Instead she got a mouthful of linen.

While she was spitting out the scarf, he took her by the shoulders and pinned her against the opposite wall.

"What are ye doin'?" he hissed behind the mask.

She smiled. "What do ye think I'm doin'?"

He released one of her shoulders to tear away the scarf. "How did ye know 'twas me?" he whispered.

"Oh, I didn't," she teased, reaching up to play with his ear. "I just have an affinity for poxy men."

He swore softly, then seized her roaming fingers, enclosing them in his hand, and repeated, "How did ye know?"

She chuckled. "Why, love, did ye think I hadn't memorized every inch o' ye? After all..." She leaned close to whisper in his ear. "I've crossed swords with ye." She took a deep breath of his intoxicating scent. "I've kissed ye." She turned her head until their lips nearly touched and murmured against his mouth, "I've made love to ye."

His shuddering breath grazed her cheek.

"I know ye...intimately," she told him, freeing her hand to draw back his hood and run her fingers through his hair. "From your wild mane..." She wrapped her leg around his and slid her heel sensuously down the back of his calf. "To your scuffed boots." She let her hand drift down his neck and beneath his shirt, stroking the thick muscles of his chest and arms. "From your broad shoulders..." Her other hand stole around his waist and lower to squeeze his buttocks. "To your firm arse."

She was rewarded with a groan of desire, but 'twas clear Drew had weightier matters on his mind.

"Oh, lass," he whispered brokenly, pushing her away and staggering backward. "We can't. We mustn't be seen together."

"Ye're right," she said, clasping his hand and tugging. "Come. We'll hide in my chamber."

He resisted her pull. "Now, lass, ye know that isn't what I...We can't..." He extricated his hand from hers. "Damn it, lass, I have to keep ye safe."

"Safe?"

"Aye."

"So ye're guardin' me?"

"Aye."

"Well, what better way to guard me than to sleep at the foot o' my bed?"

"I'm not goin' to—"

"Shh," she warned, placing her finger over his lips and frowning at some imagined noise. "Hurry."

She wasn't about to take nae for an answer. Taking his hand again, she pushed open the door and half-dragged him in.

In the end, 'twas Josselin who slept at the foot of the bed, but only because they made such a chaotic mess of the linens that 'twas impossible to tell which end was which.

Chapter 44

Josselin was still glowing when she arrived at the Musselburgh course the next morn, but she was careful to avoid looking at the cloaked hunchback hanging at the back of the knot of spectators. In faith, she thought Drew was being overly cautious. After all, he didn't know about the incriminating missive, which, thanks to her cunning, was no longer incriminating. As far as he knew, there was no evidence tying him to any espionage.

But by now all of Musselburgh was well aware that the Highland champion had gone home, so she had no choice but to go along with the ruse. She supposed 'twouldn't be so bad, as long as that pox-riddled old man visited her chamber once in a while. She smiled at the thought.

Her reverie was suddenly interrupted when a nobleman in black emerged from the throng at the beer wagon to hand her a triple-notched tankard. She dutifully turned to fill it, feeling under the bottom of the cup for the missive. 'Twasn't there.

She quickly scanned the ground at her feet, fearing she'd dropped it. There was nothing.

"Hurry up, wench!" someone barked.

"They're almost ready to tee off," another added.

She didn't know what to do. Perhaps the contact had dropped the note. Deciding swiftly, she turned back to him and placed his empty cup on the counter.

"I believe there's a crack in your tankard, sir," she told him slowly, hoping he'd comprehend her message. "Perhaps ye can find another and come back."

She started to turn toward the next patron, but the man in black snatched her wrist in his gloved hand. She gave a little gasp and glanced up into a pair of merry gray eyes.

Loudly enough for the bystanders to hear, he said, "Here's a coin for your honesty, lass," slipping a note into her hand. Still gripping her wrist, he leaned forward to whisper, "'Tis meant for *ye*."

Then he released her and turned to go, leaving his tankard on the counter and vanishing into the crowd.

She shoved the missive into her pocket. There would be time to look at it later, when there were fewer witnesses about. But it rattled her to have a contact speak to her directly. And it troubled her even more that she'd taken a good, long look at him, and she'd never forget his face.

The young nobleman was quite handsome. Beneath his black velvet cap with the black feather, dark, curly hair framed his swarthy face. He had a straight nose and an easy grin, but most memorable were his remarkable gray eyes, which gleamed like warm mercury, jolly with mirth and charm.

He seemed the most unlikely spy.

But then that was the point, wasn't it? The best spies were the ones who looked like beer-wagon wenches and merry noblemen.

Gradually, most of the crowd dispersed to meander

over the green, and Josselin finally had an opportunity to read the missive. 'Twas brief and to the point.

> *J—*
> *Send driver back tonight. Meet me at Sheep's Heid. Come alone.*
> *—P*

She ran her thumb over the *P*. 'Twas Philipe's mark. She folded the missive and tucked it away.

'Twas very mysterious. What could it mean? Why did Philipe wish to see her alone? Had there been a surge in Reformation activity? Had a Knox plot been uncovered? Were her services required in some new, exciting capacity?

She hoped so. To be honest, she was growing rather weary of serving beer to wagering fools.

Josselin's hackles had gone up the moment she arrived at The Sheep Heid and encountered, not Philipe, but the handsome nobleman in black from the golf course. Spying was a risky business, and surprises were most unwelcome, even when they came with laughing gray eyes.

Nonetheless, she greeted him politely, taking a seat at his table while he ordered an ale for her.

"Philipe sends his apologies," he confided. "Some royal business came up, and he was unable to get away."

There was no reason not to trust him. But somehow she didn't. "I see."

"He entrusted me to pass on his message."

"Aye?"

Her ale arrived, and she took one sip, then set it down. She sensed 'twould be best to keep her wits about her.

"First, he wanted to commend ye on your good work so far," he said, smiling broadly. "He says ye've done your country a great service."

She warily returned his smile. "'Tis no more than any loyal Scot would do."

"Loyal, aye," he said thoughtfully. "Philipe has in mind to reward ye for your loyalty."

"Indeed?"

"Aye." He gazed at her a little too long, then shook his head as if to stir himself from a dream. "Forgive me, lass. I never expected ye to be so bonnie."

His remark was unsettling, but she didn't wish to give him cause for suspicion. So she lowered her eyes in feigned shyness and ran her fingertip idly around the rim of her cup. Meanwhile, her mind was working furiously. What kind of spy would say such a thing? What kind of spy would be so easily distracted by a woman's beauty?

"And now I've made ye blush," he apologized. "Can ye forgive me?"

Did the fool think he was putting her at ease? He wasn't. In fact, she was growing impatient. She wished he would get on with Philipe's message.

"O' course," she said sweetly. Her patience might be limited, but she knew better than to annoy noblemen.

"Philipe said ye were one o' his most valuable assets," he continued, "that 'twould be a shame to lose ye."

She glanced up in alarm. "Lose me?"

"Aye," he said, crinkling his eyes with pleasure. "Ye see, Philipe has great plans for ye."

Despite her wariness, she couldn't help being intrigued. "Great plans?" Already she could imagine commanding an army of spies or serving as the queen's personal guard.

"Oh, aye," he assured her. "Ye know, I started out much as ye." He chuckled, then leaned forward. "I wasn't born a nobleman."

"Nae?"

"Nae. 'Twas an honor conferred upon me for loyal service."

She raised a brow. "And were ye a beer-wagon wench before?"

He laughed. "Ah, ye're a woman o' wit, Josselin."

She flinched internally. Why did he know her by name?

She took a sip of ale to ponder that. Philipe must have told him. But anonymity among spies was sacrosanct. It troubled her that he'd used her name so casually.

"A great wit," he repeated, "with a lively sense of humor."

He'd scarcely met her. He couldn't know anything about her sense of humor.

She decided to play into his game. She flashed him a bright smile. "So what are these great plans Philipe has in store for me?"

"Eager, are ye?" He gestured to her tankard. "Finish up your ale then. Ye'll need a ride back to The White Hart, won't ye? We'll talk about it in the privacy o' my coach."

Privacy of his coach? Josselin didn't like the sound of that. Now she knew she didn't want to drink another drop. "I'm far too excited to finish," she gushed. "Why don't ye just tell me now?"

He glanced around the room. "There are too many ears here."

He stood and took her by the hand, bringing her to her feet and escorting her toward the door as if they were lovers.

She was tempted to pull out of his grasp, to demand

that he stop being coy with her and deliver his message without delay, and to tell him she'd bloody well find her own way back to The White Hart. But she knew one had to be careful with royal contacts. She'd already made numerous mistakes with Philipe. She couldn't afford to offend his agent.

Drew scowled into his ale. Following Jossy to The Sheep Heid had been risky. 'Twould be a miracle if the innkeeper didn't recognize him, regardless of Drew's hunched back, his bad limp, and his pox mask. But he'd taken that risk to safeguard the lass.

The fact that she'd come, not to an assignation with Philipe as he'd expected, but to sup with the handsome nobleman from the golf course...

He smirked beneath his mask. In his heart, he knew Jossy couldn't possibly like the smug popinjay, but she was certainly making a good show of it. She smiled coyly at the fellow, running her finger around the rim of her tankard, and laughed at his remarks as if he were the most brilliant wit, while jealousy gnawed at Drew's gut.

It appeared he'd worried for nothing. This man was no assassin. He was clearly interested in courting Jossy, not killing her.

Having seen enough, Drew was about to push up from the table when he saw the nobleman take Jossy's hand. Her brow furrowed as the man glanced surreptitiously around the room, as if checking for witnesses. When the man stood, lifting her to her feet, Drew felt the hairs rise at the back of his neck.

Drew recognized the look in his gleaming gray eyes. The man wanted to get Jossy alone. He intended to lull her into trusting him so he could seduce her and avail himself of her charms.

Drew told himself that Jossy was a grown woman who could handle herself, that she knew damn well what she was doing, that she loved Drew and had no intention of letting the rogue have his way with her.

He told himself that, but it didn't keep him from following her when the nobleman escorted her out of the inn.

The hour was getting late. 'Twould be dark soon. But when Josselin and the nobleman stepped outside 'twas still light enough to see there was no coach parked there, only a cart and horse and two lone cobs.

At her hesitation, the man tucked her hand into the crook of his arm and led her along the perimeter of the inn.

"I left the coach around back," he explained.

But when they reached the rear of the building, there was no coach there either. And when his arm tightened around her hand, she knew there'd never been a coach.

He'd lied to her.

With her free hand, she drew her dagger and prepared to lay it against his throat. But to her shock, in the next instant she felt cold steel against her own neck.

"Drop it," he said.

She hesitated, and he pressed the sharp tip against her flesh. She winced as she felt a sting and a tiny trickle of blood. Reluctantly, she dropped her dagger.

"That's a lass," he said, as cheerily as before. "Now come along. 'Twould be a shame to bloody your gown."

For a fleeting moment, Josselin wondered where Drew

was. After clinging to her like iron to a magnet for the last two days, he'd picked a fine time to let her out of his sight.

Then the man wrenched her forward by the arm, and she had no choice but to be dragged along. All the way, she silently cursed her foolishness. She should never have believed him. He probably wasn't even Philipe's man. Whoever he was, he knew enough about her to trick her into following him.

As they ventured farther and farther into the shadowy wood, Josselin started to wonder about his intent. What the devil did he want? Was he going to kidnap her? Hold her for ransom? Ravish her?

And where the hell was Drew?

The man finally stopped at a small clearing in the middle of the woods and turned to her.

"I don't believe I ever properly introduced myself," he said with a polite dip of his head. "I'm Donald, Donald Syme."

The name didn't mean anything to her, except that 'twould be burned into her memory forever when she survived whatever he had in mind and reported back to Philipe.

At her lack of response, he clucked his tongue and shook his head. "I took ye for a master spy. But ye're not very observant, are ye?"

She didn't know what he was rambling about, didn't know and didn't care. She was busy thinking up ways to disarm him.

"And ye're a troublemaker, aren't ye?" he said. "A wee troublemaker who can't keep her nose out o' other people's affairs."

Hoping to catch him off guard, she jerked her neck

away from his blade and, with a sharp blow of her hand, knocked the weapon from him. Then she tried to sweep him off his feet with a kick to the back of his leg, a move she'd learned from Angus.

But somehow he anticipated her movement. He dodged her foot, and his hand shot out to seize her by the throat. He shoved her up against a tree, slamming her head against the trunk, pinning her there with the weight of his body.

Dazed, she scrabbled at his fingers.

"Well, ye might be a wily kitten," he murmured cheerfully, inches from her mouth. "But ye're fightin' a lion now."

She spat in his face.

He casually whipped a kerchief from his jerkin and wiped the spittle from his cheek, then banged her head hard against the trunk again.

Her head throbbed, and her vision swam, but she managed to muster a fierce frown. "Who are ye?" she growled. "What do ye want?"

He pouted in mock injury. "I told ye who I am. Have ye forgotten so soon?" He clucked his tongue. "As for what I want, does the name Ambrose Scott mean anythin' to ye?"

She gasped. Everything fell into place.

Ambrose Scott was Queen Mary's alias. 'Twas the name Josselin had cleverly forged onto the secret message, knowing 'twould do no harm, since Ambrose Scott would be completely above reproach. But if the man in black had read the missive, if he knew that Josselin had changed the name...

Donald Syme, he'd said his name was.

D.S.

Bloody hell. This was the spy who'd been tracking Drew. Now she prayed to God Drew wouldn't show up.

Chapter 45

Drew entered the clearing, throwing back his hood, tearing off his mask, and brandishing his sword before him. "Unhand her!"

He hadn't known what he intended when he followed the pair out of the inn. He wasn't certain until he stepped outside to discover that they'd utterly vanished. With one hand on the hilt of his hidden sword, Drew searched the premises. When he ventured behind the inn, he found Jossy's dagger lying in the grass.

He recognized at once she was in trouble. Jossy wouldn't unsheathe unless she felt threatened. And she certainly wouldn't leave her dagger behind.

Scowling, he'd straightened, tossed aside his walking staff, drawn his sword, and followed the trail of bent grass into the woods.

And now, glowering fiercely at the brute who had his filthy hands on Jossy, he knew exactly why he'd followed them out of The Sheep Heid.

The man, startled by Drew, glanced over his shoulder, and in that instant, Jossy jabbed him hard in the stomach with her knuckles.

The man doubled over, releasing her at once, and Drew focused his attention and the point of his sword upon him.

"Well, well," the man managed to wheeze, still bent in half, looking up at him. "Drew MacAdam. I thought ye'd left us—hied to your Highland home."

"Get away from her now, ye filthy bastard," Drew ground out, not even caring how the villain knew his name, "or I'll run ye through where ye stand."

To his surprise, 'twas Jossy who objected.

"Nae, Drew," she said. " 'Tisn't your fight."

The man in black was just as surprised. "Ye *are* a wee spitfire, aren't ye?" he rasped out. "Philipe said as much."

Philipe? Drew tightened his grip on his sword. He *was* Philipe's man. Which meant he had much more than seduction in mind.

"Stand aside, Jossy," Drew said.

"Nae," she stubbornly replied, holding out her hand. "Lend me your sword."

Drew cursed under his breath. Sometimes Jossy's willfulness was infuriating.

"Do ye know this man?" he asked her.

"I do now."

The man raised one hand in a weak wave. "Donald Syme."

D.S. Drew had feared as much. "And do ye know what he's after?"

"What I'm after?" the man said with a forced chuckle. "Ah, I see. Ye think I mean to swive the lass."

Drew seared Syme with a burning glare. "Nae, I think ye mean to kill her."

Syme half-laughed, half-coughed. "Kill her? Hardly. I'm here on royal business. I only need to collect a wee bit of information from her."

Drew knew he was lying through his teeth.

"This is my fight, Drew," Jossy said. "And I know the cost."

Drew frowned. 'Twas just like Jossy to throw his own words back at him.

"Ye mean to cross swords with me yourself, lass?" Syme asked, straightening with difficulty. "Well, my dear Josselin, aren't ye the devoted mistress? First ye change the name on the missive to protect your lover here, and now ye're offerin' to fight in his stead." He sarcastically pressed a gloved hand to his black heart. "'Tis touchin'."

Could it be true? Drew gazed at Jossy in wonder. "Ye changed the name on the missive?"

She shrugged as if forging a royal document were the most natural thing in the world. "I had to. It named Drew MacAdam as a traitor spy."

"I know."

"Ye know?"

He quirked up one corner of his mouth. "Why do ye think MacAdam had to hie home so suddenly?"

"But how could..." Her eyes widened as she realized the truth. "Ye read the missive."

"Aye."

"All this time ye've been able to read?"

He arched a sheepish brow. "I never actually said I couldn't."

Her gaze softened. "Ye stayed by my side, knowin' ye were in peril."

His heart swelled with love. "How could I leave ye?"

Syme wiped at his eye in mockery. "Please stop. Ye're bringin' tears to my eyes."

"Quiet!" they barked simultaneously.

"Or what?" Syme said on a chuckle, casually drawing his sword and pointing it toward Jossy. "Are ye goin' to throttle me with your bare hands, lass?"

"Jossy," Drew said, "let me squash this weevil." As much as he despised duels, there were some things in life worth fighting for, and Josselin was definitely one of them.

She shook her head. "Not on your life, golfer. Toss me your sword."

Syme's eyes gleamed in amusement as he made lazy circles in the air with his blade. "Oh, aye, who'll fight me then? Will it be the lovesick English golfer or the wee scrap of a lass from Selkirk?"

Drew narrowed his eyes. He knew this was Jossy's moment to prove herself, and she was right—this wasn't his fight. She needed him to believe in her, to give her the respect she was due. But damn it, Drew loved her. He couldn't stand idly by and watch her be killed. This wasn't just any opponent with a blade. This man was an assassin.

'Twould be a duel to the death—hers or Syme's. But there was one thing about killing a man that Jossy didn't know, something Drew had discovered long ago, something that had probably cost Jossy's mother her life. Drew had to be vigilant. He couldn't let Jossy make the same mistake her mother had.

"Ye know 'tisn't a fair fight," Drew muttered to Syme.

"I think the lass would beg to differ," Syme said.

Jossy straightened and lifted a haughty brow, confirming his opinion. Damn Syme—he was right. Jossy was a

proud Scots lass—too proud. She'd never back down from
a fight, never admit she'd met her match. And knowing
Jossy, the moment Drew tried to convince her otherwise,
she'd dig in her heels even deeper.

"Fine," Drew said on an exasperated sigh. He reversed
his sword and tossed the weapon to Jossy, who caught it in
one hand, giving the blade a flashy whirl.

He couldn't miss the eager gleam in her eyes, and
already he regretted arming her. On the other hand, Jossy
was skilled, probably more skilled than Syme would
expect. Drew had fought her. The lass *could* hold her
own . . . to a point. Maybe Syme would be caught off guard
and Jossy could seize the advantage.

Still, 'twas not a fair fight. Not only did Syme have the
clear benefit of size, reach, and power, but he had a history of killing.

Like Drew, Jossy might have been trained in chival-
rous combat, but nothing could prepare her for the atroc-
ity of real battle. As in love, in war there were no rules.
War was ugly and desperate and inhumane. There was
nothing noble or decent about it.

Drew had learned that painful lesson when he'd slain
his first opponent. War was literally a double-edged
sword. It might cut down one's enemy, but it also carved
large pieces out of one's soul.

He couldn't let Jossy pay the price of that lesson. He'd
fold his arms and let her fight, and he'd not distract her.
But the instant he perceived the battle was nearly finished,
he intended to be ready with Jossy's dagger, which rested
just beneath his itching fingertips.

Chapter 46

Josselin's blade whistled through the air. She loved Drew's sword. 'Twas beautiful, and it had perfect balance and weight. After she settled this dispute with Syme, she'd ask Drew where his father had gotten it.

Her confidence was high, and her spirits soared, fueled by Drew's love and trust and respect. And now she was eager to show him just how deserving she was of that respect.

She kicked her skirts out of the way and faced Syme with narrowed eyes. No matter how much she wanted to impress Drew, she didn't dare let him distract her. This battle would take all her concentration.

She whipped her blade twice through the air, testing its performance, while Syme waited with a smug smile on his face, a smile she intended to wipe off in another moment.

She wasn't going to kill him. After all, they both worked in the service of Queen Mary. He was only doing what he thought was in the queen's best interests. She just meant to teach him a lesson, proving to him that she was no timid mouse, that she knew what she was doing, and that she was not to be trifled with. All she had to do was

drag him from his lofty pedestal long enough to talk some
sense into him. Once Syme realized that she was Mary's
loyal servant, that Drew was not a dangerous enemy, that
she'd not been compromised, she was sure they would all
shake hands and walk away in peace.

So, with a lightness she hadn't felt in days, Jossy flexed
her knees and prepared to engage the spy.

He thrust swiftly forward, and she deflected the blade.

He grinned and nodded his appreciation, then slashed
downward in a savage arc that would have chopped off
her head if she hadn't dodged aside.

'Twas immediately obvious that, despite the light-
hearted twinkle in his eyes, he was taking this duel
seriously.

So could she.

She replied with a low slash that grazed his shin just
enough to scar one of his black leather boots, which
dimmed his smile considerably.

He attempted another killing blow, but he was too slow,
and she sneaked in a matching slice for his other boot.

Now the grin disappeared from his face, and she could
see by the flare of his nostrils that he was displeased.

He jabbed forward, and she let him come, pulling his
sword arm further forward with her free hand, using his
own momentum against him. He stumbled forward past
her, and she swatted him on the arse with the flat of her
blade.

His face flushed red with fury, and his gray eyes looked
like smoke from a fire raging inside. He lifted his sword
high, looming over her, and charged.

She ducked under his arm and came up behind him,
this time thwacking him on the back of his head.

He roared and turned on her with murder in his eyes. Josselin wasn't afraid. She'd dealt with men of temper before, and Angus had shown her how to use an opponent's anger against him.

If he barreled forward, she need only deflect that motion from herself to send him careening into the bushes.

Predictably, he did barrel forward, and she sidled away, intending to shove him past. But her foot slipped on a patch of mud, and she didn't move out of the way fast enough. The edge of his blade caught her shoulder, slicing through cloth and flesh.

She didn't feel the cut at first. But from the corner of her eye, she saw Drew's arms come out of their fold before he could stop himself, and she knew 'twas bad. Quickly, before the pain could register, she regained her wits and her balance and came at Syme with a series of aggressive slashes.

She managed to back him against a tree before the pain surged in her shoulder. It stung like the devil, and she sucked a sharp breath through her teeth. Blood was surely dripping down her arm, but she didn't want to look at it.

She winced, and Syme used that instant of vulnerability to attack, slicing low as if to cut her legs out from under her.

Josselin leaped up and dove over his blade, rolling forward to come up beside him. But before she could strike, he jabbed her viciously with his elbow, which she caught in the ribs. She grunted and stumbled backward, and he brought his blade straight up, earning her a nick at the point of her chin.

She scrambled back and braced herself for another

attack. He came at her with blow after blow, which she easily anticipated and was able to counter. But though his strikes were predictable, they had a heavy, ruthless quality that was quickly taking a toll on her stamina.

She was lighter, quicker, more agile. But he was determined, tireless, and brutal. More than once she suffered bruises from his pummeling elbows, and he didn't hesitate to deliver rough kicks to her legs at every opportunity. She could only skip out of his way so often before her strength began to flag.

Though she'd enjoyed the challenge of battling him, 'twas clear to her that she needed to look for a way to finish the fight before his violent blows broke one of her arms or legs or ribs.

Breathless and sweating, Josselin retreated to the edge of the clearing to allow herself a moment of respite. She flipped the hilt over in her grasp and pushed her damp hair away from her face with her forearm. Then she prepared to engage him again.

This time she drew him in, enticing him to continue his measured strikes by exaggerating their impact upon her, while carefully evading his blade. She gasped and winced as his slices came closer and closer, lulling him into overconfidence. Then, when he swung with lethal force toward her torso, she suddenly dove for the ground, rolling sideways at his feet.

Like a cluster of skittles upended by a barreling ball, he tripped over her and fell heavily, losing his weapon and lolling onto his back. When she came up again on her feet, she was able to whip her blade around, placing it at his throat.

With a cocky grin, she stared down at him, squirming

there at the point of her sword. Now she had him. Now she could make him understand.

"Kill me then," he ground out, his eyes no longer dancing, but full of cold hatred. "Kill me. But know this. I'm not the only one after ye. Ye're not long for this world, lass."

She frowned. "Quit with your threats. I don't mean to kill ye. We're kin, ye and me. We both serve Scotland and the queen. But I want ye to understand how 'tis with me, with us," she said, gesturing toward Drew, "and if I have to do it with a blade at your throat, so be it." She took a deep breath. "Ye're right. Drew MacAdam is no Highlander. He's an Englishman. But he's no spy. He has no interest in royal intrigue. He only came to Scotland for the golf."

Syme may have been listening, but 'twas hard to tell. His eyes smoldered like live coals, ready to ignite at any moment.

"My identity hasn't been compromised," she assured him, "and I've revealed no secrets. 'Tis true I forged the name on your missive, but 'twas only to protect an innocent. I changed nothin' else, and if ye've seen the letter, ye know that. I'd never do anythin' to endanger Mary."

She let up slightly on the pressure against his throat. Syme was a reasonable man. Surely he'd realize it had all been a misunderstanding. There was no need to risk pricking a fellow servant of the queen.

"Here's what I propose," she told him. "Ye'll tell Philipe ye were mistaken about my disappearance. As far as identifying Ambrose Scott as a possible agent," she said with a smirk, "I'm sure the queen will be pleased to know her disguise was able to fool—"

Without warning, Syme slapped her blade away. Before she could gasp in surprise, he rose up, grabbed her by the front of her bodice, and tossed her aside like a sack of laundry.

"Jossy!" Drew cried.

The breath was knocked from her, yet she managed to gasp out, "Stay back, Drew!"

She scrambled back to her feet at the same time as Syme.

"He's mine," she told Drew, pinning Syme with her gaze.

She might be swordless, but her da's had taught her to fight with her fists and feet as well. She still had plenty of weapons in her arsenal to battle the brute. The last thing she needed was Drew coming between them.

Still, she silently cursed herself for her misjudgment. She'd let down her guard for an instant, and Syme had seized the upper hand. Apparently, he wasn't ready to listen to reason.

Syme circled her like a predator, his gray eyes now as flat and dull as clay.

He lunged forward, and she skipped back out of his reach. He lunged again, and she spun, coming around with a high kick that caught him in the side of the head.

He staggered but didn't fall, then charged forward with fists clenched.

She ducked two punches, but a third caught her in the ribs, and she bent forward, wheezing in pain.

"Jossy!" Drew yelled.

"Nae!" she protested.

Syme towered above her, his laughing face now a mask of grim satisfaction. While she cradled her bruised ribs with her arm, he laced his fingers together and cracked his knuckles.

Will had taught her to use a strong man's strength against him. When Syme swung for her chin, she pushed his forearm aside, knocking him off balance. There was no time to reply, but she at least gained freedom as he stumbled past.

He turned on her again, growling like a raging bear. She flexed her knees and put up her fists, ready for him.

This time when he approached, she gave him a kick to his midsection followed by a punch to his chin.

Temporarily slowed, he wasn't stopped. With both hands, he seized her by the throat and began to squeeze.

"Jossy!"

Josselin brought her fists up between his arms, splitting them apart, simultaneously kicking him hard in the ballocks.

Fury kept him from responding to the pain, and he continued to advance.

She drove the sole of her foot into his knee, and he twisted but didn't fall.

She stamped her heel upon his other foot, and he grunted but didn't stop.

He managed to bend his arm around her waist, trapping her against him, and clamped her tightly, crushing her battered ribs.

She drove her elbow up hard into his throat. With an agonized cough, he released her, then staggered off, nursing his collapsed windpipe.

Exhausted, Josselin hunched forward, bracing her hands on her knees, preparing for the next onslaught.

She didn't notice that Syme had recovered his dagger,

and she didn't see the flash of silver until 'twas almost too late.

"Look out!" Drew barked as Syme lunged forward with his blade.

She dove sideways, rolling atop and reclaiming her own discarded blade, then coming to her feet, sword in hand.

Syme's underhanded attack was like a sudden awakening slap. Josselin realized he didn't want to listen to her, to negotiate, to hear the truth. He wasn't just a spy. He was an assassin. He meant to kill her. What had before seemed a contest of skill was now a fight to the death. And 'twould not end until one of them lay bleeding on the ground.

She clenched her jaw and prepared to engage him in earnest.

In effect they were now evenly matched. Josselin's longer blade equalized Syme's superior reach. What Josselin lacked in strength, she made up for in dexterity. And while his attacks were more powerful and lethal, he fought like an assassin, accustomed to slaughtering helpless victims, not opponents who could defend themselves.

Thus, the battle continued at length as Syme hacked away at her and she dodged and nicked him, neither of them able to do much damage.

Eventually, Syme made a fatal mistake. While Josselin kept him busy, blocking her slashes, he forgot about her agile feet. She pumped her left leg forward and kicked hard at his wrist. The dagger sailed from his grasp.

This was her moment. He was at her mercy. She had to kill him now.

She drew back her sword, preparing to plunge the blade into his heart.

Suddenly, the world seemed to slow impossibly around her, and everything came into sharp focus. She saw her own hand, grimy with soil and sweat, gripping the swept hilt of Drew's sword. Her gaze followed the long, bright blade as it shivered in the dying light of day. She saw Syme's black doublet with its ebony buttons, smudged with mud, and the seams that perfectly tailored it to his frame.

Her eyes drifted upward as if weighted by lead. His pulse beat sluggishly in his neck, and she could see every bit of black stubble on his chin. His lips were parted, and they trembled as he sucked in a long breath. His nostrils flared, and she watched a drop of sweat roll slowly down his brow.

She looked him in the eyes, and there she saw the spark of human life, the spark she intended to extinguish.

'Twas then the impact of what she was about to do dealt her a crushing blow. Her heart sank to the pit of her stomach. The breath caught in her throat. And her arm began to tremble. While the world moved on in its strange lethargy, Josselin stood paralyzed.

She heard Drew call her name, but the sound was muffled, as if he were underwater. Slowly, she turned her head toward him. Drew was scowling, lumbering toward her as if he were moving through honey.

Josselin didn't know exactly what happened next as she was yanked abruptly back into real time, but all hell broke loose.

It had nearly killed Drew to watch Jossy battle the assassin and not to intervene, and he had the white knuckles to prove it. But now his moment had come.

While Jossy faltered with her sword, unable to make the killing thrust, Drew saw Syme's left hand steal down his thigh to extract a slim rondel secreted in the top of his boot.

Drew warned Jossy, but she seemed dazed as she turned curious eyes toward him.

As he'd planned, Drew whipped out her dagger and flipped it in his hand, gripping the blade between his fingers. He hurled the dagger forward, aiming for the assassin's chest.

And missed.

Drew cursed as the blade sank into the flesh of the man's dagger arm, slowing but not slaying him. Now what?

Syme's discarded sword lay on the ground between Drew and the combatants. If he could claim it in time...

He hurtled forward. With not an instant to spare, he slipped the toe of his boot under the hilt of the dropped sword and flipped it up into his hand.

As the desperate assassin drew back his injured arm, preparing to thrust the deadly blade between Jossy's ribs, Drew charged forward, pushing Jossy aside, and plunged the sword into the man's black heart.

Chapter 47

For once, as he watched the assassin sink lifelessly to the ground—the man's gray eyes dimming in his sallow face and blood trickling from his death-pale lips—Drew didn't feel a shred of the nauseating guilt that had accompanied killing before.

Instead, a powerful surge of relief and justice filled him. Jossy was alive, whole, and unharmed.

He turned to her. Her sword fell from her fingers, clattering on the ground, and she looked bone-pale, as if she were about to faint. He lunged forward to catch her, sweeping her up in his arms.

"Oh, Jossy," he said with a fierce hug, "ye're safe, lass. Ye're safe."

He touched her all over, as if assuring himself she was real, and pressed his lips again and again to the top of her precious head.

After a moment, Jossy moaned softly, then squirmed against him and scrambled out of his embrace. Her face white with panic, she stumbled to the edge of the clearing and retched into the bushes.

Drew knew exactly how she felt. This was her first taste

of real war, and 'twas far more bitter than she'd expected. Some could stomach the violence. Others, like Drew, could not. For now, Jossy needed to recover. Later, she'd decide whether she had the fortitude to live by the sword.

The battle was finished, but Drew feared their troubles were far from over. There were things that needed to be done now, and quickly—loose ends to tie up, decisions to make, lies to tell. And Jossy was in no condition to take care of them alone.

So while she hunkered over the bushes, shivering, Drew dislodged the sword and tossed his cloak over the body, shielding Jossy from the gruesome sight. That done, he came up behind her, gently placing his hands on her quivering shoulders.

"I couldn't do it," she lamented. "I couldn't kill him. I froze."

"I know."

"Why?" she asked, turning to him in anger and distress. "Was all my trainin' for nothin'? Am I just a coward, unfit for battle? A disgrace to my mother? Bloody hell, why couldn't I finish him?"

He cradled her bleak face in his hands and demanded her gaze. "For the same reason your mother died on the battlefield. The same reason I won't go to war."

"Why?"

"Because, my sweet Jossy," he told her, "ye have a heart."

She frowned in disgust.

"'Tisn't a bad thing," he assured her, licking his thumb and wiping away the smudge of blood on her injured chin. "Ye're a great fighter. Ye held your own against him. And I've never seen such agility—in man or maid. But there's much to war that ye don't understand, much more than any amount of sparrin' can prepare ye for."

As he spoke, he checked her briefly for injuries.

"War isn't bonnie or noble or fair," he said, examining her arms one at a time. The flesh was reddened and scraped, but there was no swelling. "When a man is fightin' for his life, there's no chivalry. And there are no rules." He turned her head to one side, then the other, looking for breaks along her jaw and lumps upon her brow. There were none. "'Tis ugly. Messy. Brutal." He probed gently along her ribs. Luckily, they seemed intact. "And if ye have an ounce of empathy, a morsel of humanity—if ye glimpse the enemy just once, not as a foe, but as a fellow man..." He shook his head. "Ye can't bring yourself to senseless slaughter."

Josselin furrowed her brow. Was Drew right? Was she too softhearted to be a warrior?

When it had come to the final blow, the taking of a man's life, she hadn't been able to look into his eyes, into his soul, without remorse. Even watching another slay him had sickened her.

"What about ye?" she challenged. "Ye claimed ye hated bloodshed. Yet ye had the stomach to kill him."

Drew's eyes grew as cold and solemn as the grave. "I do hate bloodshed. But I'd kill anyone who threatened the woman I love."

The intensity of his threat gave her chills, even as his words warmed her like mulled wine.

"I owe ye my life," she realized. Were it not for Drew MacAdam and his dogged guardianship of her, she'd be dead now at the hands of an assassin.

"And I owe ye mine," he said. He shook his head in amazement. "Ambrose Scott? I can't believe ye risked forgin' a royal missive for me, and with that name."

She raised her chin to give his words back to him. "I'd risk anythin' for the man I love."

His smile was gentle and grateful, and it heated her to the core. When he slipped his hand along her cheek and leaned forward to press his lips softly against her brow, his kiss was like a salve for her wounds. Reveling in his tender caress, she no longer felt the cuts and bruises of battle. Bathed in his loving light, she forgot her aching legs and twinging shoulder, her scraped arms and battered ribs, and surrendered to the balm of his affection. His touch soothed the violence from her blood, replacing it with a mellow elixir of love and peace and harmony.

For a moment, she almost forgot her troubles...the royal note she'd forged...the Englishmen with whom she'd fraternized...the assassin, who lay in a pool of blood a few yards away.

Then, as if a great milldam burst, all the implications of their actions flooded her brain at once. Drew and she were in grave danger. And there was little time to lose.

She broke from Drew's embrace, pushing him gently away.

"God save us," she muttered, "we've murdered the queen's man. What do we do now?"

Drew bit the inside of his cheek. Jossy might have shrugged off Syme's dire warning as an empty threat, but Drew knew better. They were no safer than before, and now they couldn't afford to make any mistakes.

They both spoke at once.

"We have to hide the body," he said.

"We have to inform Philipe," she said.

"Nae!"

"But we *have* to," she said with a scowl.

"Philipe...can't be trusted."

She planted her hands on her hips. "He's the bloody secretary o' the queen. If he can't be trusted, who can?"

He placed his hands on her shoulders and fixed her with a sober gaze. "Listen, I know ye don't want to hear this, but it has to be said. Syme was sent by Philipe."

"What!" With a sneer of disbelief, she tossed off his hands. "That's impossible. Philipe had no cause to suspect me of anythin'. I handed the missive to him myself. If he didn't believe my story, if he didn't trust me, why would he return me to Musselburgh to spy for him?" She shook her head. "Nae, if anythin', that missive cast doubt upon Syme. Syme was the only one who knew 'twas a forgery. Which is why he came after me."

"Do ye think Syme wouldn't tell Philipe 'twas a forgery?"

"And admit that he'd let the missive fall into enemy hands? I don't think so. Syme came after me because I made a fool o' him for namin' the queen as an English spy."

Drew might have believed that, if not for Syme's threat. But how could he prove his suspicions to Jossy?

"Think, Jossy. What made ye come to The Sheep Heid?" he prompted. "Why did ye agree to meet with Syme?"

"I wasn't supposed to meet with him. Accordin' to the note, I was supposed to meet with Ph—" She stopped short, realizing what he was insinuating.

"Philipe?" he prodded.

She scowled, reluctant to acknowledge the truth.

Drew continued. "Was Philipe's mark on the note?"

"Aye," she admitted, bristling. "But that could have been a forgery."

He answered quietly. "Ye don't really believe that."

She was silent. He could see she was digesting the painful possibility that Philipe had betrayed her.

He took her hand in his, and though she resisted, he refused to let her pull away.

"What did ye sign, Jossy? That first day when ye met Philipe in The White Hart. What did ye sign?"

She compressed her lips.

"Was it an oath?" he asked. "Did he make ye swear to kill yourself if ye fell into the hands o' the enemy?"

She gave him a quick startled glance, then averted her gaze.

"That's why ye tried to take your life in the forest, isn't it?" he asked.

Her stone silence was answer enough.

"Philipe," he told her, "Philipe means to finish the deed. He means to murder ye."

"Nae!" she snapped, trying to pull away.

He held on firmly. "I know it hurts ye to hear it, Jossy, but in the royal game o' chess, ye and me, we're only pawns. When it comes to the safety o' the queen, if there's any doubt whatsoever about your trustworthiness, Philipe would sacrifice ye without battin' an eye. 'Tis his duty, and he's very good at it."

Jossy broke loose of his hold and rounded on him in fury. Despite his efforts, despite the overwhelming evidence, the loyal lass simply couldn't accept that the country she'd vowed to defend with her last breath and the queen to whom she'd pledged her life now wished her dead.

" 'Tisn't true!" she cried. "I won't believe it."

She began pacing in agitation, as if she could outrun the inevitable truth.

"Jossy, listen to me!" he barked in frustration. "We don't have much time."

"But I'm a faithful servant o' the queen," she countered. "Philipe knows that. Mary knows it."

"Damn it, Jossy! Did ye not hear what Syme said? He's not the only one after ye," he bit out. "He told ye so himself."

She stopped pacing abruptly. Her brow creased as she searched her memory for Syme's exact words. "Nae," she breathed.

"Remember? He said ye weren't long for this world," Drew insisted, "and aye, he told ye he wasn't the only one after ye. Who else is a threat to ye, Jossy? How many others want ye dead? How long before Philipe sends another man? Before another assassin comes to finish what Syme started?"

Chapter 48

Josselin's heart, which had sunk to the bottom of her stomach with the dull ache of betrayal, now bolted into her chest, clearing her head and awakening her instinct for survival.

There was no time to dwell on misplaced loyalties or broken vows or crushed dreams. Drew was right. Philipe meant to kill her.

She couldn't blame him. He was only doing his duty. He had to eliminate any threats to the queen, and if that meant having his own spies assassinated, he was honor-bound to do so.

But that didn't mean Josselin had to sit politely and wait to be killed. Her life was at stake. Assassins were on her trail. She had to flee...now.

She eyed Drew, wondering if she had the strength to do what was right. She had to let him go. She knew that. She couldn't let Drew, dragged into the danger through no fault of his own, come to harm for her sake.

"Go!" she commanded. "Go back to England."

"Not a chance."

"This isn't your battle."

"Damned if 'tisn't," he said, arching a brow.

"I don't want ye here," she lied.

"I don't much care."

Shite, the man was infuriating. "I can't..." The words stuck in her throat. "I won't watch ye be killed for my sake."

His gaze softened. "And I won't watch *ye* be killed, darlin'. Which is why we're goin' to fight together."

She gave him a disapproving scowl, but she couldn't stop the secret relief that filled her at his promise. The odds might be stacked against her. She might be walking into a hopeless, suicidal mission. But unlike her mother, she wasn't going to the battlefield alone.

They lingered long enough to drag the assassin's body into the bushes. Syme might have been a God-fearing man, worthy of a proper burial, but according to Drew, the backstabbing bastard deserved to be eaten by wolves. By the time they kicked leaves over the bloody sod, the moon was rising.

They dared not return to The Sheep Heid or The White Hart. There was no telling who was friend or foe. So they crept through the moonlit streets of Musselburgh, crossed the links, and walked down to the shimmering firth, stealing along the shore until they came to a low cave carved out of the sandstone wall. 'Twould be a safe enough haven for the night to attend to Josselin's injuries and hatch their plans.

They huddled together on the sandy floor of the cave, gazing out at the hissing sea.

"What if everyone were led to believe that Syme completed his mission?" Drew suggested. "What if he *did* kill ye?"

He lifted her bare arm to tie the makeshift linen bandage around her wounded shoulder.

"I can't die," Josselin insisted, watching Drew dress her wound. "'Twould kill my da's and Kate. Besides, where would I go? To your fabled village of Tintclachan?"

"Ye could flee with me to England," Drew said, though she could tell from his bleak voice that he didn't want to leave her beloved Scotland any more than she did.

"In the company of a man deprived o' his precious golf for the rest o' his life?" She chuckled ruefully. "Nae, thank ye."

Drew finished tying off the bandage, and Josselin sat forward, hugging her knees to her chest in thought. There had to be a way for them to remain in the Lowlands, under the noses of the royals, without being discovered.

"What if we disguise ourselves?" she pondered. "I can dress like a young man, and ye can dress like an old wo—"

Drew silenced her with a scathing glare, then wrapped his fingers around her ankles and dragged her legs down straight so he could continue his inspection.

She sighed and leaned back on her elbows, letting him pull up her chemise and wincing as he pressed at the tender places between her ribs. She supposed 'twas too much to expect Drew to live the rest of his years as a woman. But dressing like the opposite sex had *seemed* like a good masquerade. Even the queen thought so.

The queen...

Josselin gazed dreamily out at the softly rippling, silvery waves of the North Sea, remembering Mary with her charming smile and laughing eyes and conspiratorial wink.

Drew was right about Philipe. He wasn't a bad man. He was only possessed of the same fierce loyalty to the queen that she had. He couldn't be blamed for protecting Mary so ferociously. The young queen's vivacious spirit enchanted everyone. 'Twas probably a nightmare for Philipe to keep Mary safe when she insisted on tugging at the royal leash and mingling with the unwashed rabble.

As she thought about her beloved Mary, Josselin began to realize that the headstrong queen herself just might be the single strand that could unravel this whole tangled mess. Slowly, thread by thread, a simple, clever, perfect scheme wove itself into her thoughts.

Drew broke into her musings. "Your ribs don't seem to be cracked, just bruised. Do ye hurt anywhere else?"

His fingers rested lightly on her belly, warm and gentle, and Josselin, suddenly happier than she'd been in days, smiled slyly up at him. She had the answer now. 'Twas as clear as a summer sky.

"That's a wicked grin ye're wearin', lass," he said, grazing the sensitive flesh of her stomach with the back of his knuckles. "What's on your mind?"

"Tell me, Drew," she said, "what's the best way to hide a weak defense?"

He smirked at her unexpected question. "*Now* ye want my advice on swordfightin'?"

"Tell me."

He let his fingers drift up between her breasts, sending a pleased shiver through her. "A strong offense." Behind his grin, his eyes began to smolder with desire.

"And what's the best way," she said, squirming deliciously beneath his tantalizing touch, "to meet a foe?"

He boldly slipped his hand beneath her chemise to cup

her breast. She gasped as his thumb brushed over her nipple. He leaned forward to whisper, "Face to face."

Despite her injuries, despite their desperate situation, despite the fact they were huddled in a cave like fugitives, Josselin wanted him. Now.

"We won't hide," she said breathlessly, gazing at him through half-closed lids. "And we won't flee. I have an idea."

She sighed in surrender, closing her eyes and letting her head fall back.

"Is this your idea, lass?" Drew said with a chuckle, lunging forward to feast on her exposed neck like a lion feasting on prey.

All reason deserted her then as a strong mélange of lust and affection rose up in her, as powerful as the tide that raked the nearby shore. She sank back onto the smooth sand and captured him by the back of his neck, guiding him to her hungry mouth.

He tasted like the sea—cleansing and commanding and relentless. But each kiss was more to her now than water for her thirst, more than balm for her wounds, more than satisfaction for her desire. Each kiss was a promise of their future together, an affirmation of their love.

She fought with his doublet, trying to wrench it from his shoulders, and he separated from her just long enough to peel it off, along with his shirt, and cast them aside.

Returning, he opened her bodice wide and dragged down her chemise, exposing her breasts, then lowered himself to warm her body with his own.

She drew in a sharp breath as his flesh melded with hers, sending hot current through her veins. She arched up, aching to be even closer to him.

Emboldened by lust, she slipped her hands inside the back of his trews to clasp his sculpted arse and was rewarded with his groan of pleasure.

As if they were well-matched combatants, he answered her with a brazen attack of his own. He nuzzled her breast, finding her nipple with his tongue, then drawing it between his lips to take strong suckle.

Every nerve in Josselin's body suddenly came alive with current. 'Twas as if he sucked all modesty and patience and reason from her, replacing them with pure need.

Seeking sweet revenge, she seized the top of his trews and wrenched them down over his hips, freeing his swollen staff.

She massaged his buttocks, and he moaned against her breast, but even as she lifted her head to flash him a triumphant smile, his hand moved stealthily beneath her skirts. With unerring aim, he nudged aside her thighs and trapped the aching place between them in his palm.

She dropped her head back onto the soft pillow of sand, thrusting her hips up to meet his hand.

He obliged her desires, deftly parting her nether lips to delve between, and she gasped in sweet distress as he teased the flesh there.

But she wasn't ready to give up the fight. Biting her lip against a wave of yearning, she snaked her hand between them to surround his pulsing cock and gently squeezed.

He arched back, sucking breath between his teeth as she drew her fingers firmly along his silken length.

She knew her victory was short-lived. 'Twould always be thus. But this was one war she didn't mind losing.

Drew flashed her a savage grin. Then, with a growl of

claiming, he tossed up her skirts, spread her legs, and took what she'd intended to give him all along.

Their lovemaking was as feral and unpredictable as the North Sea, and Josselin clung to Drew like a storm-tossed ship, trusting in him to steer them both through the squall.

The current of their passion grew stronger and stronger, the surf more intense, until she feared to drown beneath the heaving waves.

As the waters threatened to close over her head, 'twas suddenly as if lightning flashed across the sky, electrifying the wide sea and sending a sizzling bolt through her body. She cried out in shock and amazement and heard her wonder answered in Drew's groan of victory. Their release was wild and powerful, like the sea pounding the sand. She spasmed in pain and pleasure all at once, fused to Drew by the heat of their passion and the strength of their love.

When 'twas over, they lay like castaways stranded on the shore, breathless and exhausted. Their clothing was damp, their hair was strewn with sand, and they smelled of sea and salt and sex.

But Josselin had never felt more content as she drifted off to the reassuring sounds of their slowing heartbeats and Drew's even breath and the soft hiss of ocean foam caressing the shore.

Her destiny was clear now.

The future was bright.

And their stars were no longer crossed.

Chapter 49

If anyone had told Drew he'd be golfing with the Queen of Scotland for a second time at Musselburgh, he would have said they needed to curb their ale intake.

Yet here he stood on this bright September morn, teeing off against Mary, accompanied by the queen's four faithful companions, two cadets, and a small crowd that had gathered for the impromptu match.

Drew had to give Jossy credit. She'd come up with a brilliant plan . . . as long as it worked. If it didn't, the two of them would likely be drawn and quartered for treason by the end of the day.

Face to face, Jossy had insisted. Nothing could be more direct than an Englishman and a rogue spy confronting the Queen of Scotland in the full light of day.

Jossy had sent a missive by way of Davey the beer-wagon driver to be delivered directly to Mary at Holyrood. 'Twas a challenge from Drew MacAdam—Highland golfer and friend of Ambrose Scott—to a game of golf at Musselburgh.

The queen, amused by the boldness of the letter and rabid for the game, had responded at once, accepting the challenge. This morn she'd managed to evade her watchful guards and set aside the responsibilities of the crown long enough to meet him secretly on the course.

"So what's to be the wager, MacAdam?" the queen asked as they stood at the first tee. Loath to attract attention, she was dressed in relatively modest attire of subdued colors. Her glorious hair was hidden, tucked under a French hood, and she wore only a simple Cross on a chain about her neck. Her brown eyes twinkled as she said, "I suppose ye'll be wantin' a piece o' land? Maybe the lairdship o' . . . Where did ye say ye were from?"

He froze for an instant, mortified, then managed to choke out, "Tintclachan."

A crease touched her pale brow. "Ne'er heard of it. I can see I shall have to do more travelin' if I'm to reign o'er this vast country."

Jossy stepped forward and bowed her head in reverence. "If it pleases Your Majesty, I'd like to name the wager."

Mary studied her, then grinned. "Ye're the beer-wagon wench."

"Aye."

"I'm guessin' ye'll want more than a thimble this time?"

Jossy smiled, obviously pleased that the queen remembered her. "If Drew wins the match, Your Majesty, I'd very much like your blessin' . . . on our marriage."

The Four Maries gasped unanimously in delight, then sighed in pleasure. Drew smirked. They were definitely French.

The queen looked just as pleased. "So there's to be a weddin', is there?"

"If ye'll allow it," Jossy said.

The queen smiled, then nodded.

The Four Maries clapped in approval.

"And if *I* win?" Mary inquired.

"What's your pleasure, Your Majesty?" Drew asked.

She thought for a moment, then replied, "I'd like to journey to your home in the Highlands. If I win, ye'll accompany me to Tintclachan."

Despite the horrible sinking in his chest, Drew managed a weak smile. "As ye wish."

Faith, he thought, giving Jossy a worried glance, he'd better win this match.

The wagers made, they began the game. The queen made the first drive, and as before, Drew was impressed with her skill. She'd obviously mastered the sport in France, and her well-trained cadets rushed to build her tees and hand her the proper clubs for each shot.

Halfway through the course, Drew was winning by three strokes, and the crowd had grown to unwieldy proportions as word rapidly spread that the young queen was playing at Musselburgh.

'Twas while they were teeing off at the Whin Hole that disaster struck.

Stalking across the green with murder in his eyes, his dark cloak swirling with each angry stride, came Philipe, finally alerted to the queen's mad escapade and no doubt on a mission to put an end to it.

Drew shot a meaningful glance at Jossy, who lingered at the back of the crowd. She'd seen Philipe as well, and she gave Drew a somber nod of acknowledgment.

A cadet placed the queen's ball upon the tee, and she lined up her club behind it.

"Your Majesty!" Philipe called, loping up in a froth, mopping his brow with a handkerchief. "Wait!"

The queen, displeased she'd been found out, sighed and twisted to frown at him. "I'm about to tee off, Philipe. What is it?"

The onlookers scowled at him in disapproval.

"I need to talk to you, Your Majesty," he said sternly.

" 'Twill have to wait," she told him.

"But I...I..." Philipe sputtered in frustration.

As he scanned the crowd, he suddenly spotted Jossy. He shot her a glare of menace, which she returned with a brow arched in silent challenge.

"Your Majesty," Philip insisted, biting out each word, "I must speak with you now."

"Not when I'm in the middle o'—"

"It is most urgent," he hissed.

The queen, clearly annoyed, withdrew her club and turned to face him. "What is it, Philipe?"

Philipe straightened and gave her a pointed look. "I fear for your safety, Your Majesty."

"I see. Well, put away your fears. 'Tis only a game o' golf, not a duel to the death."

The bystanders chuckled, and Philipe flushed in anger. "I believe," he announced over their laugher, "there is a traitor in our midst."

The crowd's levity turned to mumbles of surprise, and the queen crossed her arms atop her club. "Indeed? And which one of these loyal Scots lads would that be?"

"Not a lad." Drew froze as Philipe pointed one bony finger of accusation at Jossy. "Her."

To Drew's amazement, Jossy stood firm, far more confident of the queen's affections than he was.

"The beer-wagon wench?" Mary exclaimed with a laugh. "I see. And what proof do ye offer o' her treason?"

Philipe drew himself up proudly. "She has been consorting with him." He turned his stabbing finger on Drew.

"O' course she's been consortin' with him," Mary said. "They plan to wed. In fact, if MacAdam here wins the game, I've promised him my blessin' on the match."

Philipe's eyes widened in horror.

"Now," the queen stated regally, "stand aside, secretary, or I'll put ye to work, searchin' for balls in the rough."

That silenced Philipe, but it didn't keep him from imposing his threatening presence upon them all, and when Drew next looked up from play, the secretary was standing close to Jossy—too close, eyeing her with a cold, calculated air of menace. As Drew lowered his gaze, he could see that in one hand, Philipe covertly gripped Jossy's arm, and in the other, he clutched a small dirk, which was pressed against her ribs.

Drew always prided himself on being able to ignore distractions when he golfed. The crowd could yell and scream, wave their arms and stamp their feet. Hell, they could set their dogs on him, and he'd not bat an eye. He knew how to shut out everything but the swing before him, to focus solely on placing the ball where he wanted it to go.

But when he saw Philipe looming over Jossy like that, his composure faltered, and his concentration dissolved like mist.

What did the man intend? Was he trying to frighten Jossy into a confession? Did he hope to intimidate Drew into throwing the match? Or would he use the protection of the crowd to plunge that lethal blade into her heart?

Drew felt sick. Jossy stood mere yards away, yet there was nothing he could do to protect her, not without raising suspicion and ensuring they both swung from the gallows.

His playing suffered—his arms trembled, his swings went wild—and no matter how many times he looked over to make sure Jossy was safe, he kept thinking about how quickly Philipe could end her life with the single thrust of that dirk.

Three-quarters of the way through the game, the score was tied. By the time they were teeing off at the last hole, Drew had fallen behind by two strokes.

Bloody hell. He was going to lose. Which meant he'd lose Jossy. Forever.

Without the queen's blessing on their union, nothing would stand between Philipe and his desire to dispatch the rogue spy and expose the counterfeit Highlander.

Josselin had had enough of Philipe's tiresome menace. She'd allowed him to take and hold her hostage, mostly because she hadn't wanted to interrupt Mary's play with the feeble complaint that her meddling secretary was poking his pointy knife at her belly.

But now the match had come down to life or death, and Drew was behind by two strokes. He had to stop blundering about and start playing a serious game. And she intended to tell him so.

So as they stood waiting for the players to tee off at the last hole, Josselin surreptitiously lifted her booted heel and brought it down with crushing strength, grinding atop Philipe's sensitive toes as if she were extinguishing live coals.

He yelped and withdrew the dirk long enough for her to wrench free and make her escape. He dared not pursue her now for fear of making a spectacle and incurring the queen's wrath. She rushed forward through the crowd to seize Drew's arm.

Drew turned, and instantly his bleak countenance brightened. "Jossy."

"Listen to me, Highlander," she whispered while Mary's cadets were mounding sand into a tee for her. "Ye'd better not be tryin' to weasel out of our marriage. I fought bloody hard for ye, and I'm not goin' to let ye go so easily."

He opened his mouth to protest, but she gave him no chance to reply. "Now I know ye can play better," she murmured. "Ye've beat Mary before. So stop muckin' about and focus on the game."

As she advised him, she went quickly through the motions herself, the way her da's did when they showed her how to fight. "Find your balance. Bend your knees. Keep your grip firm, but not too tight. And for God's sake, keep your eye on the target."

She suddenly noticed the crowd had gone silent and was watching her.

Mary was grinning. "MacAdam, ye ought to make the lass your cadet. She knows almost as much about the game as ye do."

Drew's heart filled with pride as he gazed at the lass he meant to make his bride. He'd forgotten how strong she was, how determined, how feisty. Hell, she could probably wrestle Philipe to the ground with one arm tied behind her back.

With her honey curls and her wide green eyes, Jossy might look soft and vulnerable, but she was clever and willful and full of spirit. She might be as tender as new grass, but she could also be as prickly as a Scots thistle.

She could purr like a kitten one moment and roar like a lion the next. And damned if she wasn't the kind of woman worth fighting for.

'Twas exactly what he intended to do.

Moments later, when his ball rolled smoothly into the final hole, a great cheer went up, and he couldn't stifle his own grin of relief. Even Mary didn't seem disappointed when he won by one stroke. But then 'twas the mark of a true golfer. For the queen, 'twasn't the score, but the love of the game that kept her coming back to the course.

Still, for once, Drew had to admit that he was glad of his winnings. And when Jossy nearly bowled him over with her enthusiastic embrace, he'd never felt so elated.

Until Philipe's stern voice floated over the crowd. "They cannot be wed, Your Majesty," he intoned, pushing his way through the onlookers toward the queen.

"And why is that, Philipe?"

"Because," he said, lifting a smug brow to make the shocking announcement, "Drew MacAdam is an Englishman."

The crowd silenced in uncertainty.

"An Englishman," the queen echoed.

Drew's heart stopped, and the silence that followed seemed to last an eternity.

Then Mary suddenly burst into laughter, and the rest of the crowd joined her while Philipe glowered in outrage.

The queen stacked her hands atop her golf club as if 'twere a royal scepter. "Don't be ridiculous, Philipe," she said with a regal air of command. "The English don't know a niblick from a fairway club. Besides, do ye truly believe that the Queen o' Scotland could be bested at the game o' golf...by an Englishman?"

Epilogue

October

Josselin popped a chunk of Kate Campbell's apple coffyn into Drew's mouth. His expression was a predictable mixture of wonder and delight.

"See?" she said while everyone at The Sheep Heid Inn cheered.

Despite their differences, which so far had amounted to little more than mild disgruntlement, all the parents had come together for the wedding—her three da's, Kate, and Drew's uncles, who, for their own protection but much to their chagrin, were forced to attend in the guise of Highlanders from Tintclachan.

And now all the guests feasted on fresh salmon and mussel brose, seaweed soup and barley bread, carrageen pudding and Kate's renowned apple coffyns.

Beer flowed like a storm-swollen stream, which was fortunate, for most of the inn's patrons were too drunk to notice that some of the Highlanders had a distinct English drawl to their speech.

"I'll make ye a bargain, lad," Kate promised Drew with a pointed glare. "If ye vow to stay in Selkirk, I'll give Jossy my recipe."

"Selkirk?" Robert barked at Kate. "Pah! Nay, they'll be coming to Andrew's home."

"O'er my dead body," Angus growled.

"Da!" Josselin scolded.

"That can be arranged," Simon muttered.

"Uncle!" Drew snapped.

Will folded his hands patiently around his tankard. "Where *do* ye intend to go, lass?"

Everyone looked at them expectantly. They definitely weren't staying in Edinburgh. After their confrontation with Philipe on the golf course, Josselin had promised the apoplectic secretary that they'd keep well away from the queen.

"Well," Drew said, "we haven't quite decided, but..."

Josselin continued for him. "We're stayin' in Scotland."

Drew's uncles groaned.

"You'd let a maid tell you where to live?" Simon spat in disgust.

"She isn't tellin' me—" Drew began.

"Why would you want to stay," Robert growled, "in such an uncivilized—"

There was a loud scrape of chairs as the Scots in the room rose to their feet.

Josselin sighed and shook her head as vile oaths and threats began to fill the inn.

"Listen to me!" she bellowed, silencing them all. "There will be no malignin' of anyone's place o' birth at my weddin', do ye understand? The next person who utters one more word of it, I swear Drew and I will both disown ye." She gave them all a withering glare. "Now sit down."

Once they were seated, she resumed. "I'm not tellin' Drew where to live. 'Twas his choice. He makes his livin' at golf, and he—"

"Can't you bat your ballocks around some sheep field in your own country?" Robert asked.

Drew suppressed a laugh. "'Tis balls, Uncle, not ballocks."

"Well, can't you?"

Thomas answered his brother. "Golf's been banned for years now in favor of archery."

"The lad should go where he can make the best livin'," Alasdair added, "and the best home for Josselin and their bairns."

"Bairns!" Kate cried with, in Josselin's opinion, far too much enthusiasm. "Ach, lass, are ye already with child?"

Simon protested. "Surely, Andrew, you won't let your son be born on Scots soil!"

Angus narrowed his eyes. "And what's wrong with our soil ... aside from the fact it's stained with English blood?"

"Out!" Josselin cried, pointing toward the door. "Both o' ye! Out! And leave your weapons here."

Simon and Angus scowled, but they did as they were told. They stood, slammed their daggers flat on the table, and shoved their chairs back, then began lumbering reluctantly toward the door.

But just as they were about to exit, the door opened, and Davey the beer-wagon driver sauntered in. He had a missive for Josselin.

Josselin took the letter from him, gasping when she saw the seal. 'Twas stamped with the royal insignia of Queen Mary. With quivering fingers, she broke the seal and, standing beside Drew, read the contents aloud.

"My faithful and good subjects, as you may find it a difficult, indeed impossible, undertaking to return to your ancestral abode at Tintclachan in the Highlands, I am determined to grant to you, by God's grace, at the suggestion of my secretary, Philipe de la Fontaine, and as a condition of your marriage, 200 roods at the southeastern limit of Scotland, including a links bordering on the North Sea. It is my dearest wish that you will endeavor to establish a course there for the pleasure of any who may come, and that you will erect a tavern nearby for the comfort of all. Furthermore, I trust that you will understand always the responsibility that accompanies the holding of a property so positioned. I pray God to give you a very happy and long life. From Edinburgh, this 11th of October, 1561. The Queen of Scotland, Marie."

While the parents blinked in confusion, Josselin grinned, and Drew swept her up in his arms, twirling her around till she grew giddy with laughter.

"'So positioned'," Drew repeated in wonder. "'Tis at the border. Everyone will be able to play there—Scots, English, Catholic, Protestant."

Josselin nodded, pleased. Apparently, Philipe had found a way to grant them the next best thing to exile.

"We'll have tournaments," he continued. "And I could start a school—a school o' golf."

"I can run the tavern," Josselin gushed. "And we'll be ideally situated to guard the border for Mary, to defend Scotland against ruffians."

While they celebrated their great fortune, Drew's uncles watched uncertainly.

Finally Simon grumbled, "I suppose, lass, you'd consider us ruffians?"

There was a pregnant pause.

Finally Josselin smiled at him. "O' course not... Uncle."

He scowled, but she could see the endearment pleased him.

Drew raised his tankard from the table. "A toast to kith and kin livin' in peace and harmony!"

"Aye," Josselin added, eyeing Simon and Angus, "and if ye ever dispute that, ye'll have to fight it out with clubs and balls on our links."

Everyone raised a cup in accord. By the wee hours of the night, the sworn enemies—their tongues and hostilities mellowed by an excess of beer and merrymaking—were toasting one another's health and swapping tales of the married couple's childhoods. When Will began gleefully relating the story of how Jossy, at four years of age, offered to defend her first love—Rane MacAllister, the lord sheriff's huntsman—with a wooden sword, she decided 'twas time to retire.

She stole up the stairs with Drew, closing the door on the festivities below. The two of them had their own celebrating to do.

The morn was halfway gone when the happy bride collapsed back onto the pillow, spent. Her chemise was halfway down her arms. Her skirts were bunched around her waist. One of her stockings had gone missing. But somehow she couldn't summon the energy to care.

Beside her, the bridegroom, too, lounged in apathetic splendor. He wore a self-satisfied smile and little else. His shirt was torn, revealing his still heaving chest. His legs were splayed casually across the bed, with his trews slung around one ankle.

If they continued much longer like this—dozing blissfully off, only to awaken again for another round—they might remain at The Sheep Heid forever and never make it to their new home.

Josselin sighed. She supposed she should drag herself out of bed. Change was in the wind, and they had a future to plan. Drew would want to inspect every inch of their seaside property to determine how to arrange the course. And Josselin had ideas for the magnificent tavern she'd build.

"The Silver Thimble," she mused, gazing at the wedding ring on her finger, which had been fashioned out of the thimble Drew had given her.

"Hm?"

"Our tavern." She turned on her side and idly ran her knuckles down Drew's arm. "We have to have a name for it."

"How about The Blue Cods?" he replied, too exhausted to open his eyes.

She gave him a light punch on the shoulder. "Ye're a filthy lad." With the attention she'd lavished on them all night, his cods were anything but blue.

He grinned with his eyes still closed.

Josselin frowned up at the heavy-beamed ceiling. 'Twould be clever, she thought, since she and Drew had overcome the differences of their birth, to unite the symbols of their two countries. "The Cross and Lion," she tried.

He snorted, countering with, "The Fig and Prick."

"Drew!" she scolded, dropping her jaw. "I'm serious. 'Tis an important consideration."

He opened one lusty blue eye to gaze at her. "Darlin', how can I consider anythin' but swivin' when ye're lyin' there, all naked and lovely and temptin'?"

She might be flushing with pleasure at his smoldering glance, but she wasn't going to fall for his flattery again. They'd been swiving all night. Enough was enough.

She gave him a chiding smirk, tugging the bedlinens up over her breasts, and he sighed in exaggerated disappointment, closing his eyes again.

Maybe the name of the tavern should reflect something of the legacy of warfare they were leaving behind and the new journey of peace upon which they were embarking. "The Rusty Dagger," she suggested.

One corner of Drew's mouth curved into a smile. "The Frisky Yard," he insisted.

She had to bite back a laugh at that one, then shook her head. Drew MacAdam was incorrigible. But she supposed that was one thing she loved about him. After all, if he was a man to give up easily, he would never have pursued the cursing, trews-wearing, brawling lass with whom he'd crossed paths on the Royal Mile. He would never have chased halfway across the countryside to keep her safe. And he would never have risked the wrath of his uncles and her da's to marry her.

She smiled. Their parcel of land wasn't going anywhere. The day was still young. And they had years ahead of them.

"I know," she said with a wicked glint in her eyes, walking her fingers down his chest. "The Withered Cock."

Drew opened his eyes and lowered a disapproving brow at her. Then he clasped his hands behind his head and gave her a slow grin as his trusty staff responded boldly to her rousing touch.

With a smug growl, he tore off her coverlet, rolled atop her, and sank into her welcoming warmth. "The Long-nose Club," he told her in no uncertain terms.

'Twas a long while before Drew and Josselin left their room at The Sheep Heid Inn to venture to their new home, but when they did, two pieces of their destiny had been determined. One was that their tavern would be called The Rose and Thistle. The other was that their first son would be born exactly nine months hence.

THE DISH

Where authors give you the inside scoop!

From the desk of Hope Ramsay

Dear Reader,

Picture, if you will, a little girl in a polka-dot bathing suit, standing on a rough board jutting out over the waters of the Edisto River in South Carolina. She's about six years old, and standing below her in the chest high, tea-colored water is a tall man with a deep, deep Southern drawl—the kind that comes right up out of the ground.

"Jump, little gal," the man says, "I'll catch you."

The little girl was me. And the man was my Uncle Ernest. And that memory is one of those touchstone moments that I go back to again and again. My uncle wanted me to face my fear of jumping into the water, but he was there, big hands outstretched, steady, sturdy, and sober as a judge. He was the model of a man I could trust.

I screwed up my courage and took that leap of faith. I jumped. He caught me. He taught me to love jumping into the river and swimming in those dark, mysterious waters, overhung with Spanish moss and sometimes visited by snakes and gators!

I loved Uncle Ernest. He was my favorite uncle. He's

been gone for quite a while now, but I think of him often, and he lives on in my heart.

There is even a little bit of him in Clay Rhodes, the hero of my debut novel WELCOME TO LAST CHANCE. Jane, the heroine of the story, has to learn that Clay is the type of guy she can always trust. A guy she can take a leap of faith with. A guy who will always be there to catch her, even when she has to face her biggest fears.

And isn't love all about taking a leap of faith?

I had such fun writing WELCOME TO LAST CHANCE because it afforded me the opportunity to go back in time and remember what it was like spending my summers in a little town in South Carolina with folks who were like Uncle Ernest—people who made up a village where a child could grow up safe and sound and learn what makes a life meaningful.

I hope you enjoy meeting the characters in Last Chance, South Carolina, as much as I enjoyed writing them.

Ya'll take care now,

Hope Ramsay

www.hoperamsay.com

♥ ♥ ♥ ♥ ♥ ♥ ♥ ♥ ♥ ♥ ♥ ♥ ♥ ♥ ♥ ♥

From the desk of Cynthia Eden

Dear Reader,

Have you ever wondered how far you would go to protect someone you loved? What would you do if the person you loved was in danger?

Love can make people do wild, desperate things…and love can certainly push people to cross the thin line between good and evil.

When I wrote DEADLY LIES, I created characters who would be forced to blur the lines between good and evil. Desperate times can call for desperate measures.

The heroine of this book is a familiar face if you've read the other DEADLY books. Samantha "Sam" Kennedy was first introduced in DEADLY FEAR. Sam lived through hell, and she's now fighting to put her life back on track. She knows what evil looks like, and she knows that evil can hide behind the most innocent of faces. So when Sam is assigned to work on a serial kidnapping case, she understands that she has to be on her guard at all times.

But when the kidnapper hits too close to home and her lover's stepbrother is abducted, the rules of the game change. Soon Sam fully understands just how "desperate" the victims are feeling, and she vows to do anything in her power to help Max Ridgeway find his brother.

Anything. Yes, desperation can even push an FBI agent to the edge of the law. Lucky for Sam, she'll have back-up ready to help her out—all of the other SSD agents are back to help track the kidnappers, and they won't stop until the case is closed.

I've had such a wonderful time re-visiting my SSD Agents in this book. And I hope you enjoying catching up with the characters too!

If you'd like to learn more about my books, please visit my website at www.cynthiaeden.com.

Happy reading!

Cynthia Eden

♥ ♥ ♥ ♥ ♥ ♥ ♥ ♥ ♥ ♥ ♥ ♥ ♥ ♥ ♥

From the desk of Robyn DeHart

Dear Reader,

There have always been certain things that fascinate me—the heinous crimes of Jack the Ripper; why cats get up, turn around, then settle back into the exact position they were just in; people who can eat only *one* Oreo cookie; and the ancient legend of the Loch Ness monster. Recorded sightings of the creature date all the way back to the 7th century, and not all of these sightings have been water-based—there are those who claim to have seen the monster walking on land.

Regardless of what you believe, it's interesting to think that there just might be some prehistoric animal hiding in a loch in the Highlands. It was this interest that compelled me to write TREASURE ME.

Another interesting tidbit about this book is that it was actually the first romance novel I ever wrote. Okay, that's not entirely true, but the concept of a couple who fall in love near Loch Ness, centered around adventure and action and danger, well, that was all in that first book—even the characters' names stayed the same. But I didn't keep anything else. When it came to the third book in my Legend Hunters trilogy, I took my basic concept and started from scratch.

If you've read SEDUCE ME and DESIRE ME (the first two books in the series), then you might remember meeting Graeme, the big, brooding Scotsman who looks and sounds remarkably like Gerard Butler. Graeme has been after the authentic Stone of Destiny for years, because he believes the one sitting in Westminster is a counterfeit. He's gone back to his family's home in the Highlands to do some research, and meets with trouble in the form of a delectable, self-proclaimed paleontologist named Vanessa. She's just run away from her own wedding and is determined to make a name for herself as a legitimate scientist.

Add in a marriage of convenience, a deadly nemesis,

and some buried treasure and you've got yourself a rollicking adventure full of intrigue and seduction that will leave you as breathless as the characters.

Dare to love a Legend Hunter...

Visit my website, www.RobynDeHart.com for contests, excerpts, and more.

Enjoy!

Robyn DeHart

♥ ♥ ♥ ♥ ♥ ♥ ♥ ♥ ♥ ♥ ♥ ♥ ♥ ♥ ♥

From the desk of Kira Morgan

Dear Reader,

It's easy to write about a match made in heaven. Cinderella meets Prince Charming, they fall in love at first sight, and live happily ever after.

But for my latest book, SEDUCED BY DESTINY, I wanted to take on the challenge of star-crossed lovers, characters like Romeo and Juliet—a man and a woman cursed by fate and thrown together by chance, who have to overcome their tragic history to find true love.

In SEDUCED BY DESTINY, set in the time of Mary Queen of Scots, Josselin Ancrum and Andrew Armstrong each have a dark secret in their past and deadly peril looming in their future. They have little in common. They should avoid each other like the plague.

She's Scots. He's English.

She likes to stir up trouble. He likes to fly under the radar.

She's a tavern wench who loves to play with swords. He's an expert swordsman who'd rather play golf.

Her mother was killed in battle.

His father was the one who killed her.

Talk about Fortune's foe...

All this would be fine if only they hadn't started falling in love. If they hadn't felt that initial spark of attraction...if they hadn't begun to enjoy one another's company...if they hadn't succumbed to that first kiss...their story might be a simple tale of revenge.

But Drew and Jossy, unaware of the fateful ties between them, are drawn to one another like iron to a magnet. And by the time they discover they've fallen in love with their mortal enemy, it's too late. Their hearts are already tangled in a hopeless knot.

This is where it gets even more interesting.

To make matters worse, outside forces are working to drive them apart. What began as a personal mission of vengeance now involves their friends, their families, and ultimately their queens. Suspected of treason, hunted by spies, they become targets for royal assassins.

The uneasy truce between Queen Elizabeth and Queen Mary is mirrored in the fragile relationship between Drew and Jossy. The lovers are swept into a raging battle bigger than the both of them—a battle that shakes the foundation of their union and threatens their very lives.

Only the strength of their fateful bond and the power of their love can save them now.

Of course, unlike Romeo and Juliet, Drew and Jossy will triumph. Nobody wants to read a historical romance with an unhappy ending! But just how they manage to overcome all odds, when their stars are crossed and the cards are stacked against them, is the stuff of nail-biting high adventure and a story that I hope will keep you up all night.

To read an excerpt from SEDUCED BY DESTINY, peruse my research photos, and enter my monthly sweepstakes, visit my website at www.glynnis.net/kiramorgan. If you'd like to read my daily posts and interact with other fans, become my friend at www.facebook.com/KiraMorganAuthor or follow me at www.twitter.com/kira_morgan.

Happy adventures!

Kira Morgan